The Outburst

Girish Jakhotiya

Vitasta

Let Knowledge Spread

Published by
Renu Kaul Verma
Vitasta Publishing Pvt Ltd
2/15, Ansari Road, Daryaganj
New Delhi - 110 002
info@vitastapublishing.com

ISBN 978-93-82711-65-0

All characters in this book are fictitious. The story, however, is so close to real life that many people may find images of themselves or of people known to them in the characters of this book. All such resemblance is coincidental.

Typeset by Vits Press
Cover Design by Geetali Baruah
Printed by Vikas Computer and Printers

Dedication

I dedicate this novel to my beloved wife Manjiri who has travelled with me on my life's journey supporting me all the way.

Acknowledgment

I sincerely thank my publisher Ms Renu Kaul of Vitasta Publications, Delhi. I also thank Ms Veena Batra for her competent editing and Mr Rajesh & Ms Freny Narvekar for their editorial assistance.

Chapter 1

"You are the home minister of the state, Mr Jadhav. If you look so helpless, what do you suppose we are to do?" asked Indrajeet, the Chairman of the Pride Group.

"Indrajeetbhai, you really must understand my predicament. Ever since the 26/11 terrorist attack on Mumbai, my senior police officers are busy tackling the public and the media. They are all working round the clock to regain the confidence of Mumbaikars. We all have to retain our power after all. You do know that the assembly elections are nearing."

"I agree Mr Home Minister. But please, you must consider what's at stake here for me. I have already invested two billion Rupees. We need 1300 acres of land for our Special Economic Zone venture. Mr Mehta, your revenue minister has already cleared our project."

"Oh Indrajeetbhai, I'm well aware of all these details. Bhojani has briefed me several times." Jadhav looked derisively at Bhojani. Dil

Bhojani was the trusted associate of Mr Indrajeet. He alone handled all the clandestine deals with the politicians.

"Jadhav Saab, you have all the information, and yet, there has been no action from your side. My people, after obtaining the support of the officers in the revenue and agriculture ministries, started acquiring agricultural land, acre by acre. We managed to acquire around a hundred acres. Our initial acquisition improved the confidence of our foreign investors. But then, a few social organisations started opposing the acquisition. They also started to aggressively provoke the farmers. It began to get ugly and our people were finally obliged to use physical force in some areas to quell the agitation...."

"And Mr Indrajeet, your people killed six farmers! My department gave me all the details."

"Minister, please don't hold my people responsible for this. Your department did not offer us enough police bundobast. Things had been going on so smoothly until a few stupid social workers started blackmailing us."

"No, no, Indrajeetbhai, they did not blackmail you. Let's call a spade a spade. I know these social organisations very well. I come from the same region after all. The point is, six farmers were killed. It is a very serious matter. Just yesterday, the Opposition raised a pointed question in the assembly. Even the media has been following the whole episode very closely," said the minister, a certain seriousness ringing in his tone.

"But I do not see why so much fuss should be made over the deaths of merely six farmers? We are a country with a population of over a billion. So many farmers commit suicide everyday," Dil Bhojani intervened.

"Mr Bhojani, don't make such ridiculous statements, at least not here in my office. Do you not understand the gravity of this entire situation? This is not a simple case of your *dalalee*!" The minister turned crimson with fury.

"Sorry sir, that was not my intention," said Bhojani glumly.

"What should we do now, Mr Jadhav?" asked Indrajeet.

"We have only one solution. Our activists will try to plead with the family members of the deceased farmers. These families will have to be financially compensated. Once that issue has been settled, the 'deaths' would have to be declared as either accidents or suicides. My activists will have to work real hard. The vital point here is that we are going to require a sizeable budget to carry out this plan." The minister glanced at Bhojani.

"How much are we going to have to spend?" Indrajeet inquired.

"Oh don't worry yourself. Bhojani and I will get together, discuss and decide. Why must you be bothered with such a trifling matter? We are here to serve you Sir!" The minister laughed hysterically. Indrajeet and Bhojani joined in.

"But Minister, what about your investment in this project?"

"I have to talk to the respected Ramesh Salunke. This is a big project we are talking about. We need a green signal from Salunke saheb."

"Don't worry Minister. I will speak with Salunke saheb directly. We shall in any case be meeting over some other projects. He has promised me a bigger assignment—an international civil aviation project. After all, my father and he were close friends."

"Yes, my dear Indrajeet, we all know that. In fact, the whole country knows about their camaraderie. Both of them grew in their respective disciplines with the support of the other," said the Minister.

"Please Minister, do sit with Bhojani today itself. Before things get out of control, I think it's imperative that we quickly settle the issue of the farmers' deaths. You know it was always the dream of my father, Shri Jagjeet, to develop a Special Economic Zone, one which conformed to global standards in terms of quality and size."

"Yes, we should indeed channelise all our efforts and realise that dream!" said Bhojani with a twinkle in his eyes.

Indrajeet then left the Minister's office. Dil Bhojani and the Minister pondered over the situation for a couple of hours. The Minister spoke with several close associates over the phone. And finally, a financial budget was decided to tackle the issue of the six farmers' deaths.

The killings were to be defined as suicides. Money would make it all happen. The families of the farmers were to be approached very tactfully. A SEZ of 1300 acres was a huge project.

Ramesh Salunke, who happened to be a very senior cabinet minister at the centre, had his own vested interests in this particular project of the Pride Group. His sustenance in the corridors of power at Delhi was threatened of late. Industrialists and powerful bureaucrats had begun to take him for granted. The restoration of his position and influence in the 'Delhi Darbar' had consequently become his top priority. Such restoration called for a lot of money.

After having had a very fruitful meeting with the Minister, Dil Bhojani returned to his house. His three sons were waiting for him at the dining table. Pawan and Charan, the elder two, knew about the meeting that was scheduled between the Home Minister and their father. Nayan, the youngest of the three, only listened to the conversations between his father and brothers out of compulsion. He was a misfit in the Bhojani family.

Pawan, with his boundless curiosity couldn't help but ask several questions about the meeting that took place that day. After all, it was a meeting to finalise a financial deal. Such deals always meant good money for the Bhojanis. Dil narrated the interesting events that had transpired to his sons. Bhojani's wife was serving freshly made hot meal at the table, reluctantly listening to discussions pertaining to yet another deal. What shocked her and Nayan too was the cover up regarding the deaths of the farmers. It was appalling! It was the height of being insensitive towards humanity. Nayan could not bear to listen any further. He quickly finished his dinner and hastened to his room.

Dil Bhojani and his elder sons then began talking about the terrorist attack on Mumbai.

Dear Shini,

Hi! How are you?

I'm sorry I couldn't reply to your earlier mails.

Let me share with you my most recent encounter with corruption. The supply chain head of my company was entertaining some custom officers yesterday. A few million rupees of tax were craftily evaded. What's even more horrifying is that a few of the papers were signed by the officers in our manager's cabin, as though the cabin itself was the Customs Office.

Shini, you're probably wondering why I work in such an office? It would be too risky to disclose everything through an email, so for now, it suffices to say that there is a big story behind my so-called employment in this outfit. I'll give you a hint though. My company belongs to the well known Pride Group. Anyway let's come to the real stuff now. How are our friends—Orango, Hu, Manzar, Sukarno and Akito? I really want to catch up with them. Janaki is doing fine in Delhi. I call her Didi these days. She's enjoying the new title since it gives her the opportunity to dictate terms to me, which I'm obliged to obey. You know her father is a senior officer in the Ministry of Parliamentary Affairs. She promised to mail me some sensitive stuff very soon. I often end up getting rather confused with all the deadly information about the power struggles in Delhi that she furnishes. She uses a punch line these days. It goes, *Life is a journey from confusion to fusion!*

How are you doing at the *Global Times*? You sure are working with one aggressive newspaper. But then again, I guess such aggression suits your nature! We have already had a taste of it here at the international workshop in Mumbai. Only you had the guts to initiate most of the debates.

Shini, for how long are we to keep emailing each other, talking about our pains, perils and probabilities of prosperity. Do you remember the last time we met we decided that we should meet at least once a year? Well a year has almost gone by now. I'm sure that by now we must both have gathered a lot of explosive information to share. I for one, certainly have a lot to share with you guys. The more I think about the future, the more confused I get.

Before I conclude, I want to remind you once again to take care, write regularly, don't forget your international friends and do not ever forget the oath we took—*let* us become *global* citizens!

As always, awaiting your reply with the customary punch of a journalist!

Yours truly

Nayan.

After having sent the mail to Shini, Nayan lunched with his elder brother Pawan. He then went into the garden and sat on a stone bench. The place had a good view of the sea. He often felt that this bench had been specially made for him as it prompted him to contemplate his future. His father, Dil Bhojani, was a very rich Sindhi. He was not always so. He had his humble beginnings like many Sindhi and Punjabi families that sought shelter in the various cities of India, having fled the massacre of the Hindus in Pakistan. The Bhojani family decided on Bombay and settled in a low-class area of central Bombay. Dil Bhojani, despite whatever adversity he faced, managed to complete his schooling and started to work in South Bombay. He found a job in a cloth shop, and despite the lack of a formal university education, he became successful thanks to his sheer hardwork and business acumen.

During that phase of his life, he chanced to meet Jagjeet Sankala, and quickly became a member of his inner circle. Eventually, it was with the help of this close team, his inner circle, that Sankala built the esteemed Pride Group of Industries. Indeed, the entrepreneurial journey of Sankala was as adventurous as it was sinful.

Dil Bhojani grew to be the loyal, trusted, dedicated right hand man of Jagjeet. He was rewarded well in many ways. Both the sons-in-law of Bhojani held very senior positions in subsidiary companies of the Pride Group. Bhojani's eldest son, Pawan, was a part of the coterie of Indrajeet Sankala, Jagjeet's only son. Charan, Bhojani's other son, was at the helm of his own five hundred million business outfit that supplied raw material to Pride Group. Dil constructed a sprawling lavish beach bungalow in a northern suburb of Mumbai, on a one acre plot gifted by Jagjeet. Since nothing comes for free, quite evidently there must have been some 'behind-the-curtain' contribution made by him for the Pride Group. Jagjeet's political clout amplified with every changing government. And Bhojani's success grew in direct proportion to that of Jagjeet. Bhojani was the key, the one who solely and entirely managed the Group's connections with the political machinery. Even at seventy, he continued to be the 'mentor' of the second generation Sankalas. One could safely say that Bhojani was to Pride Group what Shakuni was to the Kauravas in the great Indian epic, the Mahabharata.

He married a Maharashtrian Brahmin girl called Namrata Gokhale. She happened to be his neighbour, way back when the Bhojanis initially settled in Bombay. She was enamoured by his alacrity and prudence in business and of course his diligence. There was a time when Dil played an important role in the Gokhale family. He guided them through their commercial ventures and decision-making. He also, in a way, became a hero by obtaining special sanctions whereby all members of the lower middle class colony, where the Gokhales resided, benefited by way of some extra residential land area. Namrata's family gained too.

Namrata came from a family that propagated Hinduism. Her grandfather and father were staunch followers of a Hindu outfit called Samiti. Samiti was known for its disciplined cadres of activists, social work, patriotism, but mainly for its self-proclaimed image as protector of Hinduism. This probably explains why there was a fallout between the Bhojanis and the Gokhales. Bhojani, upon joining the Sankalas was engaged in dubious business activities which the Gokhales could not tolerate. It was an ideological clash that could not be redressed for years. Namrata was cut off from her family on account of this and it took a toll on her health. Time turned out to be the best healer. It wasn't until more than a decade later that Namrata's brothers rekindled the connection. After Nayan's birth, last in the tally of three boys and two girls, Namrata's health rapidly deteriorated. Dil Bhojani was plunged in his money-making racket totally consumed by his work. Namrata struggled on but finally agreed to have Nayan grow up with her brothers. Though Bhojani did not appreciate that, he accepted that Nayan would come back once his schooling was over. Little did he know then, that Nayan would grow up to be a different entity, totally different from his other siblings.

Nayan, during his formative years, lived amid the Gokhale clan. The Gokhales shifted their residence to Pune and so did Nayan. Every vacation he would come down to Bombay (Mumbai as it came to be called) and spent time with his mother. He was compelled to grow up in a confused state on account of the cultural differences between the Gokhales and the Bhojanis. The former were simple and straightforward, with limited ambition, whereas the latter, the Bhojanis, unflinchingly displayed their regard for politics, economics and business with a definite thirst for success.

Nayan grew up attending the Hindu Samiti cultural classes. He was exposed to the literature of Veer Savarkar, Tilak, Chanakya and many other Hindu philosophers. His upbringing was one of a middle-class Brahmin. The Bhojanis were unhappy about it. However, once Nayan finished his schooling, he came back to Mumbai, where he enrolled in a reputed college for higher education. All of a sudden, he was exposed to the business world, the kind that was hitherto unknown to him. Business deals, political connections, intense discussions, rough, violent business conversations were a part of life at the Bhojani Residence. Nayan could never be really comfortable with this kind of existence which his father and brothers were quite accustomed to. However, intuitively, he realised and even recognised that life, as the Bhojanis defined it, was pretty much a reality. He kept wrestling with these two extremes that formed an integral part of his life thus far: the beautiful and the ugly, the placid and the violent, the same way that the yin contrasted with the yang in Chinese philosophy.

The childhood impressions of the Hindu Samiti had made

Nayan's thought process quite rigid. Like any other conformist Hindu, young Nayan too thought that Hindu Samiti alone was the most patriotic and disciplined organisation. He believed that all the working offshoots of the Samiti were essentially non-corrupt. This belief translated into a sense of self-exaltation in the youngster's mind. One could sense a kind of arrogance in his demeanor which proclaimed—Hey there, I am the flag bearer, the protector of India's cultural heritage. All that came to naught when he discovered that the Hindu Samiti wasn't sacrosanct after all! A few of the politicians, bureaucrats, social activists, business folk submerged in unethical practices with his father were members of that same Hindu Samiti. Among those who visited the Bhojani residence, the most frequent visitor was Madan Joshi, a Minister from the Nationalist Hindu Party [NHP]. Joshi grew to become closely associated with the big man – Jagjeet Sankala, so much so, that he became a household name for the Sankalas. As a matter of fact, Jagjeet blindly followed Madan Joshi to curry a few political advantages, and to gain some political mileage which would later prove to be detrimental. Their symbiotic relationship led to Sankala getting political exposure and Joshi amassing funds. The Sankala family donated hefty sums to many trusts that were privately run by Joshi. Also, several members of the NHP often waited outside Bhojani's office to seek a meeting with Jagjeet Sankala.

Nayan realised the poignant truth that the Hindu Samiti was unable to eradicate corruption from the Indian society. Enrolled in the Metro College, a cosmopolitan institution, he understood the concepts of plurality. The multi-cultural exposure did not help him and his ideological confusion—only compounded it. No one amid the Bhojanis offered him conceptual clarity, and the Gokhales were away so had their limitations. Nayan had to find himself a 'friend-philosopher-guide' for his life.

His close friend Deepak Sathe had shared a bond with him right from the college days, those 'ragging' days, when he had shielded Nayan. Needless to say, Nayan accepted legitimate criticism from him on various occasions.

He journeyed back in time to the International Residential Workshop on Culture and Humanity. It was Deepak Sathe who had urged him to attend that workshop. Sathe was at that time working for a radical thinkers' group as an editor of a weekly called *The Reminder*. Quite clearly, he wasn't welcome at Nayan's Residence, a fact overtly indicated by Nayan's folks. It was a sore point for Nayan who valued Sathe's thinking and his devotion towards the masses. In fact, Nayan clashed on this issue very often with Pawan. They would have heated arguments on the subject. Pawan once blasted Nayan. "Look here Nayan, once and for all please note that people like Sathe can neither create wealth, nor generate employment. They only serve to instigate, provoke, and drive the masses to protest." He dismissed Sathe as a person smitten by syndicalism and went on to call him a mad man, a trouble-maker and an obsessed anti-capitalist. Nayan had so much to say in defense of his friend, but could not express himself freely out of respect for his elder brother. Also, psychologically he always felt small, ineffectual and in some way at the mercy of the Bhojanis.

The workshop on International Culture and Humanity was a real eye-opener for Nayan. The workshop, with forty participants from eleven countries, gave him a wealth of knowledge—with its PowerPoint presentations, film shows, one-act dramas, drawings, poetry and folk dances.

The two most important features of this workshop were lectures by eminent speakers on International Culture and Humanity, and inter-personal discussions between fellow participants in the evenings.

The most enlightening and engaging lecture was by one Professor Aditya. He seemed a perfect blend of a corporate personality with real social concern. Aditya's lecture was difficult for Nayan to assimilate in totality. However, there was this intense chemistry between the professor and students in terms of wisdom, courage, creativity and human concern.

There were in all forty participants in that workshop; of them only seven struck Nayan as friendship-worthy. Somehow he had this feeling that these seven ought to gel and bond to become true friends. Shini Herel from US topped the list. Shini was the daughter of a Jewish father, a leading attorney in the city of New York. Her mother was a British educationist. Shini had the good luck to debut with the prestigious *Global Times*. Her talent as a journalist was impeccable and she hit the bull's eye very often. She did not have to rise up the ladder gradually. She started off as the executive secretary of the chief editor. Within no time she was given the position of a junior reporter on political affairs. Nayan was sure that within a year she would be in a position to handle an independent portfolio. She was blessed with extraordinary communication skills. Small wonder, she was rated very highly.

And then there was Janaki from Delhi who shared a special bond with Nayan. He grew to like her and appreciate her as an elder sister. She worked as an assistant editor of a magazine particularly committed to the cause of women. She was a graduate in Sociology.

Pawan went to receive his father at the International Airport. Either Pawan or Charan went to fetch their father from the airport after the 'conquest' by the old man at his secret mission, this time in Dubai. As far as this deal was concerned, Dil Bhojani attended the meeting merely as a mute spectator. Indrajeet, the man in command, presided over this special mission and Dil was the escort. Pride Group was open and vulnerable to terrorist attacks, especially its plants. Terrorists across the border threatened Indrajeet directly. Though the government was quick to assure security, Indrajeet doubted the government machinery's competency. Some risk management experts even advised him to enter into a dialogue with the major terrorist groups and 'buy' peace for a price. He was uncomfortable with the prospect of bribing, in case it became a regular repetitive practice. On the other hand, the terrorist network was strengthening. Gradually, Indrajeet realised that the terrorist outfits were conscious of the ill-gotten wealth that Pride Group had amassed over the years. The same terrorist organisations did not even remotely threaten the Bhadralok Group, which had at its helm none other than Mr Bhadralok, a Parsee industrialist, a gentleman at heart, known for his ethical business practices and service unto the human race.

Dubai based Mafioso of international repute, Rehman Sheikh, agreed to broker the deal between Indrajeet and the terrorist groups. A meeting was arranged in Dubai. It was coordinated by the Pride Group office in Dubai. Dil Bhojani accompanied Indrajeet to settle the transaction matters resulting from the meeting. The negotiations were conducted by Rehman. Wisely, Indrajeet insisted on a one-time settlement, which, as expected, was refused by the terrorist group. After all, why would they kill the cow and eat it just once, when they had the option of milking it on a daily basis? The Pride Group's growing prosperity was a long-term, regular assurance of cash flow. Finally the two parties arrived at a decision—that of an annual mode of payment. Subsequently, Rehman Sheikh, without wasting time asked for his pound of flesh! He insisted on Bhojani leaving the room. The disappointed Bhojani had little choice. The sum involved was astronomical and the payoffs obviously had to be commensurate. He suddenly found himself envious of Rehman who could broker deals on a giant platform whereas he himself was the small guy, on the small stage, handling small deals!

Pawan saw his dad amble out of the airport, with a long peeved face. Things didn't seem quite right he thought. It took little time for Dil Bhojani to pour it all out to his son and his confidant. Pawan knew his father very well. He was certain about what weighed on the old man's mind—his yet unfulfilled desire to create the 'Bhojani Industrial Group'—a dream yes, and an achievable target, or so Dil believed. Pawan tried to cheer him up with an interesting bit of information he had on hand.

"Dad, you need not wallow in that Dubai hard luck; just check this out—a new window has opened up for us. A neat way of making some quick big bucks!"

"Uh? What did you say? Really?" Dil continued, "Didn't look like there was an opportunity lurking in the very near future."

"Cool it, cool it, dad; this is a very recent development. You are aware that Indrajeet got hold of new mining licences from the NHP that's governing the south."

"Yes, I myself brokered that deal. How could I forget? Pride Group financed the NHP during the Assembly elections. You can safely say, almost fifty per cent of the NHP candidates are on the pay-roll of Indrajeet till date."

"Dad, now see what I am getting at. There is a twist in the tale! Most of these mining licences I am talking about are illegal. The environment activists and members of the Opposition are questioning the very credibility of the present government. It is all happening dad, can't you see? Now Indrajeet will have to spend on 'people management'. And that's when my dear dad's job starts! A big opportunity to broker coming your way real soon dad." Pawan watched his father's face light up albeit a little bit.

Nayan went to his room and sat down to check his mailbox. As expected, Shini's brief mail was starring at him.

> Hi Nayan ol' pal – Christmas is round the corner but the spirit is far from peppy.
> We've got to arrange for a meeting after these Christmas festivities. Be a pet meanwhile, and organise our next meeting with the rest of the gang. Where do we meet, for how long... with what agenda? Nayan please, I trust you to take the lead. Heavens there are so many burning issues. I'm confident you'll coordinate and manage things.
> Now time for some spice: My newspaper is fostering a forum to oppose the Government's stance of shielding the guilty who failed our economy. Things may be difficult but not impossible!
> Ciao until the next + luv to u – Shini

Nayan felt revitalised by the mail. *Things may be difficult, but not impossible!*— didn't she say that? Nayan went on thinking, mesmerised by her words. He sensed a growing respect for her. His heart beat wildly as he reflected on his mail exchanges with her. He wound up his mails with 'yours truly' or some such clumsy correct thing, and she, she just didn't hesitate using endearing words.

Nayan had to share his feelings with her mom that evening. He shared the mail with his mom. It was a reminder and an assurance to her all at once. A reminder that Nayan's attending a cultural workshop of that magnitude had transformed his life, his goals, his entire perspective as fresh horizons had opened up for him. The assurance was that he was becoming his own man, about to formulate his own ideology and course to move ahead. His global reach with his new found cultural workshop friends was steadily going to shape his future. Whether he was a Bhojani or a Gokhale, time would tell.

Nayan was pleased to share with his mother the issues that were close to his heart—his initiative in coordinating a gathering of his new global friends. He showed her the video of his discussions with them. With the exception of his mother, no one in the family had any interest whatsoever in such unproductive discussions.

He was working on the primary details for the get-together. He was terribly focused about it and wanted the meeting to hold a serious sense of purpose, to be valid, to be meaningful and result in something concrete. Shini had already indicated her expectations, though her topics of interest were not clearly defined. Nayan now had to interpret expectations from other members.

On one occasion Nayan awoke late. As he came down he realised that all the family members were already seated for breakfast. Pawan saw Nayan enter and he called out mockingly, "Here comes our beloved prince. Frankly, mom and dad, you two have pampered him beyond redemption; now he is actually proving to be dumb and dumber day by day. Dad, you for instance, always keep preaching the good of working fifteen to sixteen hours in a day, just like our late leader Jagjeet. Then how come you allow our little prince to kill time unproductively?"

"Pawan, you don't have to be so harsh on him. He is currently working on his job at Pride Retail, and he is learning," said the father, quite unpersuasively.

"No, there I don't agree with you dad. At the age of nineteen, just nineteen, I started my own business of supplies to the Pride Group. And look at it now – it is a five hundred million Rupee company."

"Yup and Nayan too is employed in the supply chain. He must learn the tricks of the trade real fast for I expect him to join me soon,"

Charan echoed Pawan's sentiments.

"Charan, we are dad's sons and Nayan is mama's boy. You got it?" said Pawan mischievously.

"Look Nayan, you may fritter away time with friends but after attending to business. Business itself should be your first companion. Look how dad and I, both of us, have made such a lot of money out of all the underhand dealings of Jagjeet and Indrajeet. After all, the caretaker of the lake is certainly expected to consume its water sometime or the other. Half of my business investment has been funded by this systemic loot of Pride Group's money. And you know, the best part of it is that Indrajeet must be well aware of what I am doing. Yet he can't hurt me—he can't hurt us, because between dad and I, we earn so much for him.

"Dad has been looking after most of the dealings with the politicians for the last so many decades. In a sense, to put it plainly, all is symbiotic. The Sankala family did not do us any favour and we did not fail them either. Ultimately wealth has to get shared, formally or informally! Nayan, we are not calling upon you to make money at the Pride Retail. What we want of you is to merely learn the tricks. Become Nayan the ruthless, Nayan the cunning." Charan virtually gave a small discourse to Nayan!

"Nayan, oh my Nayan, your brothers are absolutely right. I too have a dream, a vision of witnessing the Bhojani Group of Industries being formed by the three of you. How long should we keep on serving the Sankalas? Why? We are equally capable of crafting a business empire of our own. Jagjeet was fortunate to have found an associate in me. No doubt he was a great businessman but without our complete commitment to *his* cause Pride Group wouldn't have been where it is today."

Nayan was listening but his mind was someplace else, crammed with a very complex mixture of thoughts. Shini's quote from her mail, *Things may be difficult, but not impossible*! kept flashing before his eyes. What *is* right and what is wrong after all? How do you define the appropriateness of a particular behaviour? If creating and generating more and more wealth was his endeavour, his reality, then why did destiny push him on the path of the chaste cultural classes of the Hindu Samiti? Nayan experienced internal conflict. All at once he was torn between two polarised philosophies—that of the Bhojanis and that of the Gokhales. And the choice was his to make!

Nayan bathed and then had a big breakfast and rushed to the office. On returning in the evening, he sent an email to Janaki.

> Hey Janaki—dunno why I say Janaki when 'Didi' is what is in my comfort zone!
>
> So Didi,
>
> How are you and everyone at home?
>
> Actually, I am about to share some personal info with you for the first time. How do I introduce the matter? Well, I belong to a rich entrepreneurial family. My elder brothers are both very ambitious. Somehow I do not think that I can fit into their design of life. This morning I was almost given an ultimatum to adopt their lifestyle. I must be clearer here—my entire family works for the Pride Group. Does that explain things? I suppose you are well aware of the Pride Empire and its modus-operandi.
>
> Shini was suggesting we meet for a week to discuss some serious matters. We can also insert a short picnic on the agenda. Give me your feedback 'cause I need to inform all our friends. Didi, you were to send me something interesting. What about that? I am waiting. How is your magazine doing?

Any interesting cover story I must know about? I think I am asking too many questions. Say a Hi to uncle and aunty.

Cheers,

Nayan

Nayan's mom suddenly rushed into his bedroom. She had been away all morning, organising the annual pooja of Lord Krishna. When she returned home, her husband mentioned to her about Nayan's depressed mood without giving her any idea of the morning brouhaha.

So she barged in worried about her youngest boy. "Nayan, how are you my son?" she asked anxiously in a ruffled tone.

"Mommy, don't worry about me. Honest to God, I am quite ok. I know what you are going through and what you've had to endure. I promise you that I'll lead my life and career the way you want. I know what you expect from me and I won't deny it to you. I won't be another Charan or Pawan. Trust me mom, my life will be different—by that I mean much better. You've performed the pooja today, now leave my destiny to him." Nayan spoke ardently hugging his mother. She wept for a while but was comforted and reassured as much by her son's words as by the warmth of his hug.

Nayan was himself surprised that he could actually console his mom. He shuddered to think that he had given a very difficult promise to her. All the same he was happy that he had taken his first step towards the goal. Nayan remembered Deepak Sathe, his true friend, with whom he had shared so much, so completely, in the past. Sathe had absorbed a quantum of Nayan's woes and difficulties. He proved to be an extremely patient listener. He was a bit whimsical but his heart was without a blemish. The situation called for a chat with Sathe.

Nayan went to meet Sathe. As he approached his house, he saw a small crowd gathered outside preparing for someone's funeral. Nayan was shocked. How come he wasn't informed by Sathe? And who must have died? Sathe's parents were quite healthy to the best of his knowledge. Anxiously, Nayan crept into the house. Sathe's father was dead. His mother stared at Nayan with empty eyes. Sathe stood up and came up to Nayan. Suddenly he burst out, "You rich fellows, you are all same. What are you doing here when your Pride Group is the one responsible for my father's death?" Nayan made a weak attempt to console and explain but it wasn't the moment. He solemnly attended the rituals. Sathe, wounded to the heart, cried out aloud. Nayan stood stoic until the funeral ceremony was over. He visited the Sathe house the next day despite the fact that he was ignored and made to feel the culprit. The third day, however, Sathe narrated his tragic story to Nayan.

Sathe wasn't financially stable enough to start his own magazine with the appropriate infrastructure. He had to take a loan by mortgaging his house. Nayan had advised him to take the loan from Instant Bank, well known for its quick processing and early disbursement of loans. Sathe did just that and launched his magazine, *The Reminder.* Since he did not have a godfather in this business the venture had its share of teething problems. Initially it was quite a disaster. The magazine was considered gossip material by some while others even called it a typical communist publication. It had its share of bad luck and was just about picking up its viewership. The poor start, and the very gradual pickup with a measly profit, were mainly responsible for him turning into a defaulter for payment of loan instalments to Instant Bank. He opted not to share his financial problems with Nayan.

To put Nayan in the picture, Sathe explained that in the last few months, in *The Reminder* he had written a series of articles on the nexus between the Pride Group and a few senior politicians including a few ministers. The exposure these articles gave created quite a furor among the parties involved. There was a connection between the Pride Group and Instant Bank, the latter being known for its 'systemic arrogance' anyway.

One evening, when Sathe's retired father was alone at home, he got a threatening call from the Pride Group's office. The caller warned the old man about his son's articles against the Pride Group. He was ordered to stop his son from writing anything defamatory to the Group and Sankala family. The caller went on to remind Mr Sathe that his son was a defaulter at the the Bank and the loan recovery folks were not far away. Initially, the Sathes downplayed these threats until a month ago when Instant Bank started measures for the loan recovery. Every call was nastier and more menacing. One morning, two foul-mouthed guys from the bank visited Sathe's house unannounced and threatened his father with physically taking possession of the house if the loan was not paid within forty-eight hours. Sathe's elder sister was the only other person in the house. She was resting inside with her infant. It was a terrible shock for the old man who had a massive heart attack and died. Instant Bank took the action but the mastermind was The Pride Group, Sankala's huge, diabolic, action force – visible or invisible. This wasn't the first case of its kind. Many an innocent Sathe was ruined by the mighty Sankalas on their empire-building march to the creation and sustenance of the 'Pride Group of Industries'.

When Nayan heard the story, he was filled with remorse and unfathomable guilt. He spent three sleepless nights. He was devastated and felt that his expensive clothes, diamond rings, branded shoes and wrist-watches were afforded at the price of that poor innocent gentleman – Sathe senior. He was nauseated at the thought that everything he used truly belonged to the Pride Group.

Consoling Sathe was not enough. Action was called for. With renewed determination, Nayan met Sathe. He convinced him that financial stability was of prime importance. That one couldn't live by emotions alone. He took Deepak to the bank and with all the 'Bhojani' influence he could muster, a reschedule of the loan payment was arranged. Both agreed that '*The Reminder*' should be discontinued for a year. For an ideologist like Deepak, it was a very tough decision. It was almost like surrendering to the Pride Group. Nayan made him understand that these draconian measures were temporary and were being taken with the obvious intention of foxing the adversary. History has recorded that many a great warrior took a step or two backwards to strategically conserve his energy and confuse the enemy. They had to try out that for survival. With a lot of effort, Sathe joined a Marathi newspaper known for its principles on journalism. He could now get some satisfaction at work.

Nayan informed all his global friends about the sad demise of Sathe's dad through the net. He did not mince words and openly indicated the reason behind this ill-fated event. His last line summed up his feelings "...unfortunately I work at Pride Retail." Promptly condolences for Sathe poured in from one and all. The following Sunday, Nayan received an interesting mail from Shini—an excellent bit of journalistic writing. Shini's literary skills and political smartness all in one small interesting report! It was on the visit of India's Prime Minister to the USA.

Hi Nayan,

Forgive me. I didn't mention about this article in my earlier mail because I wanted it to be a surprise. This particular article is scheduled to appear in our special weekly magazine releasing tomorrow. In a sense, through this mail, I am attaching an advance copy of my article which is a political story based on the meeting between your prime minister and our president. Of course the article is laced with some amount of believable fiction to make it vibrant and light-hearted. We Americans love vivacity and enthusiasm in every walk of life … but what about our present day picture? There seems to be dullness 'every-single-where'! This story of mine is a small effort to reduce this dreariness.

I have also mailed it to Janaki. Since she works in Delhi, a politically happening city, it would be interesting to have her take on it. You may please ask Sathe to send me a formal mail specifying the reason behind his father's death. India is an important country for us now. Personally I feel that business houses like the Sankalas should be globally exposed.

Nayan, please delete this mail asap from your mailbox. Trust you get what I mean. You tread the danger zone and may be hounded by the Sankalas! Send me your critique.

Remember to get set for our gathering. Take care.

Ciao & all my luv,

Shini

Nayan couldn't contain his curiosity any longer and he rushed to open Shini's attachment titled *The American Engagement.* He read the story over and over highlighting sentences of importance. He couldn't fathom how she could lay her hands on all that sensitive stuff. She had blended reality with fiction so craftily that it almost felt like you were witnessing the entire episode unfold in the White House.

The American Engagement

"Mr Prime Minister, we are both in a rather similar spot. The nature of our problems may be slightly dissimilar but the level of their intensity runs pretty much parallel."

"Mr President, are you suggesting we are sailing in the same boat?"

"Mr Prime Minister, I think, there is a difference in the problems but the intensity is certainly comparable. You are facing socio-political terrorism and I am exposed to a near economic collapse of my country."

"To an extent I agree Mr President. But this economic growth cannot surpass the ill-designed terror plots of our neighbour!"

"Yeah I know. To put it bluntly, we Americans know your neighbour better than anyone else! I dare say, its because we kept them engaged for so many decades."

"That is what I call the American modus-operandi Mr President!"

"Well then we have a great opportunity of working together to wipe out the roots of terrorism in and around your country. We could spin out a strategic plan mindful of the advantage of knowing Pakistan from an angle different from yours and closer as well."

"Mr President, I am curious to know your strategic planl!"

With a gentle nudge, the President led the Prime Minister to his chamber -- the kind of gesture that serves as a reminder of American magnanimity. The President finally announced to his Indian counterpart, "Mr Prime Minister, I invite your country to join us in the war against Iran and also our march towards anti-China diplomacy. In return you are promised a reasonable share in Iranian oil and an eventual role in Iran's reconstruction."

The Indian Premier was stunned for a moment.

He exchanged many revolutionary ideas with his American counterpart. Both leaders were engaged together for four sessions on three consecutive days along with their entourage of very brilliant associates.

After the Indian leader left, the President met top industrialists, bankers and other diplomats to discuss his course of action. Among the Americans who attended this significant conference were the mighty heads of oil companies, weapon manufacturers, auto giants, investment bankers, economists and political diplomats. In the President's group, the most aggressive were Lubert (CEO of Global Oil Inc) and Lynch (CEO of Western Coke). Lubert and Lynch were known for their entrepreneurial leadership. Lubert was better known for his 'behind the curtain tactics', and Lynch was admired for her killer instinct. She represented the American culture of survival of the fittest. Both Lubert and Lynch were American media friendly. They were the iconic Americans who very often mesmerised the brightest of management students from all over the world. They hosted quite a few international seminars and shared their wisdom of creating wealth. However, for the past two years these 'wealth creators' have been subdued, speaking those unimaginable words of 'economic caution'. The content of their discourses has altered with the inclusion of a few spiritual punches, suggesting a new economic world order and defining challenges before the American industry. Lubert and Lynch were extra cautious in their public meetings especially after the consecutive collapses of some of the most powerful American banks and corporations.

The President conducted several meetings with them to reach a reasonable consensus about America's new economic discipline. American indiscipline had eroded public savings. Earlier America had engaged a few countries in war and sorted out her economic crises. This time around, the same was not possible as the American destiny took a different turn. You can fool some people sometimes but not all the times!

The President and his associates could not reach any viable and sustainable solution. His idea of engaging in a war with Iran impressed Lubert, the shrewd British European, who was at the forefront criticising the President during the fabulous democratic election show. Lubert always represented the old school of thought that European whites were meant to rule America, and therefore logically, the globe. He championed the oil algorithms and created his image as an 'oil magnate'. The Iraq war was in effect Lubert's brainchild. He was big, and the President could not ignore him however much he wanted to.

Shini's observations about American arrogance and self-centeredness were so apt and obvious. She was brazen and presented the truth candidly. Nayan was surprised at her gumption at having the article published in an American magazine. When would this forthrightness come to India he thought!

Nayan got a mail from Janaki. She kept her communication very brief, just a couple of thoughts.

Dear Nayan,

Read Shini's *The American Engagement*. Absolutely brilliant piece of work, simply outstanding! Phenomenal style and very daring indeed! Hats off to her and the American people in general! That's what I call real freedom of speech and expression. Shini's article inspired me to write my story, which I have attached here. Mine is called *The Indian Drama*. It clearly describes my purpose in attending our gathering.

By the way, Indrajeet Sankala is presently in Delhi. I am told his team of fifty-odd executives has made base in Delhi for the last couple of months. I guess they are working towards something very big indeed. Apparently the mandate of the team is to get the government machinery on its side and it has been making impressive inroads into the government. This is just another mechanism of how these people manipulate the government.

That's all for now. Please read my story and give me your thoughts. Also pass it on to Sathe and let me have his feedback as well.

Ciao and take care.

Didi.

The Indian Drama

Delhi is cold, unfeeling—a city that does not belong to anyone emotionally. No sentiments, no emotions, no 'my city' no 'great city' – just a place where you make it or break it, where you take on jobs, convert deals, render, deliver, succeed and fail. Business sentiment, acumen and trade is in the blood of its residents, big and small. From the most insignificant rickshaw driver to a successful businessman, everyone indulges in 'deal-making' or facilitates its making. By virtue of being the political capital of the country, it houses many powerful and well-connected people of India using clout and influence every step of the way.

The Prime Minister of India called an urgent cabinet meeting. He briefed his colleagues about his visit to the US and his meeting with the President. This Indian government is a coalition of eight political parties with different regional identities and ideologies. The meeting was followed by heated arguments, especially on the delicate issue of backing the US against Iran. Surinder Singh, head of the Socialist Party vehemently objected to it. In his high pitched shrill tone he protested, "How can we dare to support an attack on an Islamic country when we ourselves have two hundred million Muslims in India? Oil from Iran can always come to India peacefully. Besides, Iran, an ancient culture, perhaps as ancient as ours, cannot be subjected to any military assault. Mr Prime Minister, it is needless to remind you that your Azad Party got the throne thanks to the Muslim support! And let us suppose we do support the US, then how, just how will we protect ourselves from Jihadi attacks? Will America run to defend us from Iranian Jihadis?"

Sunil Shah, the petroleum minister and a loyalist of the Azad Party was clearly irritated at Sunder Singh's outburst. Although the questions were directed to the Prime Minister, Shah took it upon himself to intrude. "Sunder Singhji, you are completely missing the point our Prime Minister is trying to make here. He is referring to a strategic alliance with US as far as the issue of Iran is concerned. We are not committing to any direct military involvement. Besides, can you not imagine the rewards that will come our way in return? We have a promise for a better deal on the issue of nuclear power. With such a deal we can come close to uninterrupted power supply in our states. That would consolidate your position for life in the northern states that you represent. If you are worried about the Muslims in your states, leave them to your Muslim colleagues. They should be able to convince the Muslim masses quite easily. There is no such thing as an 'Islamic brotherhood' on a global basis. If it were true, then Saudi Arabia wouldn't have supported the Americans on various occasions in the past."

Sunil Shah was otherwise a man of suspect credentials. His closeness to the Azad Family had got him a seat in the Prime Minister's cabinet. Though that may have been the case, his true power, which was in effect the frightening side of this man, was his connection with the Sankala clan, especially Indrajeet. It was rumoured in Delhi that Shah was Sanakala's man in the ministry and his mandate was to protect and promote the family business interests. It was Sankala who had set up Shah in the ministry. The fact about ministers serving as a front or a stooge of some or the other industrial bigwig was an absolute reality. These Ministers were the veritable mafia, though they masked themselves to be 'of the people, for the people and by the people'.

Sukumaran, the shrewd veteran from Kerala was quick to add his two-bit. "Yes, I absolutely agree with Mr Shah. I know these Muslims very well. My state has thirty three per cent Muslims and I manage them pretty well. After all, they are the ones who bring in all those petro-dollars from the Gulf. My state's economy survives on the money these people bring home. Let me tell you, these chaps have absolutely no emotional bond with the Arabs. They would be least bothered about what happens to Iran, as long as their cash flow stays unaltered. It is a mere 'master-servant' set up, nothing to speak of." Mr Sukumaran made his point loud and clear. Being power hungry, his eyes were set on the home ministry.

Ramesh Salunke remained a silent spectator through these cabinet proceedings. He was a wily character, enjoying unrivalled leadership all over western Maharashtra. This strong 'Maratha' politician had built his empire with the help of Maharashtra's sugar lobby. Over the last decade, taking advantage of economic liberalisation, he had been able to attract the following of three more lobbies: education, special economic zones and builders. Salunke's old friendship with Jagjeet Sankala was no secret. Jagjeet the great architect of the Pride Group of Industries, the ruthless face of the new-born Indian entrepreneurship, cherished the dreams he realised with the support of Salunke. Salunke used his charismatic 'son of the soil' image to acquire political patronage for Jagjeet. In return, Jagjeet guaranteed perpetual financial assistance to all of Salunke's political ventures. In parts of western Maharashtra, where Salunke was the 'uncrowned king', his reign of terror had no boundaries. Under the pretext of 'special economic zones', Salunke's henchmen annexed thousands of acres of fertile land, forcibly wherever necessary, from the poor farmers of the region. These farmers were promised 'just' compensation, morally appropriate payment for their lands, which these farmers, riddled with famine, drought and mounting debt would at times willingly, but most of the times unwillingly, accept out of compulsion. Just how 'just' the compensation really was could have very well been contested. What was disgusting was the aura of a 'messiah' credited to Salunke in all of rural Maharashtra!

The Prime Minister turned to Salunke for his opinion. Salunke was known to be a person who never gave direct answers; his reactions were always guarded, weighing all options available. The sly fox that he was, his response to the PM was, "Joining America in this war against Iran would be a strategic decision, one that would entail a good deal of thinking and analysis. I estimate that a special team should be constituted, which could assess the commercial aspects of this engagement and only then can an informed decision be taken." His answer came as no surprise to many in the cabinet. Knowing his connection with the Sankala camp, some of his colleagues viewed his suggestion with a lot of skepticism. The sarcastic looks cast at him did not bother him at all. On that note the cabinet meeting was inconclusively adjourned. The PM left the meeting to brief the party high command.

Nayan finished reading Janaki's story. Very excited, he was of the opinion that this story was more explosive than Shini's. The title, *The Indian Drama* was so apt, he thought. He was so impressed that he thought Janaki should chuck her magazine's editing assignment and work for a bigger cause. Her allusions to Ramesh Salunke's crafty, cunning persona reminded him of his visit to Bangaon. While studying at the university, on Sathe and Mohite's insistence, Nayan had visited various places in rural Maharashtra to experience the election fever there. At Bangaon, Salunke's constituency, he was addressing a public rally, championing women's rights, when all of a sudden his estranged daughter-in-law publicly confronted him. That was a big blow to Salunke. He was caught on the wrong foot.

Whether she had come on her own or was prompted by someone from the Opposition was not known. In the middle of his address, she cried out aloud, "Salunke, please stop all this nonsense. You are a predator in disguise and women like me are your prey. As your own daughter-in-law, I never got the kind of love, respect and affection you are showering these women with. Why are you fooling them? Shame on you! Tell them that all you care for is their votes." Salunke was taken aback. He regained his composure but faltered nevertheless. In the commotion that ensued, his daughter-in-law was quickly whisked away from the scene.

He continued his address and incorporated that little drama. "My friends, this is a true manifestation of how women power is wasted in India. I suggested to my dear daughter-in-law to contest this election in my stead. She refused, only to stage this attack in the hope of maligning my candidature. Quite obviously the dear child was misguided by my opponents. It is my misfortune and I alone have to deal with it and mend it as I hurt…" He took off his glasses and wiped the tears that welled up in his eyes. This gesture worked to his advantage and some of the activists roared in unison, "Salunkeji, don't worry, we are with you. You are our only leader and our saviour." Thunderous applause automatically followed. Salunke had successfully won the day.

What followed this episode was absolutely disgusting. He reconciled with his daughter-in-law—but how! Not only did he find her a seat in the Maharashtra assembly but also developed an illegitimate relationship with her. Salunke's son, for whom neither his father nor his wife had any respect, merely walked out on his unfaithful family to dwell in isolation and shame. People gossiped and then they gossiped no more. Time is always the healer. Janaki's story had a loud and clear message. If such leaders governed our country, why should those blazé ones like the Sankalas, who made no tall claims of being saints, be punished?

Nayan concluded that a gathering of his global friends was required to discuss all these issues. He abruptly lost his chain of thought as his mother entered the room. "Nayan, my dear son," she said, "Since the past couple of days it seems like you've been glued to the computer. No time to talk to mom?"

"No mom," he replied, "I've just been really busy attending to all the emails from my friends around the globe. I've also been engaged with all the preparations for our gathering."

"Oh yes, I know. Anyway, your dad and I are leaving for Matheran this weekend. I spent the whole of the last week caught up in the planning and preparations for the international conference for Sindhi women. I really do need a break. We hope to set out for Matheran this Sunday morning. That's of course if your dad doesn't get last minute urgent business calls." Having said that, his mother left the room.

It was yet another hectic Sunday for Dil Bhojani. He had just received a message from Indrajeet Sankala. An urgent meeting had been convened. It was to be held at the Sankala residence. The subject of the meeting was not revealed to him. He however sensed that the meeting was very critical. They had been careful not to disclose the matter to be discussed during the meeting. It had to be something serious, he thought to himself. He knew that Salunke had returned from his recent visit to Delhi that very Saturday.

Bhojani hurried over to the Sankala mansion on Marine Drive. It was one of those ultra-modern, multi-storied real estate extravaganzas—a twenty-first century palace. As he entered, he observed Salunke and Indrajeet sitting opposite each other. The two seemed to be engaged in an intense, animated conversation. Indrajeet appeared to be very excited. Salunke, who had just noticed Bhojani's presence in the room turned towards him and cheerfully greeted him. "Bhojani! welcome, welcome. You are perhaps the only person I greet so enthusiastically. I suppose there are two other great personalities I receive with similar enthusiasm—my bosses—the Prime minister and the High Command." Bhojani saluted Salunke in his typical style. This *salaam* had a specific significance. It was not a gesture for any and everybody. He reserved it only for the people he considered high and mighty.

Indrajeet quickly briefed Bhojani about the proceedings and the outcome of the cabinet meeting that Salunke and he had attended in Delhi. There had been discussions about India joining forces with the US in a strategic war against Iran. In return for India's backing, USA would agree to give India part of Iran's oil and also some projects in the rebuilding and post-war rehabilitation of Iran. The acquisition of oil and the reconstruction of a war-torn Iran presented great opportunities for the Pride Group. Salunke promised Indrajeet that he would have a big part to play.

There was only one real obstacle that presented itself before them, threatening to foil their designs—resistance from Opposition parties. Salunke made it clear to Indrajeet that he would have to use his networking skills to influence the Opposition and to subtly make them sway his way. Networking requires tact, talent and big bucks. Bhojani amply possessed all these. Networking was in fact quite routine for him. After Salunke took leave, Indrajeet and Bhojani had a discussion concerning funds required for such networking. They did a quick cost-benefit analysis. When the meeting was finally through and both men had shaken hands, Bhojani left the magnificent manor with a growing zeal within him. He had just been presented with an excellent and wholly irresistible opportunity to make money, and so much of it. Greed consumed him. It had always been his dream to create his own empire, a 'Bhojani group of industries'.

He reached his house shortly. He wasted no time and left almost immediately for Matheran with his wife. There was much reason to celebrate. He felt exceedingly optimistic. The trip, he was certain, would be wonderful. En route to Matheran, Bhojani spiritedly told his wife about the meeting. She, as always, listened patiently. As soon as they reached the bungalow, he fixed himself a Bloody Mary, his favourite cocktail, and sank into a comfortable armchair on the porch. His wife called for lunch from a restaurant they both liked. They spent a nice lazy afternoon in each other's company, and in the evening they set out for a long walk on the narrow and dusty roads of the hill station. They strolled together breathing in the crisp evening air and watching the sun set in the horizon. Bhojani had a good feeling about things. The bungalow where they were staying had always been lucky for him. All ventures that he had planned in that house, in the past, had been successful. He was convinced it would be no different this time around.

At some point between midnight and the wee hours of morning, Bhojani heard his wife crying out for help. He instantly rushed to the adjacent bathroom, only to find his wife slowly vomiting what appeared to be white foam. She was unable to say anything intelligible. Quite suddenly, before he could comprehend what was happening, he perceived from the corner of his eye a slight movement by the window. He reflexively turned his gaze towards the window. What he saw, struck him with horror. It was, he was certain, a cobra stealthily creeping out of the window. He was momentarily aware of the sudden and distinct rush of heat felt deep in the gut that comes from morbid fear. For a few seconds, he stood still, unable to decide what to do. Then suddenly he began to shout out for help.

But he soon realised that it was a futile exercise for they were in a bungalow isolated from the nearest colony. He then remembered that his chauffeur had been resting in the car somewhere on the outskirts of Matheran and his next impulse was to contact him and ask for assistance. Four wheelers are not permitted on the roads of the eco-conscious Matheran. Bhojani tried calling the chauffeur on his mobile, but much to his despair, there was no reply. He supposed that the phone might have been left on silent mode. He then dialled Charan, who fortunately answered on the first attempt. Bhojani frantically recounted the events that he had just witnessed. Charan urged his father to lose no time and rush his mother to the nearest doctor, reminding him that cobra bites were known to be fatal.

Bhojani, who was obviously deeply affected by the incident, felt as though logic had temporarily abandoned him. The panic had left him disoriented. He once again tried his chauffeur's number and was once again unsuccessful. He finally ran out of the house in desperation to look for aid. He had run half-a-kilometer before he reached the nearest house. He anxiously knocked several times on the front door until the owner appeared. He breathlessly informed the man about his predicament. The stranger quickly understood the gravity of the situation. It was not long before both men set out and hurried back to the bungalow. They hastily carried Mrs Bhojani to the taxi stand. "Oh God, please help me," cried Bhojani, trying hard to suppress his panic. He shook the taxi driver out of his slumber and instructed him to drive them to the nearest clinic. Unfortunately, when they reached, no doctor was available. Time was ticking away fast, too fast. He had to keep from falling to pieces. Finally Bhojani decided to drive down to a local hospital in Karjat, a nearby town. The resident doctor at the hospital carefully examined Mrs Bhojani. His expression was far from reassuring. The cobra was deadly and a good hour-and a-half had passed since the bite. The doctor gave her two injections. Her skin however, already appeared cyanotic. The poison was spreading rapidly. A half-hour passed. Bhojani sat pale and pathetic, too drained for tears as the doctor emerged. The doctor's statement was emotionless and cold, cold like the body of his deceased wife. The words resonated inside him. "I'm sorry Mr Bhojani, we could not save her." The sons, Charan, Pawan and Nayan, who had already left for Karjat, arrived at the hospital, only to find their mother's body laid out motionless on a stretcher. Nayan was completely devastated. He cried hysterically. He loved his mother dearly. She had always been very special to him. One could even say he was a mama's boy.

They arranged to have the funeral in Mumbai. As is the custom, for fourteen days, the family mourned the loss of Mrs Bhojani and performed all the traditional rituals. Indrajeet attended the funeral and participated briefly in the rituals organised on the fourteenth day. A few donations were made to charitable trusts, social organisations and temples. Charan announced that a charitable trust would be formed in his mother's name. The trust would also institute a special award for the 'best woman entrepreneur'. Ironic, especially since Mrs Bhojani never had any interest in her family's entrepreneurship.

On the fifteenth morning, Nayan walked up to his father's room. He paused and watched as his father sipped his morning coffee. Nayan had decided not to mince words. He walked into the room, intrepid and calm, and stood before his father. He said, "Dad, do you not think that the black cobra personifies the black business of the Bhojani family? Would you deny that mom ended up paying for your sins with her life? Now she won't even be there to watch as your dreams materialise. With Jagjeet's support, you amassed a truly vulgar quantum of wealth. But that was by exploiting the poor and innocent people of our country. What's so great about this ill-gotten wealth? Dad, even a prostitute earns. She does what she does because she has little choice and out of compulsion. But you and your people have needlessly and conveniently, and ever so shamelessly, turned our whole nation into a big filthy brothel. I am ashamed to say I am your son. You and my brothers are quite literally industry mafias, all collectively working for a Don whose name is Indrajeet. And you all work under an innocuous disguise which makes you so much more dangerous." Nayan had said enough. He did not bother to wait for any reply and stormed out of the room.

***

Chapter 2

Nayan packed the rucksack for his trip to Matheran conscious not to omit the laptop, a picture of his darling mother, and a copy of the holy Bhagavad Gita. He sent an sms to his dad informing him about his intended trip requesting that he be left alone there, in peace, for a few days. He recalled how harsh and inconsiderate he had been with his father the other day. Nayan wondered if his dad felt the same kind of emptiness as he did after his mother's sudden and cruel passing away. But then, his dad was chasing his big dream. Surely he would find his way out of this void and get preoccupied once again. In fact, Nayan wasn't even sure if his father had any space for his mother in his big empire-building scheme. All these years, she had been the typical Hindu traditional wife, the woman behind the man, duty-bound, only waiting to serve with devotion the man of her life, irrespective of whether he actually was worthy of so much dedication. Destiny has strange ways—the cobra finally liberated her from her marital obligations. Nayan recalled how at the funeral rites the Brahmin priest had pronounced – "The soul is imperishable, it cannot be destroyed. Only the body dies, the soul perpetuates by changing its body." The thought of 'perpetuity of the soul' however did not seem comforting enough to Nayan. The fact that he would never see his mother again hurt him so badly. This orphaned feeling was for real and the scar in his heart would forever remain fresh.

Sathe, meanwhile, had conveyed the tragic news of Nayan's mother's demise to all their friends. Coincidentally, Shini was to visit India for a story on a multi-billion dollar American investment advisory firm (found guilty of perpetrating a huge scam amounting to fifty billion dollars) at about the same time as the tragedy. The scam had vaporised the life savings of many average, middle class, honest and hard-working Americans. There was a cascading effect with a new American debacle of varying magnitude being reported almost every week. This triggered worry among the economic pundits, putting America's economic future on the anvil. Things began to look gloomier with each scam that surfaced. Shini had requested Janaki's assistance to investigate the 'Indian' connection related to her particular case. Janaki, ecstatic, happily accepted the proposition as it would give her a fantastic platform from where she could see her career leapfrog towards greater success. Janaki's story, *Indian Political Drama* was well received by Shini and her circle of friends. With great expectations, Janaki and Shini, both landed in Mumbai in the week that followed.

Nayan was 'soul searching' in Matheran, alone and away from people, with only the Holy Gita and his broken heart. After a lapse of about a week in his isolation at Matheran, he received an sms from his dad asking him to call back urgently. The concept of urgency or emergency was always reserved for Pawan or Charan, not Nayan. How strange then, he thought, as he dispassionately dialled his father's cell. The old man's voice betrayed sadness and remorse.

"Nayan, my son, how are you feeling now? Your silence worries me. I can understand your anger—you being closest to your mother. But please try and understand my position."

"Dad, please come to the point. In your Bible, time is invaluable; it's not like you to make small talk. Please say what you want to say."

"That's real sarcastic Nayan. That is very harsh. It's not only about you. I too am depressed. I always thought I had the gumption in me to do all I wanted. But your mother's death has shaken me totally. I feel traumatised."

"So that's it! It has always been about you—your confidence, your arrogance, your power that mattered. It's the egotistic you. There is no place for anyone else in your life, least of all mom. It is not mom's death that is distressing you. Just tell me the true reason for your call; no point in cosmetic rephrasing. Come, please disclose your real agenda."

"Ok. Let's talk straight. Nayan, your brothers wish to know about your level of involvement in our business. They fear that you might have chosen a different career path, and hence they seek clarity."

"But dad, tell me, why do they feel so?"

"Son, you have been in Matheran for an entire week now, away from your work. And besides, a true entrepreneur, a Karma Yogi doesn't take a long leave of absence whatever the nature of hurt or distraction -- he bounces back to work. Nayan, my boy, don't you think your holidays are over and it's time you are back at work?"

"Stop it! Who says I am on holiday here? It's you who got mom here for a holiday and that's the reason I lost her … and all of yours and the Pride Group's wealth put together could not save her."

"Nayan, Nayan, calm down, and let us focus only on your decision. No point in bringing in other things. At the outset, I only wish to caution you against prejudices you hold against me, your brothers and the Pride Group in general. Take for instance the bungalow where you presently are living – it is a result of my association with the Pride Group. The other day you choked me with your moralising and some philosophical garbage where you equated my business with prostitution! Sorry for being blunt son but it is time you squashed your baseless prejudices. An open mind is always the healthier option, as also understanding other peoples' points of view."

"Why? For one, I am quite relieved dad that you actually are aware of my prejudices, and secondly, by the fact that you wish to clear them. But what a price I paid for all this? My mom's death! In any case, I am certain you cannot erase my prejudices as you call them. They are my opinions, and mind you they are based on facts and experiences, not on imagined notions, and therefore you can't just expunge and wipe them out."

"Nayan, please listen to me. Do you or don't you know Mr Avdhut Deshpande, the corporate relations head of the Pride Group?"

'Who wouldn't know a trickster, a con artist, a go-between like that, dad? Someone you'd call a 'fixer'?"

"Now this is what your problem is Nayan. It ultimately doesn't matter what you call him. Philosophically, we are all 'fixers'—fixing, arranging—it is nothing but networking!"

"Dad, let's not mix philosophy and business. It is preposterous. It is Deshpande we are talking about."

"Nayan, if you agree, I shall be more than happy to 'fix' a meeting between you and Avdhut. You would be surprised, yes, but he is known to be a staunch member of the Hindu Samiti. He too, like you, has attended the Samiti's shakhas in his childhood. Incidentally he headed the Mumbai branch of the Samiti's student wing and later went on to join the Nationalist Hindu Party. He would be happy to discuss with you, given your common backgrounds and the culture that you both have been exposed to at the Samiti. As a matter of fact, I have already spoken to him about you and he's looking forward to meeting you."

"Uh hum! Why ask me then since you have already 'fixed' it? Drop the pretenses dad! I know you are not doing it out of any special concern for me. But fine, I shall meet him nonetheless and on my terms."

"Granted son! You name your conditions and I'll satisfy them," said Bhojani, all excited.

"I shall meet him along with some of my friends. I'd expect him to tell us the complete truth without the slightest fabrication. He should not withhold, formulate or twist facts. The truth is all I need to get from him. And mind you, primarily he needs to give us enough time, all the time we need to get clear-cut answers, to our satisfaction."

"Sure! by all means. I don't see any problem there. Deshpande has all the time in the world. He used to be a close associate of Jagjeet, but now he looks after the educational trust set up by the Sankala family. He is damn nice chap and I am sure you will have some fruitful conversations with him. When should I arrange your meeting with him then? Nayan, I can't tell you how much I am looking forward to the day when you will join our business, and as God is my witness, I hope that day arrives asap. My plea to you is to let go of the shackles that are binding you. Give a chance to pure entrepreneurship." Bhojani sounded emotional.

"Great! Why not meet this Sunday? My friends and I could meet him here, in Matheran. A couple of days wouldn't harm anyone and should be good enough to have fruitful, uninterrupted discussions. Besides, philosophy vis-à-vis prejudices, indeed requires an environment of meditation and peace, wouldn't you agree?"

"I shall ignore the touch of sarcasm only because I have hope. I am quite confident that Deshpande will allay all your fears and misconceptions, at least to a great extent. I understand that things such as these don't change overnight, but even if the process kicks-off in the right direction, I would be very happy. Good luck to you my son. I will make sure that Avdhut reaches Matheran on Sunday. Let us hope for the best."

"Yes dad. Let's hope for the best. I am extremely eager to meet 'The Avdhut Deshpande', old and trusted associate of 'The Great Jagjeet Sankala'."

On that note the conversation came to an end. Nayan spoke to his friends Sathe, Janaki and Shini. All three accepted his invitation of coming to Matheran to meet Deshpande who was known as Jagjeet Sankala's very close associate. Such an opportunity was not to be passed over and Shini agreed to even extend her stay in India for this. The Pride Group was a well known entity internationally. The prospect of getting to know the story of the amazing financial success achieved by a son of a modest mine worker who built an industrial empire in one single generation, and that too with inputs from his very close associate and confidant, was too hot to be missed. Deshpande had stood by Jagjeet through thick and thin, through good days and bad ones and obviously had first hand information on the Group's meteoric rise. Shini was of the opinion that they discreetly record all their discussions with Deshpande without the latter's knowledge. This meant that Bhojani, Nayan's father too was to be kept in the dark. Nayan was initially not quite comfortable with the idea, but however reluctantly agreed to do so on the condition that the recordings wouldn't be used for any purpose without his knowledge and consent.

When Pawan and Charan learnt about Deshpande's meeting with Nayan and his group of friends, they were extremely annoyed. They feared the meeting could prove to be counter-productive. However, they trusted their father's expertise in matters such as these and went along with the plan of wily old Bhojani. If Deshpande were to succeed in bringing over Nayan to their side, it would mean a great bonanza for the Bhojani family. If the youngest hunter would rejoin the pack, what a formidable team of wild predators the Bhojani family would make! The Bhojani-Empire-dream would then come closer to reality. So all hopes and expectations were pinned on the skills of Avdhut Deshpande.

Janaki, Shini and Sathe reached Matheran late in the afternoon on the eve of the meeting which was scheduled for Sunday. Together they discussed and decided on what the agenda of their discussions would be. Janaki's miniature, yet very powerful microphone, generally used by journalists while on sting operations, was also thoroughly checked before putting it to an acid test the next day. They prepared themselves for their meeting with the man whom they hoped, was to divulge sensational information about the Pride Group. Later in the evening they went for refreshing walk around the many natural trails that Matheran has to offer. They slept early to be rested for their meeting. They wanted to make the most of it.

Avdhut Deshpande, as scheduled, reached Matheran at 10am, the next morning. He was a tall, fair man with an aura of intelligence and a phenomenal alacrity of mind. His entire persona was befitting of an astute corporate executive of international standing. Shini sensed a slight stoop in his bearing, which Sathe joked about as being the burden of the sins that he had been carrying all through his years with the Pride Group. After an exchange of the initial courtesies they settled down to a good breakfast, where Deshpande probed into the backgrounds of the youngsters before him. Hiding their actual agenda, Nayan and friends told him that they were all MBA students pursuing their respective programs at different universities. Contrary to their expectations, Deshpande came across as a warm, affable and a jolly old man, one with whom they could readily connect.

"Friends—that's what I would like to assume we would be at the end of our meeting. Nayan, I think I can understand your apprehensions. To be blunt, I think you fear I am here to 'brainwash' you and manipulate you into become a 'thoroughbred-Bhojani', given that I am here under your father's instructions. However, that is not what I shall do." Having said that, he sat back, awaiting the reaction from the youngsters. Nayan stared at the old man wondering whether his intentions were as honourable as he had projected them to be. Deshpande gauged it all. "Nayan," he said, "I know about your ideologies. Believe me; I am here for simple and honest discussions."

"Uncle, that sounds encouraging and will surely make things easier for all of us. It will also make me very happy. But…"

Deshpande interrupted Nayan and added, "Nayan, please be frank. I can almost imagine your next question. How can you trust me, you don't even know me."

"No uncle, it is not a question of trust or the lack of it. What we have here is a sense of purpose. You are on an assignment, a designated one where your job is to brainwash and convert my ideologies to match those of my clan – the Bhojanis."

"Nayan, it wouldn't be wrong of you to say so under the circumstances. But you see, I am seventy-five now. I've come a long way, and now I am at a point in life where there is no more winning or losing! I am sure you must be thinking, rather believing that mine is a story of laurels and success all of my life. Any why not? Logically you may infer so – this man Deshpande, having worked at such close quarters with none other than the big man, the late Jagjeet himself, and at the helm of Pride Group – could he ever have known failure? No, it seems logical he wouldn't. But that's not true. Likewise, if you take the story of Jagjeet, a mineworker's son turning from rags-to-riches, transforming into a mega-industrialist in just one lifetime – that story too defies logic!"

Deshpande rambled on. "So I give the impression of always winning eh? I thought it too. But fate—fate is a leveller. I'll give you an analogy in cricketing terms. My story is like that of a fast bowler taking the most prestigious wicket with a sparkling performance. As he sores up to the sky in gleeful conquest the umpire calls it a no-ball. Yeah, my dear friends, this is what happened to me. I leapt for joy and joy was no more." His face cringed, his eyes closed and his voice cracked as he went on. "Albeit late in life, around the age of forty-two, I was blessed with my only son. My Aakash grew to be a tall, strapping handsome fellow. Got his MBA from Stanford …"

Shini interjected with, "An MBA from Stanford! It translates pretty much like: your-life's-made-forever! 'Twas my dream too." Affectionately looking at Shini, Deshpande went on to say that his dear Aakash had fallen in love with an American girl.

Nayan interrupted, "An American Indian?"

"No, no – a white American," Deshpande replied. Nayan and Shini had a quick exchange of glances. The old man went on in a trance, "White or black or brown makes no difference. Did we ever think of a black American president? It happened, it was ordained! My Aakash married at twenty-eight, left for a honeymoon in the city of romance, Paris, and then decided to drive up to Manchester to see a friend before returning to US. Don't know much more than the fact that he had a head-on collision with a trucker and he was killed on the spot." His face contorted in pain as he continued, "Poor Helena miraculously survived the crash and came to Mumbai with the mortal remains of my son for his funeral. She stayed with us for three months and was ready to live with us, her new shattered family, forever. She declared she did not wish to remarry. But it would have been unfair, so my wife and I, we insisted she went back to the US where she belonged." Deshpande opened his eyes and his gaze fell on Shini. The youngsters were sitting numb, mouths-open, moved by the poignant story of the old man. Shini, fighting back tears, excused herself to help serve water to everyone.

"It wasn't really a question of an American girl or an Indian one. For anyone to come to a decision of abandoning the pleasures of life on losing her spouse, to devote her life to his aging parents, only speaks volumes of her genuine love for her young dead husband. She loved my son so intensely that his memories alone would be the staff, the force to guide her through the rest of her life! Actually this is what power is—this is control and this is ultimate gumption. And what did I do all my life? I gained power and wealth. Wealth through power and power through wealth." Saying this Deshpande excused himself and rushed to the confines of the toilet, when he could let tears of sorrow roll down his cheeks in private. Nayan felt disturbed as he turned to his teammates and said, "Hey guys, don't you think it wrong to misguide Deshpande about our true identity and intent for the meeting?" Janaki, with all her caution, insisted it was perhaps yet too soon. "Let's not plunge into it. We'll need some more time to gauge him and then ... we can always apologise and reveal ourselves later. If he is truly the nice person he portrays, he'll understand us."

Deshpande was back from the toilet, sheepishly excusing his abrupt departure as an old age problem.

"Children, I confess, I started contemplating life per se only when I lost Aakash. Till then, I was invincible, amassing wealth. Now the world is empty, so empty, with my son gone. My wife too is so devastated, she speaks only in prayer. She spends her entire time reading the *Bhagavatam*, I guess to seek solace.

"So Nayan, what is your take on life? All that I deemed correct suddenly came to a naught. My own destiny had to teach me! Hurtful, I say painful, but truly the baggage of a corrupt, ruthless life is too heavy a burden to bear. Try hard as you may to dump it, Mother Nature has its amazing ways of making you carry it." This overt outspokenness astounded the youngsters who weren't ready for it. Of course, genetics plays a role, and so Nayan, with his father's guile in his blood, could not readily believe Deshpande.

"Allow me to narrate my bit of the story about Jagjeet Sankala—how I came into his life and fitted in. That's what you are curious to know, and as I tell you my part, you'll be in a position to place things in proper perspective. My father was a staunch follower and an active member of the Hindu Samiti. As you must be aware, the Samiti has many facets such as religion, culture, education, tribal development, cooperation, social publications etc. Its recent most branch or wing is political in nature, called the Nationalist Hindu Party (NHP).

"Upon completing my engineering degree, my father suggested I devote five years as a full-time activist, participating in building a strong Hindu nation. Having conducted many cultural assignments during my college days, I could readily turn into a full-time activist in charge of growing and developing the student's wing of the Samiti. My leadership qualities were so evident that the Samiti gave me the challenging task of supervising the activities of the newly established

NHP, which was groomed to become the formidable opposition to the Azad party. The communists failed and were out of the fray. And the Shoor party remained a regional group of local politicians. On the other hand, NHP was set to become a major national party."

"But uncle, the Hindu Samiti was never into politics. Why then was NHP created?" Sathe asked.

"Building up a strong Hindu nation would require our presence in power. It dawned on us that the political processes of spreading Hinduism were quintessential. If you wielded political power, you could perform miracles, certainly in a country like India."

Deshpande looked for Shini's reaction and she promptly obliged with, "No uncle, not just for India. The concept holds good for any country. In the US too, politics is a potent profession."

"Coming back to the NHP—we did win a few local and regional elections. But our presence at the centre in Delhi was negligible. There the Azad Party marched on exploiting Hindu innocence, fomenting feelings of insecurity among the Muslims and instigating an identity crisis of the Dalits."

"But uncle weren't there a few Hindu industrialist giants like the Guptas, Mehtas, Karlas etc. Couldn't they support your party financially?" Nayan questioned.

"See, the thing is they supported our religious activities. However, they were not confident of us coming to power. So who'd bet on a losing horse? Not an industrialist, of course. By choice, the business community always remains closer to those in power." Deshpande paused and continued, "Most ministers in Maharashtra were from one single community – the high-caste Marathas. Nothing new, for caste-based politics is common in all states other than Maharashtra too. However, here, a Brahmin like me had no place in politics. When we came to power in Maharashtra, we came in jointly with the Shoor party. Our trump card was 'Hinduism'. My team and I put in all the hard work but did not get any recognition. My activists anticipated that I would be made minister. That did not happen because I was a Brahmin. The Hindu Samiti was of the opinion that I should not enjoy power directly or indirectly. We were only supposed to promote heroes, put them at the helm and not savour an iota of power ourselves.

"Initially this system worked well; that of promoting leaders and not directly or indirectly wielding power. Nonetheless, gradually 'power' started stimulating the minds of innocent activists too. Even those who were ideologically robust started succumbing and surrendering to the greed of power. Here Lord Acton's dictum comes to mind—*'Power tends to corrupt and Absolute Power corrupts absolutely'*. Standing in the capacity of a political supervisor, I was obliged to render favours, however petty, for the activists of the Hindu Samiti. The Shoor party political activists were already on track exploiting their bit of power in the partnership. The ministers representing them distributed licenses, memberships of powerful committees, subsidies etc. to their political activists and supporters. With the Shoor party pursuing such methods, the NHP's ministers obviously came under tremendous pressure to follow their footsteps. In this way, even the innocent activists of NHP gradually transformed, shed off their purity, put aside ideological restrictions and got into a power-crazed tempo." Deshpande continued, "The youth of NHP were so possessed with this power frenzy that they started ridiculing the old ideologues of the Hindu Samiti. A Brahmin like me felt sidetracked. As a matter of fact, many Brahmin activists reconciled to the new situation and joined the bandwagon of power brokers. These activists now became 'systemic agents'. They got free entry to the power corridors. Thus a chain of political entrepreneurship was created." Deshpande sipped his glass of water.

The butler, at this opportune moment, served hot puris and pakodas. Deshpande went on, "I felt humiliated by my junior colleagues who were in power. They evidently enjoyed more clout than those innocent activists, since they were in a position to do them a variety of small favours. I felt silly; I felt compromised because on one hand I knew the ropes, I worked hard, but the credit went elsewhere. I was thus forced to change myself. I too started along that stratum, currying favours for some of the senior activists of the Hindu Samiti. In this way, I started ingratiating myself to that class of people. NHP's ministers then started inviting me for their close-circle discussions. It was almost a euphoric feeling! By then I could safely tell that the NHP and Shoor party were deeply involved in a money-making racket with much higher stakes."

"But uncle, why then did the Hindu Samiti not object to the growing corruption?" Sathe asked.

"The Samiti did try to put a tab on it on several occasions. But each time the customary reply was: 'politics requires money, lots of it; hence money-making assignments are unavoidable!' Most senior activists of the Samiti did not understand much about politics and economics. They merely knew how to conduct social reforms and run social organisations. Politics was never their cup of tea. Thus NHP, though an off-shoot so to say of the Samiti, could not conduct itself with the Samiti ethics, and so gradually set out to ape the Azad party and its ethos of corruption. Assignments, commission, elections, big projects funded by international institutions etc. became the core business for the members of NHP. Every young activist of the Samiti aspiring to become a politician learnt to join the 'students' wing and subsequently sought direct entry to the NHP!" Deshpande reflected.

"Simply a-m-a-z-ing! In the US, we think only Americans know how to network and engage people. We should stand corrected for in networking the Indians beat us hollow," Shini said.

"You are quite right Shini; this political networking here surpasses even our business networking. My dad always articulates that politics is a big business. He goes a step further calling it political entrepreneurship," responded Nayan.

Deshpande picked up from there saying, "So ... with the growing Maratha influence in my own political party, I was getting restless. On several occasions, I was the subject of taunts. I was mocked and called a coward, vegetarian, toothless Brahmin. Gosh, my blood boiled and how! The problem was that there weren't many ambitious Brahmin politicians in NHP. Senior Brahmin activists of the Hindu Samiti were gradually losing their shine. The socio-political environment of India was fast changing. In the name of what they called 'inclusive politics', every damn caste was entertained by the NHP. Only the Brahmins were seriously neglected. As far as the Hindu Samiti was concerned, power had to be retained at any cost!" Though everyone had became more or less comfortable with the old man, a certain amount of restraint was maintained.

"In one of the meetings of the core members of NHP, Jagjeet Sankala, a budding industrialist was invited. The state elections were drawing close and the party needed a huge flow of funds. Five years in power had translated into an abundance of 'money-making' opportunities. How much of those earnings really got deposited in the party's treasury was a big question though. Jagjeet attended that meeting with Bhojani, Nayan's father. That was our initiation into the corridors of power. It was also about the same time that I was exposed to Jagjeet's astute personality. It was impressive when you actually saw the powerful ministers riveted, listening to Jagjeet, patiently and politely. One Maratha minister, known for his arrogance, was seated next to Jagjeet trying to grab his attention and portray himself as a close associate of the Sankala family! It was quite a great drama.

"Sankala and Bhojani presented some financing plan. At the end of the meeting, Jagjeet brazenly made a nasty remark on the political leadership. 'Most of you guys, supposedly the 'sons of soil'—what have you in effect done for your community? Show me? Look at my community and my village and the tremendous work we have done without the backing of any political power! Allow us to manage the state for a year or so and see how the Pride Group will turn the tide and win back the original pride that belonged to the state.' The ministers swallowed this with a half-hearted, docile laugh. What else could they do anyway when Jagjeet was to be their fund raiser? They needed his resources to win the next elections. That was the day Jagjeet turned into a hero for me, the solid fellow who could thrash ten opponents single-handedly and squash them! My decision was made then. He was the man whom I'd join.

"I arranged to meet him, offered my candidature humbly yet convincingly, that I was the right man for him and left the rest in the hands of God. Jagjeet, known for his networking, had already learnt about my potential. He was quick to discern that of all the politicians around him I would be the most loyal and trusted. My close association with the Hindu Samiti was perceived as an added advantage. Jagjeet knew how to seek out useful people. He strongly believed in paying the right price for such people. The day I joined him as his PRO, my title alone commanded respect, amusingly even from those arrogant, silly ministers. After all, I was Pride Group's PRO –a persona with many sensitive assignments to conduct! Gradually, I became Jagjeet's right hand man.

"Steadily, under him, I learnt the politics of entrepreneurship. By joining him, I got the opportunity to take my personal revenge on many. The Maratha lobby stopped calling me names like the 'weak coward Brahmin'. The senior activists of the Hindu Samiti suddenly started calling me 'Avdhutji', the suffix 'ji' was added after my name. Bureaucrats from various ministries started following me like 'loyal dogs' and the activists of the NHP Students Council started respecting me as Jagjeet's indispensable man. I realised the importance of being a 'money-spinner'. For that you need some power. Being powerless could be disastrous. I was up and down the streets of Mumbai, Delhi, Kolkata, Pune, Chennai, Ahmadabad and many other important cities. Voila! Avdhut Deshpande called the shots because he was 'boss'. Interestingly there came a transformation in my language as well. When you change culturally, you change totally."

"Uncle, is that true? Did your language really alter? I was of the opinion that language serves as a man's ultimate identity – and it never changes," Sathe exclaimed.

"Yes and no. I agree with you but partially. My language somehow became more offensive. Progressively, I used abusive, foul, tainted language. Asshole, son-of-a-bitch, sister-fucker were words on the tip of my tongue! Sorry to offend you with such profanities, but power consumes you, mesmerises you to a point where you see no need to control yourself. Pushed to prove my mettle and in a bid to conceal my traditional Brahmin weakness, I turned non-vegetarian. Needless to say, wine was the next step. Those despicable ministers and politicians started calling me Avdhut *bhau*. *Bhau*, was meant to imply a mastermind, a Mafioso, or a leader of the gang. I learnt one important thing—that most politicians are cowards at heart. They try to project themselves as intelligent and smart. You could at best call them street-smart. That's why I grew to admire Jagjeet. He wasn't like that bunch full of second-raters. He was the tiger—a shrewd, alert, ruthless hunter, an epitome of intelligence, a networker of unparalleled skills."

"He was a blood-sucker, a parasite that thrived on innocent masses!" Nayan squirmed with agitation. Deshpande stared at Nayan with a straight face and then smiled with a tinge of irony. "Yes, yes indeed, but I realised that too late. And it cost me dear. Jagjeet, all of his Pride Group and his political puppets exploited our country with all the cunning they could muster, shamelessly and ruthlessly."

"Yet, you accepted my father's request to come here and brainwash me? My father is very much a member of Jagjeet's entourage," Nayan said.

"Son, I have told you this once, and I shall reiterate the fact, that I accepted your father's request only to use it as a platform to lessen my own burden. I wanted to present to you the picture closest to truth as I understood it. Trust me this is how the story goes. You are indeed free to arrive at your conclusion."

"Nayan, don't rush him. Give the man a chance. Let him complete his story. At least he could get himself to speak to us so overtly about his life and times with Jagjeet. His account appears quite plausible," Janaki hastened to add, not missing the man, nor the moment.

"The business of Pride Group is spread over many states in India and abroad. In a particular state where the group doesn't have political clout in the government, too bad, the group will allign with the Opposition to espouse its cause. So what ideology, what manifesto, and what rubbish allegiance to parties are we talking about? Party is only a name, x, y or z. The package is different, the content the same."

"What does that mean uncle?" asked Sathe.

"For eg, if we have some work in Karnataka where the ruling party is the Azad party, all we have to do is point out our requirements to the ruling NHP in Maharashtra to find a way politically. No sweat! NHP, that is in Opposition in Karnataka will appoint the agent, the bureaucrat who will do the needful. In fact, they are many rogue bureaucrats that run these sort of operations. Nobody crosses them. They make it or break it for your corporate house. Even powerful ministers steer clear of their kind." Deshpande admonished.

He went to the toilet. Janaki whispered, "Guys, let us just reveal our true identity to the old man. He is so open with us. Don't you realise what we are doing is pure deception? We've got to tell him who we are and what we are doing professionally."

"No Janaki, do not let your emotions sway you. I know how the members of Pride Group excel at laying traps … they are quite the masters of the art. Let us wait for an appropriate moment. You see, by virtue of the fact that he happened to be a close associate of my dad, I had this kind of reverence for him. However, now I am learning to respect him much more after appreciating his genuine frankness. But please, let's wait for some more time," Nayan appealed.

Deshpande returned to the room and continued.

"Where do I start? Jagjeet's father, Chimanbhai, was an illiterate villager from the Maharashtra – Goa border. His forefathers came from north of India in search of occupation and lodging and they settled on this border. Chimanbhai eventually moved out of this village and sought work at an iron-ore mine, south of Goa. The old man worked very hard for a paltry remuneration. A third of his salary was grabbed away by the mine's union leader. Chimanbhai had four daughters and one son by the name Jagjeet. Obviously, with his meagre income he couldn't afford any education for his daughters even if he had wanted to, but for Jagjeet, his male heir, he made arrangements for him to attend school. What you wish often does not culminate, just like what is preordained never changes! Jagjeet was never happy or comfortable with the formal way of learning. He somehow managed to finish his primary schooling. He was very gutsy right from his childhood, and was crooked too! Ruthless as he was, even at a tender age, he wouldn't flinch to harm others for his own petty gains. He was unfeeling; he had no heart, no emotions, no care or thought for anyone other than himself. He didn't believe in emotional relationships. For him, money was everything. On his giving up schooling, his father set up a job for him in a tea stall just outside the precincts of the mine. Jagjeet made extra money by selling unaccounted cups of tea to the mine workers. He was indeed very proud of his manipulative mind.

"At the age of fifteen, he went to Australia with a group of young workers. They all managed their entry into Australia illegally. In quite the same manner, they got jobs in one of the Australian mines. The white supervisors habitually humiliated the young Indians. Young Jagjeet was a rebel every step of the way. One day, his supervisor asked him to clean-up the toilet. Jagjeet was outraged and he slapped the white, tall, well-built supervisor. Jagjeet was short, weak and black. Workers were stunned to see him slapping his master. He was imprisoned for a month and subsequently deported to India. He returned to India brimming with ideas. He had the big Australian mines experience, ideas of how they were managed with advanced technology in contrast to the Goan mines which were very small and ill-managed.

"He abruptly left for Orissa to join an iron-ore mine there after briefly announcing his plan to his dad. Jagjeet's tact, cunning, and acumen in the field impressed his boss. His boss was a thorough gentleman. He trusted Jagjeet and shared with him all his technical skills and know-how. One ill-fated Sunday, the boss died in an accident. Not much was known about this accident. It was only later that Jagjeet confessed how he had strategically planned that accident! He perhaps narrated it to instill fear in us. That was his technique, a clear message – *you serve me, my purpose, efficiently, and you are safe. You cease to be of use to me, or worse still, become a hindrance and you'd simply be eliminated. The ropes are in my fist to pull!*"

"How brazen, this is simply ghastly. The rascal learns all the tricks of the trade and then kills his trusting, innocent superior once the purpose is served," Janaki spat out with indignation.

"Yes, his philosophy was very clear-cut. Any threat or disturbance in the way of his personal growth had to be obliterated. After that so called accident, as per his diabolical designs, Jagjeet was promoted to the position of his boss. He was just twenty years old at that time. There started his nefarious journey of becoming Jagjeetji Sankala from mere Jagjeet! He was aware of the connection between the union leader and the local mafia there. The Mafioso was none other than the brother-in-law of a very powerful politician. Jagjeet realised that the union leader was going to be his ladder to success. He started working for this man who realised that Jagjeet was made of different stuff. A lot of the mafia money was lent to the poor workers at phenomenal rate of interest. This lending business was managed by the union leader. Jagjeet selected his role and started working as a recovery agent. He improved recoveries very fast. Obviously the mafia noticed him, and impressed by his performance gave him bigger assignments. The next big assignment was that of recovering and managing the loans given to the small mine owners. Let's not forget there were many small mines in Orissa owned by the 'sons of soil'. These small miners used to live a lavish life. However, they carelessly never tallied their revenue with their expenses and therefore foolishly borrowed heavily. Banks being rigid, the only easy source of borrowing was from the mafia."

"But uncle, what was the source of the mafia money?" Sathe asked naively.

"The mafia always has many sources. The main source here was the politician's brother-in-law. The second important source was the business of running a few hundred brothels. Many mine workers, staying away from their families, were the natural customers for these brothels. Drug trafficking was the support business. Good money was also made in the lending business," Deshpande explained.

"So you mean to say that it was a sort of self-supported local economy. Capital moved around in the hands of those few nasty people?" Shini questioned.

"Yes, a cent per cent self-operated economy based on total exploitation of the innocent workers and their helpless families. This new assignment opened the doors of destiny for Jagjeet. This was the turning point in his life. Of course, he was ready and hungry for the big game," said Deshpande.

"What about Jagjeet's marriage and family?" urged Janaki.

"He married a little late. That too is an interesting story in itself. For a long time the guy kept himself sexually satisfied skipping from one brothel to another. As expected, to him sex was not an emotional exercise. It was physical, a natural need. He was blasé about it, as he bluntly expostulated that sex and emotions, never combined. No relationship was worthy of emotion and therefore every relationship was mechanical, structured, calculated. So for Jagjeet, a prostitute was just a machine, a means to an end," Deshpande explained at length.

But Janaki went on, "But what happened to his marital relationship? How did he manage his relations with his wife?"

"I'll come to your question very soon. I am unfolding a complete character called 'Jagjeet' step by step," Deshpande assured.

Everybody exchanged glances.

As if every sentence was to be challenged Janaki went on, "But uncle, Jagjeet was so intelligent at the mere age of twenty! Isn't it?"

"Yes, a version of perverted, destructive intelligence!" Deshpande groaned closing his eyes for a few seconds. "Let me come back to his story. He performed well in his new role as the close associate. On a few occasions, he met the mafia's politician brother-in-law too. Craftily the bloke never spoke about the politicians. Perhaps, he was eyeing that post for himself as a long term goal, so why reveal the itsy-bitsy details prematurely. The mafia empowered him further and allowed him to make deals with the small mine owners. The politician's black money was invested in these deals. These were not formally recorded with any government authority. And of course, Jagjeet made good earnings for himself out of these deals. He used the mafia's tool: terror, and the politician's clout to regularise bogus deals. The bugger was ruthless with mounds of gumption. His risk-taking ability was limitless. He always pushed us to take risks and wind up several sizes bigger. In just two of his deals he managed to transfer the ownership of two small mines to his name! He made documentary proof of his domicile in Orissa. The spirit of corruption underlining the complete government machinery made the likes of Jagjeet blossom. One particular ruse he was quick to learn was that every cadre, every level in the government setup had to be saluted and respected, right from the peon to the politician himself. This he did diligently to reap the ultimate harvest. Amazing foresight!"

"But uncle, he got two mines transferred in his name. Was that acceptable to the politician?" Nayan asked.

"Yeah! That's exactly what I am telling you. He took that risk. He had a plan ready in his mind – all the pieces of the puzzle in position. He brought a few of the mine owners together and took their delegation to the leader of the Opposition. He then bitched about the heinous activities of the mafia and his politician brother-in-law. He went along and promised the Opposition leader financial support from the mine owners at election time. The master stroke of course was the vote bank of mining workers."

Deshpande continued, "The mine owners engaged private commandoes for his protection. Such a big risk it was! The next regional elections of the eastern districts were won by the Opposition. Jagjeet was a formidable player. With one stroke he fell many an oak. He diluted the dominance of the Communist party by transferring the vote bank to the Opposition. He improved the level of confidence put in him by the mine owners. Almost half of were were tribal leaders who had never cast their eyes beyond their native Orissa. And Jagjeet had the weapon; he used to mesmerise them with tales of his childhood, fact or fiction, nobody would dare check. Knowing that the new government wished to make a statement, do something new, something different, our man Jagjeet suggested to the minister of steel industry to invest in a steel factory on a cooperative basis. Things were stirring, things were happening, and the small mine owners were ready to become shareholders in this new cooperative venture. They were assured a good price for their iron-ore. Steel was a very lucrative business not likely to fail. It being a cooperative venture, the government agreed to finance as much as twenty-five per cent of the total capital required. The minister became chairman of this new factory, and Jagjeet, the man of the hour, became the director! It was Jagjeet's baby, and he was in full control, as the minister got busier in his own line of politics.

"Jagjeet never looked back. He grew rapidly. Calculating and smart, he did his homework properly. He visited a few select steel factories to understand the ropes of the business. Very strategically, he poached some brilliant managers from the government owned steel factories and offered them bigger, more lucrative positions. The factory was built on the east coast. This suited him as he could now get iron-ore from Goa too. In fact, knowing Jagjeet, he must have master-minded this set up. Marine transport was and is cheap. By getting ore from Goa and south Maharashtra, he re-established his links with the mine owners of western India. Jagjeet Sankala thus became a formidable name—a force to reckon with!" Deshpande stopped as the youngsters whispered in awe.

"Nayan, umh ! How shall I put it? I am definitely not swinging but all this has lessened my bitterness towards that colossus Jagjeet. What a strategist, a bloody intelligent courageous rapscallion!" Janaki shook them all with her statement.

"Are you out of your mind? He is no rapscallion—he's a disgusting giant rogue—nothing short of that. Janaki! I thought you had more sense. How can you be swayed by evil even if it happens to be an intelligent one? Don't you get it—even Ravana, the demon from Ramayana, was a very intelligent brute. For that matter, Hitler was once hailed as a hero and strategist. Janaki, can't you tell the difference?" Sathe implored.

"Yup, but all said and done, there is no denying Jagjeet's unique personality and calibre. It's his gall, his bluff, his profound sharpness, and finally his thirst for the kill, his hunger for more..."Janaki maintained as if mesmerised.

Deshpande continued, "An old Goan mine-owner approached Jagjeet for managing his three mines in Goa. He was a tribal leader. He knew about Jagjeet's conquest in Orissa, especially his efforts in building the cooperative steel factory with assistance from the tribal mine-owners. For Jagjeet, this Goan offer was a golden opportunity. He had always dreamt of a chance to go to the west coast and try his luck.

"Soon after he started managing the Goan mines, the inevitable happened—the clichéd, the predictable, and the to-be-anticipated!

He fell in love with the mine owner's daughter and went ahead and married her. She was the only child of her parents. He was lucky. He got three mines, two big bungalows on the banks of rivers Mandavi and Zuari, and of course a status among the tribal leaders of Goa, north Karnataka and south Maharashtra. He floated his first corporate entity by the name 'Pride Mining Corporation'. He created a corporate office in Mumbai and a branch office in Panjim. For speedy growth, he wasted no time in contacting a Maratha politician from western Maharashtra."

"Wasn't he Ramesh Salunke, uncle? Tell me I am right..." Nayan interrupted impatiently.

"Yes, my son. Ramesh Salunke became Jagjeet's close associate, business partner and what not! Both grew together very fast, sponging on each other's support. Salunke at that time headed the ministry of mining and marine development. He needed a trusted, dashing entrepreneur who could exploit to the fullest his political standing, to their common advantage, and in return, support him financially. Perhaps, this was the second major milestone in Jagjeet's life. With Salunke's help, Jagjeet obtained a few mining licenses in south Maharashtra. Here too, he displayed foresight, his mastery in the field. He first got the mining areas surveyed by his technicians and then purchased enough land in the precincts keeping in mind the future possibility of constructing a steel plant. He then marched on acquiring land at throw-away prices with the help of Salunke's agents. Salunke's few smart political followers started working for the joint ventures of the Salunkes and the Sankalas.

"Here, let me highlight the few distinctions between the basic characteristics of these two personalities. Jagjeet Sankala maintained humility whereas Ramesh Salunke was arrogant. On account of his haughtiness, Salunke made hidden and open enemies within the Azad party and outside. As a seasoned warrior, Sankala battled on political and entrepreneurial fronts, whereas Salunke, who ought to have been infused with diplomacy, at times was too blunt and forthright. Sankala covered up and saved Salunke on a couple of occasions in Delhi. Delhi politics is very different, which this 'Maratha' never fully understood. Many a times, Salunke indulged in petty quarrels forgetting his standing as a central minister. His opponents never missed the opportunity of ridiculing him as a 'district minister'. Even his followers knew the plain reality that he could never become the prime minister of the country. Business houses and businessmen like Karla, Gupta, Modi etc. had developed the core competence of managing the government during the license and quota raj.

"Jagjeet had his own innovative style of using the government. Where his predecessors only broke the law or arranged to interpret it to their advantage, he simply *changed* the law."

"What does it mean, uncle?" asked Janaki.

"I'll tell you Janaki, this strategy has been outrageously used by some of the huge corporations in the western countries. They lobby with the politicians and somehow arrange to change the law to suit themselves. The judicial courts are obliged to execute these new laws—they have to comply for various reasons."

"Jagjeet was very smart at this. For instance, he managed the politicians, got a new law introduced, and then himself acquired huge acres of land for mining operations before his competitors could get a whiff of this new law permitting the purchase by a private holder. His strategy was to take advantage of the new law, consolidate his position, and then allow the law-makers to go back, choke up and revert back to the old law as some uncomfortable scrutiny would definitely start. Jagjeet had this uncanny knack; he used to do this so craftily—introduce an out of the spectrum law, legalise his stand,

and swiftly before his competitors could as much as prick up their ears, get the law undone, modified, cancelled, whatever—and in such a way that he alone had his way lawfully while the light dawned too late on his competitors. He crushed competitors ruthlessly.

"I'll tell you yet another anecdote about his brutal approach to the competition. There was this Gupta Group that wanted to put up its steel plant of a mega capacity in southern Gujarat. This investment was to be financed by the Instant Bank. Jagjeet got wind of it and promptly kindled a good relationship with Rooda, the CEO of the bank. He bartered a position in the finance ministry for Rooda in exchange for delaying the financing of Gupta's steel-dream. Rooda, hungry to rise, couldn't resist the temptation. He abused his knowledge and banking skills to thwart Gupta's steel plant and delayed things beyond economically viable limits. Those were the days of capital shortage. Bankers, with their arrogance and bureaucracy, could make it or break it for you. The government machinery functioned in much the same way too. With correct networking and funds to brandish, Jagjeet spelt doom for Gupta's plant." Deshpande paused.

"Uncle, is it the same guy Rooda who attempted to lend huge sums of loans to a few business families without proper documentation?" Nayan asked.

"Yes, my child, that same rascal Rooda. Jagjeet advised him to lobby with a few influential business houses. This was necessary because Jagjeet's recommendation alone wasn't enough to get Rooda a place in the finance ministry. But Rooda was not destined to live his dream. There was a rumour in the market that Jagjeet himself was not very keen to see him join the ministry. Hence, his behind the scenes activities defined Rooda's fate. Jagjeet could never let any of his associates or friends achieve bigger positions or social importance than him. He was terribly self-centred, an egotistic rogue. Though we were his close associates, we were morbidly careful while presenting ourselves on public platforms even though we represented the Pride Group. For him, we were the subjects and he was king," Deshpande declared flatly.

"Oh uncle, you had to face such humiliation!" Nayan remarked.

"No Nayan, it is how you take it. I, for one, never felt humiliated. It is because associates like me were completely ensnared by his financial power and glib talk. That guy knew how to make you feel special. Despite his regimented work schedule, he would personally make time for our family celebrations, attend our functions etc. I'll give you an example. Salunke's mother was once seriously sick back in the village. Our man Jagjeet went and stayed there all of three days in the rustic environment without his usual comforts! The great Salunke was so emotionally moved he'd pledge his life for him I thought. This is what I mean when I say—Jagjeet knew how to treat his people. He had the personal touch! No sorry, he had that savoir faire of showing 'personal touch'," Deshpande acknowledged.

"Yes Uncle, this is it. I am curious to learn about Jagjeet's prowess at Public Relations and his people-handling skills," said Janaki.

"Jagjeet created a large network of a variety of people. Every year he would felicitate a spiritual leader, an artist, an author, a social reformist, an editor and a woman entrepreneur. He had created a family trust – the 'Sankala Foundation'. This foundation conducted many philanthropic activities. He donated handsomely to some of the social organisations in Orissa, Karnataka, Goa, Maharashtra, Madhya Pradesh and Bihar—wherever he had his mines, mind you. These donations covered up for his crimes against environment, child-labour, power thefts and thefts of other minerals. Editors of some select and well-known magazines and newspapers were on his payroll. That his clout was vast you could tell as artists, authors, editors often got national awards upon his recommendations. In short, he gathered intellectual puppets around him. Some of the reputed newspapers had standing instructions to their reporters to cover Jagjeet exclusively in a favourable light. Any news against his business was first to be reported to the editor."

"Uncle, I just want some confirmation on this -- I am told one of Jagjeet's subsidiary companies is also an investor in some of the publishing companies?" Sathe queried.

"Yes dear, that is quite obvious. His power and ambition doubled when his son Indrajeet joined him in business. This youngster longed feverishly to use his father's position and plunge amidst the mega global scene. Indrajeet, though a chip of the old block in shrewdness and cunning, could not attain the old man's standard in oratory and glib talk. However, he proved to be a better strategist than his father. Jagjeet was a risk-taker. You know friends, when you do not have anything to lose, naturally you are not afraid of taking risks. Jagjeet, to begin with, didn't have money, name, property or emotional relationships to lose. In contrast, Indrajeet got things on a platter by way of inheritance. So his plan was to safeguard the wealth and make it grow cautiously. 'Money brings money, size brings size and power brings power'—that is the Sankala maxim. Size plays a very important role. If you have size, you can crush others. Yet another dictum—You grow only when you crush others—was Jagjeet's favourite. He swore by it, never believing for a minute in team or group or collective leadership. There could only be one solitary leader, that's it, period."

"Uncle, what I am very curious to know is about Jagjeet's journey to the top on the global front. And what about Indrajeet? Please throw light on him too," Shini pleaded.

"Now it'd be nice if you guys can excuse me. I have had quite a day and am really tired. I wish to rest. I do appreciate your anxiety and curiosity to get to know Jagjeet further. But let's put it off until tomorrow. I shall be fresh tomorrow morning and can make the story even juicier than you expect. I prefer to sleep early these days." Saying this Deshpande retired.

The young team too decided to take a break and breathe some fresh air in the open expanse of Matheran. So the group went for a walk.

After returning, Janaki switched on the news channel, and voilà the first irksome news flashed: Indrajeet got the 'Best Entrepreneur of the Year' award from the National Business Forum (NBF). For the past few years the NBF had been giving this coveted award to the 'worthy'. Its editor-in-chief was the chairman of the selection panel. And interestingly, Mr Rooda too was on the panel. While selecting the right candidate for this award, thirty per cent credence was given to votes from select personalities. Nayan said the obvious. "These voters must have been suggested by Indrajeet's PR agency. A few years ago, his father Jagjeet was the recipient of this very award apparently voted through high-handed coercive tactics. A newspaper belonging to Jagjeet's rival group printed a big story in a few episodes. However, habitually, Jagjeet's PRO denied all the allegations and the story died out."

"Oh, 'award fixing'—something like 'match-fixing'," Sathe said.

Shini flipped the channel and got hooked on a live international summit that was being aired. "Hey guys, look at that! Professor Aditya is addressing a large gathering in Tokyo. See what the banner behind him reads – *Here's what Japan must learn from the Indian family system.*" Everyone from the group started listening to the professor's speech.

All of a sudden Shini pressed the mute button on hearing Deshpande shout at somebody. Everyone dashed out. He was reprimanding an old man. "Baburao, aren't you sixty-nine now? Don't you have a bit of shame left in you, still indulging in your dirty old business? How long will you go on with it? Please for God's sake take up some decent work worthy of your age. Maybe now you should sit and pray to the Lord Almighty for the better part of the day!"

"Sir, tell me how can I do that on an empty stomach? My children have abandoned my wife and me. They are enjoying life in Mumbai. You could say they have disowned us. I agree, I spent all my life running a brothel here. But I did that to bring up my children. I continue in this business solely to earn my bread and butter. I thought that some of you guys may need some entertainment. The brothel is now flourishing and it is run by a local politician. I don't own it, I only represent him. There is a young Sri Lankan whore available. I thought you might like her. Sir, when Salunke *saab* and his young colleagues used to come here they always visited us. Salunke *saab* had a thirst for variety. I was his trusted vendor. Now I can see things have changed," the old man said with resignation.

Everyone was stunned. Nayan staggered in astonishment. His father's bungalow was used by that lecherous Salunke and others for sexual gratification escapades. Why? It made sense because the bungalow was conveniently tucked away, concealed from the main town. His head was spinning with disgust as he slumped into a chair. His eyes were full of tears. Revulsion crept up in him. He wished to throw up! The sofas, the beds, the pillows, the carpets, the bed sheets—everything repulsed him. Sweat trickled down his forehead. He felt smothered. Suddenly a morbid thought came into his mind and he leapt up to see if he could catch the old man who was perhaps still engaged in conversation with Deshpande.

"Wait, just a minute uncle. I need to talk to Baburao. Here, I need you to tell me something. Salunke was your customer, you said? What about Dil Bhojani? Was he also your customer?" Nayan asked, his body shaking.

Baburao laughed and replied equivocally, "Young man, a customer is a customer. He doesn't carry any name tag. In our business, even girls are not recognised by their names. We call them Bengali, Khani, Chipali, Sri Lankan, Russian, Magdhi and so on. They are actually given regional identities, which offer their description to the customers. About Dil Bhojani, if I remember right, he used to ask for a Magdhi girl. But he was not a regular customer. I also remember, Madan Joshi in recent times used to come here often. Madanbhai always wanted Russian girls. His friends used to call him a 'foreign fucker' or a 'white fucker'."

"Stop it Baburao, enough of your descriptions. Now take this money and scoot and don't you ever show your dreadful face at this bungalow any more. Tell your politician counterpart that no filthy creature will be staying here henceforth," shouted Nayan. Baburao took the money, turned to look into Nayan's eyes, gave him a smile and left. Nayan went in and everyone followed him.

"Nayan, just forget whatever transpired here," advised Deshpande with paternal understanding.

"No uncle, what is there to forget? This bungalow needs to be thoroughly fumigated or better still, destroyed. Those poor terrible prostitutes must have cursed this place all over. And that sinister black cobra must have, with its accursed venom, taken my mom's life. Tell me, why is it so in our mythology that every time a man commits a sin an innocent woman pays for it?" Nayan said feverishly.

"Look my son, there is no point in talking about things which are beyond our control or about sins that were not committed by us. This bungalow is beautiful. You are a reasonable young man; you can't blame this place. Yes, no doubt it was horribly misused, abused you could say. But can't you see, presently we are using it with the best of intentions? Why don't you contemplate the sheer destiny which has brought us here together? I too was a part of them until I was struck so badly that I could see the better path. Will you throw me out of this bungalow because I was a part of Jagjeet inner group? Actually you can and you wouldn't be wrong. I deserve worse!" Deshpande tried pushing sense in Nayan's mind.

Sathe put on the television and they had their dinner watching a comedy serial. Everyone enjoyed the Maharashtrian food. Deshpande swore the curry was heavenly. Shini too liked the food very much. After dinner the whole group called it a day.

The next morning, with the exception of Deshpande, everyone went on a long wonderful walk.

After a gratifying Gujarati style breakfast, the team sat down to listen to Deshpande. Nayan said, "Uncle when we split last evening, you were to tell us about Indrajeet's contribution towards the Pride Group's global reach."

"Quite right son, we'll take up from there. Indrajeet was smart. He had that uncanny sixth sense and he warned Jagjeet to give up excessive dependence on Ramesh Salunke. In any case, Salunke was not doing well in Delhi. He just didn't have the big vision. Once again dame luck didn't run out on Jagjeet and the NHP came to power in Delhi. As if that wasn't enough, Madan Joshi took over as the Minister of industry. Jagjeet, the man with foresight, knew that a healthy bonding between the two Marathi Brahmins, Joshi and Deshpande, would be useful and promising in the larger interest of the Pride Group. If Jagjeet conceived it, I'd say Indrajeet executed it. He steadily and securely nudged us to the same arena, not as opponents but as a team. With the Hindu Samiti standing tall as our common background, our connections strengthened with the passage of time.

We, Joshi and myself, started to, in your modern day terminology, 'gel' famously. Madan used all his politico-economic muscle to promote the Pride Group and let it expand its steel manufacturing capacity, of course at a price, and simultaneously ensured that the government-owned steel factory could not grow. In order to guarantee Pride Group's success, Joshi typically incorporated the necessary changes in the 'steel industry policy' to suit the Group. So, on one hand, things were authentic, and on the other, competition was crushed, and Indrajeet became the 'king of steel' with complete monopoly."

"Uncle, I get that, but what happened to the steel company of the Bhadralok Group?" Nayan asked.

"Oh, that Parsi Group, what shall I tell you son. You really have to understand the Parsi psyche. They are very ethical at all cost. They can never match the great duper Jagjeet with his arson of cunning tactics. The Parsis are basically straightforward people. Now, in our typical political set up, how can you even dream of growing big with just your straightforwardness? Bhadralok has no talent for fixing or managing the government," Deshpande replied resignedly.

"But I remember Prof Aditya's positive comments about the Bhadralok Group," said Sathe.

"Are we talking about the same Prof Aditya who once refused an award instituted in the memory of Jagjeet Sankala?" inquired Deshpande.

"Yup, correct. It is the same professor. He said, 'your competitors, your government, your dealers and suppliers may all become unethical, but you, you must be staunchly ethical.' Such a situation becomes a non-workable and a troublesome combination," Nayan replied.

"So what else did the professor have to say?" asked Deshpande.

"Well, basically the professor reiterated that you seriously and unfailingly have to be alert, innovative, aggressive and hardworking, especially when your motto is to be ethical. Just to harbour that wonderful attribute of being 'ethical' you've got to pump in everything you have. There is no harm in aggression when you are genuine. It's not a bad quality nor does it bring down your ethics."

"The funny thing is, Jagjeet and his Pride Group were always so jealous of Bhadralok and his business empire. Jealousy, pure envy, can push you to a point of insanity. Jagjeet tried and he struggled to overtake the Bhadralok Group because of its public image. How can you ever touch the untainted Bhadralok? He unashamedly tried to malign the company's image through his media-might which too failed him! In a secret survey Bhadralok got a score of 9.2 out of 10 to Jagjeet's dismal score of 4.3," said Deshpande.

"I am really glad that the people of India genuinely try to differentiate between the ugly and the beautiful," Janaki reacted gleefully.

"But Janaki, that is not enough. The beautiful must survive, succeed and know how to grow," Shini commented.

"Yes, we really must thank Deshpande uncle for his efforts to show us the right from wrong and the good from bad and utter evil," acknowledged Sathe reverently. The group split for a short break. Shini, as usual, got busy mailing on her laptop. Janaki called up her father and sounded overly chirpy. Sathe couldn't hide his curiosity about Janaki's sudden excitement.

Janaki said, "My father's friend works at a private international intelligence agency. He is working on the explosive story of Swami Gunanand."

"Oh, the same spiritual guru, I mean thug, who is very well respected in Delhi's political and business circles!" Nayan questioned.

"Yes, he is very powerful alright," said Janaki.

"He is all-prevailing because he himself is a power broker. I'll come to that later. Indrajeet sought to develop fruitful relations with the Socialist Party, ruling the three northern states. His focus was to get into the business of SEZ – Special Economic Zones. Thousands of acres of land needed to be acquired in these northern states. Madan Joshi could not arrange any meeting with the head of the Socialist Party, Mr Vikram Bhan. Bhan was conscious of his Muslim Vote Bank. The Muslim factor could never let these two leaders see eye to eye. There came Swami Gunanand to the rescue of Indrajeet. Vikram Bhan suggested that the Pride Group establish its identity in the northern towns by sponsoring some mega spiritual gatherings of the Swami. After all, when innocent people see and believe that you are spiritually inclined, they are likely to be less judgmental of you. In fact, they accept you as benign, thereby making your task of eventually hoodwinking them simpler," Deshpande explained.

"Indrajeet, Gunanand and Bhan played the same trick on the credulous masses. Huge spiritual seminars were conducted in a few towns. Image building was done to the hilt. Pride Group then announced its mega SEZ plan and started acquiring possible cultivable land from the innocent farmers. A lump-sum was paid to each farmer without a thought for their future. Wherever land could not be easily acquired, Bhan's political activists would use coercive tactics and arm twisting. A good number of retired government officers were put in action to handle these acquisition processes. These officers were offered handsome commissions, and of course their infamous past records were put on the table to coerce them into action whether they liked it or not. In a few socially sensitive towns, Bhan's henchmen arranged for social riots between Hindus and Muslims. Riots essentially implied destruction of slums and consequently the release or setting free of a few hundred acres of land. Pride Group would get the land, Bhan his money and Gunanand adequate exposure, popularity and perks through the spiritual events. This is what socio-political, socio-spiritual and socio-entrepreneurial networking is all about!" Deshpande explained this masked dimension of corruption.

Nayan felt it time for atonement. "Uncle, will you please let us express our apology to you. From the outset we were so suspicious of the whole meeting at my father's behest that we thought it best not to reveal our true identity. Of course, through dad you know about me, but not about my friends present here and their purpose for participating. I am guilty of withholding all that from you."

Deshpande laughed and responded, "Children, frankly speaking, your identity makes little difference to me. It shouldn't be of any consequence. I am happy I could share the maximum possible information with you."

"Please forgive us, and it will make me feel good to quickly re-introduce my friends. Shini works as a senior journalist with a reputed newspaper in New York. Janaki edits a magazine devoted to the cause of women. Sathe too works as a senior reporter with a well-known Marathi daily, the *Lok-Vani*. Your guidance and words of wisdom will certainly go a long way in conditioning our existence and our level of maturity." Nayan went on with a lot of emotion.

Deshpande interrupted, "Children, I am not yet finished. There are few more things left to be discussed. I have one question for you; could you please answer that?"

"Sure we'll try to, to the best of our ability," Janaki quickly responded staring at the other three for support.

"What do you folks really think of me, my life, my family and my innumerable misdeeds? God alone knows if I would ever have dared put that question to my son were he alive. But children, please give me your frank answer. I'll accept all negative comments graciously without a grudge. I assure you that," Deshpande said despairingly.

"Uncle, please, please stop saying that. We are already so indebted to you; I don't think we have a moral right as such to pass judgment on you. But one thing is certain, that if there is any way your son were to know about you, he'd be proud of you—the way you have stood humbly revealing your darker side and sharing your experiences in order to warn and enlighten us with the sole motive of helping us. You're just too good uncle!" Shini replied emotionally.

"You children are so mature. You are so nice to me. God I am so fortunate that I met you wonderful bunch of people! God is great. He showed me the way … He gave me that one ray of hope," said Deshpande.

"Uncle, before we got talking about this you were planning to tell us some more details … What was that about?" asked Sathe.

"Oh yes, that is about the financing of Pride Group. Initially a few small fictitious companies were floated in the Gulf, through which a lot of capital was channelised and returned to the Indian operations of the group."

"Returned? What do you mean by that?" asked Janaki.

"The black money belonging to Jagjeet and his political henchmen was sent to the Gulf through the 'hawala' system. It is a racket, a parallel, illegal, mostly invisible system of transferring funds from one country to another. Normally the mafias control such systems. In their own way, they observe discipline and transparency in their network. You can't go wrong there, nor can you cheat or you'd pay with your blood. Quite a few politicians, corrupt bureaucrats, industrialists use this system for illegal remittances. As per a broad international survey, almost forty per cent of the global transactions are carried out through the hawala network," replied Deshpande.

"Good Heavens, don't tell me—as much as forty per cent!" exclaimed Sathe.

"Jagjeet was an expert at hawala. Four or five big ministers invested their unaccounted funds in the Pride Group through this. The black money transported through hawala would become 'white capital' belonging to a few bogus companies in the Gulf. The same white money, what you formally call accounted capital, was then reinvested here. Worldwide, quite a few governments, rulers, royal families, dictators, so called social organisations and trusts use the hawala network. I am told, a few so-called spiritual leaders too collect crores of rupees in illegal donations, which get routed through the same hawala arrangement. The Pride Group uses many coercive tactics to exploit its suppliers, dealers, vendors, ancillaries and contractors. On paper, it commits to pay within fifteen days, but on an average, no payment is made earlier than a hundred days. The group uses the capital of small business partners without interest. It also utilises huge bank finance of a few select banks by bribing their senior executives. These days, quite a few corrupt bureaucrats park their funds directly in the Pride Group's finance company. All this is done brazenly with bogus evidence."

"But uncle, however illegal an activity may be, it would somehow require a suitable organisational structure to function. Am I not right?" asked Nayan curiously.

"You are right there. The Pride Group structure I'd say is endowed to suit its culture. Indrajeet and his close coterie take care of all the strategy formulation and hurdle management."

"Now, what is this hurdle management? It sounds interesting!" Janaki asked.

"No, it's not interesting, it's just crass. In other terms, it means bribing the politicians and bureaucrats at a wholesale level! It means that the Pride Group wouldn't have to bribe at every level in the government hierarchy. Bribes are offered to the leaders of the system – period. Retail bribing becomes dangerous because it is mostly visible and time consuming as well. The entire mechanism works for you if the leader at the top is indebted to you in perpetuity—that's the principle. The coterie also takes care of competitors and critiques. These are constantly, ingeniously and indirectly harassed. As I have told you, Pride Group maintains a separate task-force for this purpose. The task-force comprises of a few hundred advocates and solicitors, private detective agencies and so-called social organisations, a separate team of crooked, corrupt retired bureaucrats. These people work round the clock, and their job is to find out slips and benign errors made by Pride Group's competitors and critiques. These mistakes are then highlighted through media by the paid journalists and advertisement agencies wanting to indulge in yellow journalism. Everything is done so analytically that neither the Pride Group's name, nor that of Indrajeet, could ever be compromised or dragged into any exposure by their rivals. Let me tell you an interesting story…."

Deshpande returned from his restroom break and continued, "It was a critical year, the year of elections for Ramesh Salunke. His reputation was at stake. The Delhi high command had given him an ultimatum – that of winning seventy per cent of seats in Maharashtra. Of course, Salunke had no plan or innovative strategies. The guy was hopeless, all at sea! And who but Jagjeet went to his rescue. Within eight days, Jagjeet could provide him with a detailed report about the electorate along with the strength and weaknesses of the NHP in Maharashtra. He also designed a strategic election campaign for Salunke showcasing how a 'professional approach' is the sole answer to achieving."

"But uncle, was Madan Joshi actually aware of all this? If he was, then how could he tolerate Jagjeet calling the shots?" asked Sathe.

"As I recall, once upon a time Jagjeet wanted to cut Joshi to size, clamp his arrogance which was unacceptable to certain senior executives of his Group. After all, no ambitious industrialist could allow a politician to parasitically thrive on him. Pride Group's business hurdles were managed by the coterie though most of them were not professionally qualified. So indeed, there would be times when a highly educated professional manager in the Group would have to take instructions from a coterie member who wasn't particularly qualified. That's all part of the game.

"Children, let me complete the last portion of my story. The Pride Group also has a few subsidiaries in London, Hong Kong, Bahrain, Bangkok and Moscow, dealing in the speculative business of metal and currency derivatives. That offers a good hedge to the group. Pride is gradually growing in the rural business of commodity derivatives as well," said Deshpande.

"So true. I am reminded of the fact that Ramesh Salunke created a serious problem for Indrajeet while making an entry into this business. Salunke, as usual, with his arrogance underestimated the potent anger of the unorganised farmers. He gave his battery of political activists to the Pride Group in order to harass those innocent farmers into selling their produce at throwaway prices. Initially, Salunke was successful. But eventually, the 'Farmer's Movement', an outfit of the Hindu Samiti, brought all the farmers together under one banner to agitate very strongly against the Pride Group, and Salunke in particular. The agitation took a violent turn and ultimately the Pride Group had to heavily compensate the farmers to quell the unrest," said Nayan.

"Yes, since then, the north Indian lobby of the Azad party has been trying to pit the Pride Group against Salunke. Delhi, right from the outset, never liked any regional leader to become too strong and belligerent," said Deshpande.

***

Chapter 3

Shini got a call from New York. As she kept on listening her face turned red. Everyone waited anxiously. As she ended the call she said, "Goodness me! My country was planning a war against Iran. But I never dreamt Iran would initiate the first step!

"Guys, it looks like there is a serious problem in New York. I just had a word with mom. She said that there have been repeated announcements on the TV about multiple gas leakages all through the city. The news says that the New York city's mayor received three emails from an Iranian group claiming responsibility for these leakages. The group claims that Iran has taken the first step in a biological war against the US," Shini said apprehensively.

"Hey girl, don't you start panicking from miles away. The civic machinery will surely arrest the problem," Nayan said in an attempt to reassure her.

In the afternoon, when Shini spoke to her mom the second time, the picture was clearer—that the impact of the gas leakage was not of a very severe nature though the city was far from being 'out of the woods'.

After the whole day's tumult and tension, as the team retired to lounge and relax on the patio, Janaki came up with a good suggestion for Shini. Under the circumstances, when life had fallen out of gear for those living in and around New York, Janaki thought it apt for Shini's parents to take a break and fly down to India for a brief holiday until normalcy could be brought back in their homeland. They could perhaps start off with an easy-going sight-seeing tour and then stay on until the 'toxic ruckus' died down.

Late evening, Dil Bhojani called up Nayan. He was hopelessly curious to evaluate Nayan's state of mind post the Deshpande interaction. The old man had already briefed him about the discussions he had had with the youngsters. He had even admired Nayan for his maturity. Dil Bhojani was expressive and generous with words. "Hello son! Deshpande told me about your intelligent questions. Atta boy! You really make your dad proud. After all whose son are we talking about eh? That's Dil Bhojani's son!"

Nayan said, "Dad, our discussions were fantastic. My friends too enjoyed thoroughly. Deshpande uncle is truly an ocean of knowledge and wisdom."

Nayan was going through his mails when he suddenly jumped with glee. There was a mail from one of his ex-professors announcing the arrival of Professor Aditya in Mumbai for a brief stay. The professor was to reach Mumbai the very next day. Nayan thought it fortuitous – right time, right place, right person, genial ambience. What more could you call it but a great stroke of luck? One could say this meeting was ordained. Nayan rushed out of his room shouting, "Hey guys listen, I am not joking but Professor Aditya will be in

Mumbai tomorrow. Mustn't we meet him?"

Shini, Janaki and Sathe couldn't believe their ears. "Voilà, my mind's made up. Meeting Professor Aditya is the decider. Destiny has indicated that I stay back to meet him." Shini was very excited.

Nayan quickly reminded her that she was to invite her parents to India for a short break. "If things coincide, it'd be great! They too can meet him."

"Nayan, how about us meeting the professor here, at Matheran itself? We could arrange for his vacation. You have good contacts in Matheran—a Bhojani like you can arrange anything and everything!" Sathe said on a lighter note. Everyone laughed at his comment.

"Sathe, that is a great idea. Let me work on it without losing time. First I'll contact the professor. I guess Destiny has *willed* it. This bungalow can accommodate all of us and more. I really consider it lucky -- a nice place for a nice purpose! I think, it's going to be a very memorable get together," Nayan said excitedly.

"Nayan, just let me work out the logistics of my parents' visit to India first. If they can reach here in forty-eight hours, that'd be swell. In fact if Janaki's folks could come down to Matheran too at this short notice, it'd be ideal. We mustn't waste this incredible opportunity," Shini squealed.

"Great! You first speak to your parents. Janaki then you confirm with yours. If all goes well, it will be a very special get together. Sathe, what do you think? What's your take on it?"

"Nayan, It's a great idea to have my mother come up here too. She does need a change. She has not stepped out of the house since my father's passing away," said Sathe.

Getting a positive response from both, Shini and Janaki, Nayan called up the professor. The professor seemed to like the idea of meeting in Matheran. Nayan assured him of a comfortable stay in that small but beautiful town. In the afternoon, Shini got a pleasant surprise from her mom. Her mother's younger brother, Robert Wood residing in London, also wanted to visit India along with her parents. He was a landlord owning hundreds of acres of land in England and was an active member of the Conservative Party. Wood was already exposed to articles authored by Aditya and was eager to meet the man.

Nayan sent out a formal mail to Professor Aditya inviting him to Matheran.

The youngsters were slightly worried about the arrangements. Of course, the Bhojani bungalow was big enough to accommodate all the guests. The youngsters were looking into every minute detail of hospitality.

Usha, Sathe's mother, was the first to arrive. With her arrival, Nayan's mood improved. She brought some delicious Maharashtrian snacks which were devoured by the youngsters in no time. Janaki's parents, Meghnath Gupta and Shanta, reached in the evening.

Nayan got a call from his father. "Dad, it's good that you called me. We are really enjoying here. Incidentally, Janaki's parents were in Mumbai, so I invited them to visit us here in Matheran."

"Very good Nayan, show the best of our hospitality to them. I am glad you are gradually coming out of your shell and normalising, so to say. My son, I know you were very close to your mother but you must have realised that the show must go on. Who else is visiting our home in Matheran?"

"Not many people, dad. Do you remember Professor Aditya? He may be on a brief vacation in Matheran. We might try to interact with him if the situation permits."

"That would be nice. I know that professor is a globally known authority on various subjects. Take his views on global economy, world-class business vision and global entrepreneurship; it'll be worth your while. Frankly speaking, I don't really appreciate your friendship with those journalists. Deshpande praised them and had good things to say about them. But Deshpande is Deshpande; we are Bhojanis!"

"Dad, why do you often compare yourself with Deshpande? Isn't uncle your close friend?"

"Nayan, he was never a close friend of mine. We were close colleagues in the Pride Group. And you know very well that I don't like people who walk around talking philosophy!"

"But dad, uncle Deshpande instructed us on entrepreneurship and business economics. Professor Aditya will also guide us on the global business ventures. You stop worrying about your son losing his business acumen on account of his journalist friends. Don't you see this is networking. Ramesh Salunke and Jagjeet became icons because the journalists supported them and made them so through the media." Nayan surprised himself by his cheekiness. For a moment he was proud he had his own little cunning to deal with his businessman dad.

"Friends, for your information the professor has just arrived in Matheran. He just messaged me," said Nayan.

The two ladies Usha and Shanta took charge of the kitchen and set up the dinner table. Young Sathe requested everyone to join him in saying grace before the meal. Shini recalled Sathe singing the prayer in baritone during the international cultural workshop. His voice reverberated as he praised the Lord to bless the food and to nourish and motivate everyone in the right direction.

Shini enjoyed the food the most. After dinner they all sat together to discuss the agenda for next few days. Sathe was to make a kind of synopsis on what they had learnt from Deshpande through his sagacious words of wisdom. Subsequently, Shini and Janaki would edit the matter keeping it ready for Nayan to dispatch it electronically to their wider circle of friends—all those who would eventually attend Professor Aditya's lectures in the near future. A proper background was indeed of vital importance if any progress was to be expected. Of course, the availability of Professor Aditya had to be ascertained.

Before going to bed, Nayan got a rather disturbing sms from Pawan. It said that Avdhut Deshpande had resigned from his honorary positions in some of the Pride Group's trusts, foundations and other projects. The reason given was his illness. Nayan was flummoxed. Deshpande was so energetic in Matheran. How could he suddenly resign on account of illness? Or was he asked to resign? Was it the Pride Group's theory of utility at work?—use and discard. Was an emotionally disturbed Deshpande now found to be useless? Some of the trusts of the Pride Group were used to convert 'black' money into 'white' systematically. One of the trusts that was supposedly conducting spiritual activities was completely into hawala transactions. Now, a detached Deshpande was perhaps not managing these important activities with vigour thought Nayan. He wanted to call up his dad to know more about Deshpande's resignation. Asking his curt, arrogant brother would be futile. It was 11 pm—too late to call his dad. Yet, sleeping after this disturbing news wasn't easy. He somehow made up his mind and called his dad.

"Dad, is it true that uncle Deshpande has resigned from the Pride Group?"

"Nayan, he was asked to resign. Indrajeet's coterie must have reported about his diminishing energy. He had recently also turned philosophical. Jagjeet always thought such moralisers were very dangerous and utterly dispensable. Just imagine I too am equally old. Indrajeet and coterie must be aware of the fact that I take home my pound of flesh when I execute deals for them. Yet, I am very much sought after in the Pride Group. Ambitious people want your utility quotient, not your philosophical speeches. My son 'utility' is the key word. Absurd as it may sound, at times you may be required to prove your usefulness through your nuisance value. Do you get the paradox? In the past I have even blackmailed Jagjeet and Indrajeet. Now of course, the Sankalas are too big for such manipulation. Forget about Deshpande's resignation. Things happen and you must learn to let them happen. You must take care of your own interests."

Bhojani senior kept mum for a few seconds and then asked, "Nayan, are you alone or are there people around you?"

"Why dad, there is no one here. Tell me."

"It is really very confidential, absolutely confidential. It was upon my advice that Indrajeet asked Deshpande to resign. You know, lately, he had started giving me his philosophical lectures – some idealistic gibberish. The thing is, he is my old rival. It was because of him that I could not get closer to Madan Joshi. Otherwise, I could have made a lot of money a long time ago. And his recent remarks alarmed me and caused me a lot of worry. Granted that he was miserable and frustrated at the loss of his only son, but that is his personal life. That cannot and should not affect his professional life, and least of all the Pride Group."

"But dad, what I don't understand is how you could manage to convince Indrajeet into removing Deshpande?"

"It's simple! I arranged to record some of Deshpande's speeches at the social programs organised by the Sankala Trust. I also recorded some of the comments made about him by his subordinates working for the trust. These assistants are ambitious and eager to grow. Deshpande was a thorn in the way of their growth."

"What type of growth, dad?"

"Oh son-o-mine, buck up! Can't you get the hint? Where is your power of deduction? What growth would you expect when you are working for the Pride Group or the Sankala family? Deshpande was slowly and surely becoming a nuisance for me. I convinced Indrajeet that he was turning dim-witted and consequently ineffective and useless to the group.I have the mesmerising ability to convince people. I got the skill from the king himself – Jagjeet!"

"Dad, don't tell me at this age you still bear grudges and harbour bitterness. Why dad—please why?"

"It is all for you people, my son. Charan needs to expand our industry. Pawan also should consolidate his position in the Group. You too have to join Charan in the very near future. Deshpande's latest spiritual withdrawal from material benefits was the first sign of him turning hostile. So why let trouble brew? Nip it in the bud, that's the only, mark my words, only answer. Don't wait to solve a problem tomorrow when you can obliterate it today."

"But dad, he spent two whole days here and guided us so thoroughly. How do I forget that?"

"Nayan, I too have helped him on several occasions. He enjoyed his stay at our bungalow. He praised you and your friends. I've told you so many times not to take relationships so intensely, so emotionally. Always remember the ultimate goal, work in that direction and stay focused. You and your brothers must make my dream come true—the dream of a Bhojani Industrial Empire!"

"Dad, I am really amused to know that at this age you could actually record Deshpande's speeches!"

"Of course I did not physically do the recording! Obviously it was at my behest that Pawan arranged for that recording. Forget Deshpande. In life you've got to march forward, not live in the past and lament. Okay? Goodnight!"

"Goodnight dad." Nayan was shocked. He couldn't believe his ears. His dad was responsible for Deshpande's ouster from the Pride

Group. One day he sits and guides me and my pals. The next, poor guy is shown the door. Was it again Deshpande's lousy destiny at play that Bhojani ditched him at the end?

Nayan thought, what goes around, comes around. Deshpande too must have ditched many people when he was in full throttle with the Sankalas.

Shini's parents and uncle reached Matheran at around nine in the morning. Her uncle was huge. The guy had clearly abused his body consuming loads of junk food. Nayan, Sathe and Janaki were quite taken aback at the sight of him. Her uncle was talking nonstop. Shini's mother, Jennifer, said, "Shini, for God's sake take your loquacious uncle in your care. We've had an overdose of his verbosity all along the journey, and I can assure you that my patience has run out!"

"Hey gal, don't you tarnish my image. I am not verbose; I'd never use two words when one would do. I am just an effective communicator. Shini must have told you that I am an active member of the great Conservative Party of Great Britain," retorted Robert.

"Well, I am your sister, not a member of your conservative fellowship, so find yourself some contemporary audience amid these youngsters," Shini's mom suggested and everybody had a hearty laugh.

"Quite true! Beware, Shini my darling," said Robert laughing.

Janaki's mom Shanta served a south Indian breakfast. Carefully selected continental items too were served in honour of the newly arrived guests. Jennifer was pleasantly surprised to see her daughter comfortably eating the spicy Indian food.

"Oh aunty, Shini is a surprise package. She can tuck away spicy Indian delights without a twitch in the face. Am I not right Shini?" asked Janaki.

Shini was enjoying the attention. Poor Nayan was racing against time, wanting to have a word with Deshpande and subsequently with the professor.

"Uncle, I spoke to dad last night and heard about your resignation. I gathered it was Indrajeet's call. The bugger showed his true colours. You spent the best part of your life helping this family and the Pride Group prosper, and this is what you get in return." Nayan could not conceal his anger and concern.

"No point blaming the Sankalas. There is no denying the fact that under their patronage I amassed a lot of wealth. It was bound to happen, and so it did. In any case, I was planning to pull out of the Pride Group myself. Maybe I would have done so in a phased manner. That it happened so quickly was God sent. I can now join my wife in her spiritual journey."

"Uncle, I pray your wishes come true, but presently I have a request for you. We, my friends and I, need your guidance and help in the days to come. Please say yes."

"Nayan my boy, what do you have in mind? I saw the spark of a rebel in your eyes. Be careful young man. Whatever path you are planning on taking—think not just twice but several times and prepare well for your journey."

"Uncle, don't you feel it's going to be tough? That's why we requested for your guidance and help. I shall keep in touch. I confess I don't exactly know when I'll call you. Our two day session in Matheran has widened my horizon," saying this Nayan paused. He finally made up his mind that Deshpande had to be taken into confidence and told the truth. "Please don't judge me from what I am about to say."

"I think I know what you are going to tell me, but tell me nevertheless," Deshpande's tone was reassuring.

Nayan had tears in his eyes when it was time to speak about

his dad's treachery. He choked and said, "Uncle, it was dad who engineered your expulsion from the Pride Group."

"I thought as much. Bhojani is an extremely ambitious man -- ambitious to the point of being nasty. I have seen this happen very many times in my career. Nothing new about it. Sometimes you are the hunter and sometimes you are thc hunted. My dear Nayan, you don't have to feel any guilt or pain for what has come to pass. In all this, what I have discovered is something special, something that gives me great pleasure -- to know that you have succeeded in staying clean and that your intentions are extremely honourable. And yes, I assure you, that for any help or guidance you might need, I am just a phone call away. Whatever you undertake, please be very careful. Be very aware of what you are taking on."

"I am extremely indebted to you. Thank you again," Nayan felt relieved he had got that off his chest. He had let down his father and he was not happy with that either. After some quick thinking, he picked up the phone to call the professor.

"Yes Nayan, I was expecting your call," the professor responded.

"Thank you so much sir. I hope you are enjoying Matheran."

"Oh yes indeed! It's very nice, very comfortable. My wife and I went for a long walk this morning – just rambling away—such a wonderful, refreshing experience! Quite a place to want to settle down and retire amid the fabulous nature." The professor's response was quite spontaneous.

Nayan thought about how he and his friends had appreciated the professor during the international conference. He was full of youth and vigour. Though fifty, his enthusiasm was that of a collegian. He talked smart, was full of life, zest, pep and gusto and had a good sense of humour—a complete package.

"Sir, how do we plan a meeting today? Shini, Sathe, Janaki and

I are staying at my father's bungalow here. Some of my friends' homefolks have joined us too. We also have another interesting guest with us, Mr Robert Wood, an active member of Britain's Conservative Party. Your participation in our discussions would necessarily imply a lot of added value and learning for us. It would truly widen our horizon. Will we be disturbing your vacation?"

"Oh don't bother about me. There comes a time in life when work and vacation blend, when you draw optimum from both. I would be more than delighted to meet your distinguished guests and of course all of you as well."

"Sir, forgive me, I do not wish to be impolite, but for how long do you plan to be in Matheran?"

"...three days for sure. As a first step we can start with an informal meeting with your foreign guests, what say you?"

"Sure sir. I shall let them know. Shini has spoken a lot about you and they are eager to meet you."

"In that case, if too much is expected from a simple man like me, Nayan my dear, you'll have to pay the price for selling everyone short!"

"Sir, you are so modest. We are all keenly looking forward to having you amongst us. Please join us for lunch today. If the vibes are good and the moment ripe, we could start our discussion post lunch. I am quite sure you will be comfortable here."

"In that case, my wife and I will reach your house at noon. Is that okay with you?"

"I am sure it suits all of us just fine." Nayan shared the news with everybody.

He then handed over copies of the mails he had received from their currently non-participating friends, outlining what each one had hoped to fulfill in their next meeting. After everybody had gone through the mails, Shini's father Mike said, "It's unfortunate that we are facing such issues practically everywhere. We in the US live in our cocoon, in a world of our own. We don't really bother about what's happening outside of our country. Reading your exchange of mails, I am rocked by your level of awareness. Your quest for knowing the globe is admirable."

Professor Aditya arrived with his charming wife Dr Sheetala at noon. Both were casually dressed—crisp and smart. Sheetala's sweet expression attracted everybody. After a round of introductions, everyone moved towards the dining table. The delicious luncheon prompted culinary discussions among this culturally varied gathering.

Post lunch, they settled in the main hall for their discussion. "Here in India, a guru is akin to God. So let the professor take the lead," said Meghnath.

"Although we have all met here informally, Sheetala and I formally thank you Nayan for this wonderful opportunity and the amazing warmth and affection extended to us." Then turning to Robert, the Professor continued, "May I take the liberty of addressing my first question to you Robert? Tell us what the current crop of British people think about contemporary India and its people?"

Robert raised a brow in surprise. How about a gentle introduction to topics, professor?—He thought to himself, taken aback. Well, if the professor was going to be blunt, he wouldn't mince his words either. "I think the British have a mixed opinion of Indians and India in general. On one hand, the young professional Indian is a phenomenon in himself. He is smart, hardworking, intelligent, his cost is less and contribution enormous. The Brits recognise that and acknowledge he is king. And then the same Brit visits India and gets a taste of corruption, discrimination and poverty in exaggerated doses and he says … oh but that's not the India I know! So you see how the dilemma germinates…?"

Robert was interrupted by Sathe. "This is the brain-drain that is forced upon the Indian youth. Our corrupt politicians, who rave about patriotism, hound the lives out of the average Indian with their barbaric political dishonesty." Sathe grumbled and rightly so.

"Strong words, young man. I can well understand you. Back home, Britain too is witnessing the growing restlessness amongst its youth. The mass sentiment is that we leaders lack the vision to take Britain on the road to prosperity," Robert responded calmly.

"We Brits are being mocked at for being the shadow of our big brother across the Atlantic. The whole world ridicules us, calls us the 'American poodle', the fifty-second state of US, which unfortunately is not entirely incorrect. We joined in the American aggression over Iraq and Afghanistan. Of course, the military association with the high-handed US tarnished our image globally. We spent too much time, money and manpower on this so-called 'war on terror', which otherwise would have been more productively directed towards nation building—agriculture, European cooperation and many other vital issues."

"But sir, for over a century, half of the globe was ruled by the British Empire and not so long ago. Then why has your economy deteriorated in just fifty years?" asked Janaki.

"This is what is happening to the Britain of today. The present generation has become complacent, tardy and lethargic. The easy availability of jobs has made our youth lazy, and they have lost their motivation for higher studies. The government's public welfare services such as public health service, pension schemes, unemployment compensation etc. have made life easier. But cumulatively all of this has had a negative impact on our youth. We have lost the momentum, we have forgotten that 'work is worship', thus our current day predicament. On the other hand, the present day Indian is extremely industrious, and diligently toils hard for recognition and wealth. Your youth do not walk out on their parents on turning eighteen. They seek support from the family in pursuit of higher education," Robert remarked regretfully.

"Mr Wood, would it be incorrect to say that low savings is the root cause for your economic downturn?" asked Nayan.

"Yes, much like our cousins across the Atlantic, we neglected savings. Our youngsters are lavish in their spending. They need to be told that smart savings will serve them well in their future. They never learnt the story of *The Ant and the Grasshopper*! They are rigid in their outlook, their bearing. Their professional skills are at best suited only for average jobs. It's time they learnt from the Indians. Back home, our boys and girls are losing jobs to hardworking Asians, causing a lot of anguish and frustration. They then tend to blame these Asians for their plight. They need to stop this blame game and start working hard, fair and square, and expect merit to rule," replied Robert.

"But shouldn't your government take some initiative to show the way to the youth?" queried Meghnath.

"You are quite right. But by the time this realisation dawned, the situation had got out of hand. As I mentioned earlier, we were busy attacking Iraq and waging this war on terror. For decades we lived with this stupid notion that the developing and the underdeveloped countries would continue to support our leadership—rather our supremacy."

Nayan suggested a coffee break to soothe their nerves. Strong, aromatic South Indian coffee made the rounds. The Professor used the break to check his emails. Sathe, Nayan and Janaki were engaged in a casual conversation. Shini's was with her dad on the gas leak in New York. Apparently the situation was now well under control.

The coffee break ended and everybody settled in for another round of discussions.

"Sir, I have a request, rather an appeal, and I speak on behalf of all my friends here as well. We would very much like to spend as much as a week with you—deliberating, discussing and clarifying all our doubts, our fears, our reservations. Your guidance will be of prime importance, giving us a strong foundation from where we could aspire to launch ourselves to face all the challenges in life," Nayan almost begged the professor.

Professor Aditya became solemn. He paused for a while and turned to the young friends and said, "My dear friends, even if I do accept your request and spend a week building the foundation that you speak of, but then what next? Our discussions may help you in your personal lives and careers but what about the innocent masses who need my guidance and help?"

Nayan and the others were taken aback by the professor's outspokenness. He was a man of principles, they realised.

"Look here folks, the question is: whose good and well-being are we here to promote? If it is for your benefit, you as a group, or you as individuals, then I am wasting my time. I have my agenda. I go where I am needed and where my presence can help create some change. You all know, or at least will learn how to stand on your own without my guidance. Sorry but I call a spade a spade." The professor did not mince his words.

Meghnath decided to intervene and diffuse the tension. He said, "Professor the kids need to be given the bigger picture. They want to bring about a change for the betterment of the society, and are seeking to enhance the quality of life of the general populace."

"Good! If you have the desire, time and energy to espouse a humanitarian cause and pursue it fervently, only then am I your man, your partner. The human race is on the brink of a social disaster. People are suffering everywhere," the professor explained.

He became sombre. "So guys, what do you think about the change required? Should we make this change possible? Do we have the inner strength and commitment to execute it? Do we believe in optimism? If you all can say a unanimous thumping 'yes', then I will share with you a story I have lived, where the 'impossible was made possible'."

Shaken by the pounding YES! the Professor actually had to wait to let the excitement diminish. Even the parents joined their children in expressing their positive response. No one noticed the young boy standing in the door waiting for instructions to serve them. Nayan smiled and called for some special herbal tea.

Everyone savoured the tea and felt refreshed. "Guys, you might have heard of our notorious minister for rural development, Mr Ramesh Salunke. He is a senior member of the Azad party and terrorises, both socially and politically, the innocent masses of southern Maharashtra. This is a story of one of the most backward districts of Maharashtra." The professor started narrating his story.

"I know some of the heinous acts of Salunke and his associates. He is closely related to the Sankala Group," Nayan butted in.

"Yes, that was a big nexus comprising of Salunke, Sankala, and some mafia groups in and outside of India. Salunke's close friend and head of the district council of the Azad party, Sampatrao Chavan, was chairman of the three sugar factories in the district. The story I am about to narrate is about the fall of this mighty Sampatrao. My participation in this thrilling event of change was by accident. This event took place three years ago when I stayed in Pune. My maid, a widow named Seetabai Shirole, is the real heroine of this story. Her husband was a small-time farmer growing sugarcane at Gangapur.

This innocent guy called Bandu Shirole supplied sugarcane to the sugar factory of Sampatrao Chavan. Mostly all the cooperative societies, government-sponsored development projects, were headed by Chavan or someone from among his kin. His father was a horrible womaniser. He exploited quite a few women. For many years, it was mandatory for every family to have Chavan's picture adorn their wall. On every festival, every family head was expected to visit the Chavan bungalow and salute this so-called leader. Even the elderly would have to bow down to young Sampatrao. That is how rogues are born !"

"But sir, how could these people voluntarily tolerate such humiliation?" asked Nayan.

"Simple people remain unaware of their rights because they are illiterate. Thousands of untouchables were wisely led by Dr Ambedkar. He made them realise that they too were human beings as important as anyone else."

"Yes, that was also done by Martin Luther King. And recently by Nelson Mandela," added Shini

"People like Chavan and Salunke ensured that no alternate leadership came into being. Power was contained and controlled by the select few 'sugar belt political families'. The masses were kept away from any radical exposure which could probably open their eyes. This was done with cruelty, divide and rule tactics and also by maintaining a group of devoted henchmen in the region. For decades in Maharashtra, the cooperative sugar factories and other societies have been run by just a few families. Chavan and Salunke used their ill-gotten money and power to bring in self-centered intellectuals from the cities."

"This goes on in the US too. Quite a few economists, academicians, thinkers, artists and scientists are kept on regular payrolls of politicians funded by big corporate sharks," Shini added.

"Yes, and here in India, the Pride Group's Sankala Foundation supports Salunke's select intellectuals. On the latest list of government award-winners, there are some of Salunke's intelligent associates—in other words his goons," barked Sathe.

"In the rural areas, whenever a few youngsters attempted to challenge these mighty powerhouses, they were eliminated ruthlessly. Some of them were branded as naxalites. A few were arrested under bogus criminal charges and imprisoned for years. A few others were socially and economically harassed. Yet others were ostracised by 'paid' religious leaders. Then finally, a few 'smart' guys would get promoted either politically or socially. In a nutshell, all possible tactics were deployed to crush any alternate leadership," said the professor.

For a few seconds there was a lull – not a word was spoken.

"Innocent farmers were systematically looted. Corruption at every stage was rampant. Sugarcane transported to the factories by bullock-carts was purchased at discounted price, showing the produce to be of low quality. All weighing machines were falsely calibrated to cheat on the weight. Sugarcane cutters, bullock-cart operators, quality inspectors, weighing machine operators were all a part of the chain of corruption. The poor farmer was cheated, and as if that wasn't enough, his payment too was delayed ever so often. Almost ten per cent of the price was deducted regularly, under some type of unknown and unaccounted cess!" The professor reached for a glass of water. The audience waited for more to come.

"Bandu Shirole, was one such farmer who was a victim of this daylight robbery. He felt frustrated and infuriated as he was a hot-tempered person. On one occasion, he asked the factory officer to re-verify the weight of his produce. The officer fearing exposure refused. If the cheating was detected the news wouldn't take long to spread across the region. During the annual general meeting of the factory, chaired by Sampatrao Chavan, Bandu dared to raise that incident again. A few other farmers supported his questioning. The factory management conveniently interpreted Bandu's reaction as a revolt against the organisation. Some of Sampatrao's political activists come to intervene and stop Bandu from challenging them further. Like bouncers in a bar, these activists are normally present at such gatherings to deal with unwanted elements.

"Bandu's misfortunes started from this episode onwards. The factory stopped buying his sugarcane. He approached another factory in the neighbouring district. There too his request was rejected. Factories in both the districts were controlled by Ramesh Salunke's associates. Hence, farmers like Bandu were easily cornered and watched. He became more and more helpless and desperate. He tried to sell his produce in the name of his relatives and friends. He failed there too, as Sampatrao's local hooligans kept a close watch on his activities. Out of fear of a backlash from the management, the villagers too started keeping a safe distance from Bandu and his family. As a last resort, Bandu even approached a member from of the Opposition. But they were weak and without any muscle. During this entire phase, even the local cooperative bank started harassing Bandu who had his old parents, his wife and three children under his care.

"One unfortunate morning, Bandu, after having tried all that his mind could possibly conceive to help his situation, gave up on his struggle and committed suicide on his farm. His children being too young and parents being old, the entire pressure shifted on his wife. Sampatrao's agent approached her and showed typical political sympathy. The bank also expressed its willingness to cooperate. Sampatrao's cousin asked Bandu's widow to work at the master's bungalow. This so called work was not defined and would possibly have had a different meaning. Seetabai, did not fall for the bait, consulted her brother and left to work in Pune instead. She had her self-respect which didn't allow her to take up the job at Sampatrao's place. She took her children and went to Pune. Her brother, a good man, gave her shelter. Bandu's parents died one after another, within six months. Seetabai managed to request her brother-in-law to take care of her farm and other agricultural activities. It was a one-sided transaction. She didn't expect any returns except that the ownership of land be transferred in her name. Her brother was not a rich man. He just gave her shelter. Her children could not attend school in Pune for almost six months. She picked up two part-time jobs with two good families, close to her brother's house. Her elder daughter too joined her in these two jobs."

The Professor paused to drink some water. He noticed that Shini and Janaki had moist eyes. "Shini and Janaki, I can understand your feelings. But Seetabai is one among a million such unfortunate cases of India. And these cases are found in almost 150 countries worldwide."

Again there was silence in the hall. Everybody was grim. "Seetabai was a brave lady. She struggled, and managed to save some money to send her children back to school. Her elder daughter had to continue working because one income could hardly do much for the four of them. She changed her job and started working at my place. Within a few weeks, she almost became like a family member. She often narrated stories about herself, her family and her life to my wife. Obviously, I got all the details from my wife.

"One morning, one of my ex-students, who was working with the government of India as a senior bureaucrat, providentially visited my house. This student, Susheel Mohite, incidentally hailed from the same town as Ramesh Salunke. During his childhood, he and his family had the misfortune of being subjected to Salunke's social dominance and coercion. Perhaps Salunke's arrogance compelled

Mohite to get an administrative job with the central government. Of course he wanted to use his administrative power, networking ability and wisdom for the benefit of the poor people. He was clearly waiting for the right opportunity to strike. When we spoke about Salunke, I told him about Sampatrao and Seetabai. I expressed my desire that she should get justice. We met on three to four occasions and decided on a broad action plan. He gave me a thorough description of Sampatrao and Salunke's rural modus-operandi. Arranging for Seetabai to get justice was both, very difficult and a terribly risky proposition. Salunke and company were known for all types of nefarious activities. In addition, Salunke being a minister had unlimited power, resources and clout. Challenging him was like breaking our heads against a wall. Somehow, our inner voice pressed us to go ahead and fight for her.

"As per our plan, our first step was to convince Seetabai that she should fight for justice and that we would support her completely. For one full month she refused to go along with our suggestion. Her logic was simple. She didn't want to become the matter of one more unsuccessful case-study. She was comfortable with her condition, although it wasn't really much better than 'pathetic'. That is what is happening with millions of Indians. They are happy with their worsening condition because they have lost their self-confidence. They are resigned to the fact that good things happen only to the rich. 'Change' is a phenomenon, a luxury only for the upper-crust.

"We brought Seetabai's brother into the picture. He, in times of crises had stood by his sister, which meant he wished the best for her. He agreed with us in principle. He questioned the process. Somehow, we convinced him that the 'Seetabai Project' would progress step by step. We assured him that if at any step we saw any unmanageable risk, we would have the project abandoned and pre-empt any damage. Of course, the project was not foolproof from risks; some uncertainties had to be there for an operation like this. My wife, Sheetala, and Mohite's wife, Sonali, too had a few rounds of discussions with Seetabai. That was crucial. With great difficulty we convinced her. In the meanwhile, Mohite and I visited her village. It was necessary to enable us to get a feel of the socio-political and economic condition of the village. The conditions were quite pathetic. No one agreed to talk to us about the activities of Chavan or his hooligans. We could feel the stress and tension of the villagers. Before anyone got alarmed with our presence in the village, we left!

"In keeping with our plan, the two ladies – Sheetala and Sonali—visited Seetabai's village accompanied by Seetabai and her sister-in-law. Sheetala went as a spokesperson of a women's social organisation. They spoke to a small group of women and told them about their desire to conduct a few educational programs on village health, family and resource management, children's education etc. We took utmost care that no one in the village would suspect their real motive.The Sarpanch, the head of the village, was very happy about the idea of educating women.

"Our strategy was to work under cover of wanting to spread goodwill in the village. So we studied the politics of the village and Sampatrao's local network while building the villagers' confidence and self-respect.

"Our humanitarian operation picked up momentum. Our team's visits to Seetabai's village doubled. There was more visibility given to our program, and around sixty women attended on a regular basis. News of this good work gradually spread to neighbouring villages. In a short while we created five small teams of young social teachers and started covering ten villages. Subsequently, five hundred women were brought under our project-scheme. We then roped in a few retired bankers who taught these women the basic fundamentals of savings, bank transactions etc.

"The next phase in our project was to create 'self-help groups'. Twenty villagers were educated and assigned to manage these groups. Members of these groups were clubbed under a small cooperative credit society. Individual savings were deposited in the society and the society redistributed them as small loans to the same members."

"But professor didn't Sampatrao and his mafia consider your project a threat to their reign of power in the region?" asked Meghnath.

"Good question. We knew that was a big possibility from the very start. Salunke and Chavan are no fools; they know how to safeguard their interests, and can smell any threat that might come their way. To circumvent that possibility we devised a perfect strategy. The self-help group's inaugural function was arranged to have Salunke chair it. We arranged good media coverage of the event in cities like Pune, Mumbai, Nasik and Aurangabad. Tactfully, we saw that Seetabai and her core team-members were interviewed by the media. This was not taken as a threat by Sampatrao, as his constituency was brought into the media limelight."

"But sir, as I understand, politicians like Chavan and Salunke are known to push their spouses and other female members of their family to control women's projects. This is done to ensure leadership from within the family and to keep a watchful eye on any development, whether drastic or minor. What was your experience in this regard?"

"Yes! We took care of that as well. We found a way out. We got the South Asia's apex body that monitors the social organisations of Pune, to issue us a circular making it mandatory for all administrative positions in the cooperative credit society to be occupied exclusively by down-trodden women. If this condition was complied with, only then the society would be eligible to avail of future benefits and wider recognition. We promised Sampatrao that for each and every project done by us we would let him get the recognition. Ever so often we invited his spouse and daughter to chair our programs. This again got local media coverage. So Sampatrao and his family members were more than happy to get the accolades without having to do any work. The moral of the story is to praise the antagonists, boost their ego, and when it is time, quickly pull the carpet from underneath their feet!"

"That's just wonderful, hats off to you! Your wisdom should go a long way in shaping these young minds. You should become the next Indian ambassador," exclaimed Robert. There was laughter in the room. The professor saluted Robert for his praise. Usha, who had excused herself, returned with a tray of Matheran's famous cookies. The youngsters, who had by then become completely engrossed in the professor's narrative, were much too excited to relish the delicious cookies in front of them.

Professor Aditya continued, "By then things had started changing. The women had got their much-needed confidence back. Even their husbands were happy and satisfied. There was a visible change in their lives. They started believing that change was indeed possible."

"My apologies for the interruption! But wasn't Seetabai working in Pune? How could she attend the village meetings so frequently? And what about her children?" asked Janaki.

"Oh I missed that part of the story! It was obviously not going to be possible for Seetabai to do both the things simultaneously. Hence, we requested three well-to-do families in Pune to sponsor her children's education till their matriculation. These families agreed and we enrolled her children in residential schools near Pune. We started contributing towards her monthly salary too. As these expenses were being taken care of, she started saving most of the salary."

"Professor, I must applaud your taking care of the smallest detail in this project," reacted Meghnath.

"If you plan well for all possible scenarios and alternate routes to your final destination, half your success is guaranteed. Incidentally, Mohite helped me a lot. He roped in a few brilliant young minds from Pune city. The youngsters were completely captivated by the project. So much so, that on a few occasions we were faced with the problem of keeping them engaged full time. We did not want to lose them. Our project had generated a lot of heat and the energy of our youngsters needed to be correctly channelised. We assigned them tasks of data collection, interviewing women-leaders of other successful self-help groups, silently observing the events as they unfolded in Seetabai's village and the ones in the neighbourhood. Some of these activists eventually presented their experiences in regional and national seminars and were lauded for their efforts." The professor paused and looked at the youngsters. He was happy that he had managed to convince them that 'change' was impending and indeed possible.

"The real challenge was to take this project to the next stage of total independence. Our ultimate goal was to free the villagers from the clutches of Sampatrao. For that to happen, the villagers needed to have their own sugar factory. But putting up a new factory wasn't possible because of certain regulations. Our proposal for a new factory would have been rejected on technical grounds. This time too, Mohite took the initiative and came to our rescue. He mobilised certain sources and found out vital information about Sampatrao's factory. The factory had been running at a loss for several years. The subsidies and facilities offered by the government were abused and there were defaults on bank loan repayments. Factory assets showed a decline in productivity—in short—Sampatrao's factory was in a lousy shape."

"Now we had a reason to apply for a new sugar factory. Four major challenges needed to be surmounted, the first being to get the villagers ready to have their own factory. Sampatrao was the second problem as he was going to create as many obstacles as he could to oppose the new factory. The third problem was of running the factory. The villagers were too naïve and did not have the professional competence and cunning to take on such a venture. The fourth problem was finance. For a few days we grappled with these problems but couldn't come up with a solution. It was almost as if we had come to an impasse. But remember fortune favours the brave!

"Our young friends, along with Mohite and myself, brainstormed for several days and eventually came up with an answer which we thought was feasible. A few new members were inducted into our group. Our number grew to around thirty. We decided to split up into sub-groups to tackle the issue on various fronts. Sampatrao was the immediate problem. The group that was to take him on was headed by a retired army major residing in Pune. He brought in fifteen more jawans who were to ensure the security needed. The second group was to get the villagers ready for the tough journey ahead. Sheetala headed this group. The third group, headed by a retired professor from the University of Agriculture, was made responsible for scouting for competent people to run the sugar factory. The fourth group was to study available avenues for financing our project. This group was headed by a retired bureaucrat from the Ministry of Finance. Mohite and I were responsible for the overall functioning of all these four groups."

"Professor, this reminds me of the famous Oscar-winning movie, *The Gladiator*. Spot-on planning, fearless courage and coordinated efforts. As I have already said, you Indians are indeed very intelligent!" Robert exclaimed.

"Thanks for the compliment. We Indians can be very intelligent when we choose to be. You follow me?" A smile flashed across the professor's face and everyone joined in the humour!

"My wife initially set up a meeting with Seetabai and some of her close associates in Pune. She gave a brief outline of the plan. Seetabai's job was to garner support from others, a job that was difficult and risky as well. We had to ensure that we had covered our tracks well. If a small whiff of what we were doing were to reach the opposite camp, it would have been extremely damaging to our cause.

"It was decided that we take into confidence a few young boys from the village who were working in cities like Pune. Seetabai carefully prepared a list of such youngsters. Of them we contacted about fifteen. Our real agenda was not disclosed to them. I was to make an objective assessment of their mindset and estimate their true preparedness for change. We decided to meet at Mohite's residence. The venue was chosen because Mohite belonged to the same culture as those youngsters. In addition, he had the rural background and had suffered at the hands of Salunke in childhood. The young villagers would be more inclined to accept his leadership more than anyone elses.

"Mohite began by asking the boys about their experience of the women's cooperative movement in the village. Everyone was quite upbeat about the program and expressed a great deal of optimism. Mohite asked the boys what their contribution towards the growth of the village was going to be. He added that their mothers and sisters had shown the way and had more than amply demonstrated that change was possible. He then suggested that it was time to bring about a big change in the village. For a few moments, no one responded.

A young boy hesitantly came forward and asked what 'big change' was being talked about.

"Mohite went on to ask a few questions. He asked the boys who their leader was. If he happened to be Sampatrao Chavan, what had he done for them till date – why was he still their leader? Why could they not rise all together? Why did they continue to let Chavan and his thugs exploit them and their families? This badgering made one meek fellow confess that Sampatrao Chavan was too big, powerful and well-connected with Ramesh Salunke the minister, to mess with.

"Mohite then asked the boys if they held Shivaji in esteem. Receiving no answer, a disturbed Mohite repeated his question in a louder tone and got a resounding unanimous Yes! He was reassured when Shivaji was equated with God himself! He shared their sentiment because Shivaji was supposed to have fought the mighty Mughals and rescued innocent people from their clutches and gallows. He eulogised Shivaji and how the latter built his kingdom on righteousness, with few resources at his disposal, with only a colossal will and dedication to plan and execute everything himself.

"A young chap, in a tone of despair, replied with resignation that they were helpless at the hands of their persecutor. Shivaji, on the other hand, oozed success purely because of his inimitable exceptional personality. Hearing that, Mohite, with a smile, appealed to the boys to have more faith in themselves. He urged them not to feel helpless and hopeless. When he realised that his words had no impact, he went on the offensive and called them cowardly and selfish for enjoying themselves at movie theaters when actually their mothers, their sisters and their wives tirelessly ran the cooperative movement in the village.

"I stepped in and said that not everybody could become the valiant Shivaji, but they could surely try and emulate the great man. I promised that we would extend our ideas, support and reasonable protection, but they should at least show their willingness to fight their own battle. What was expected of them was not a bloody war but the gumption to go ahead and collectively own a sugar factory. It was time they stopped blaming their destiny and started working in order to shape it. I asked them to indicate how their lives were any different from the time they were under the British rule. In those days they were ruled by the British and currently they were ruled by the Salunkes and the Chavans.

"My forceful argument began to have its effect. I could see their dejection turn into some kind of introspection. It was time to reach out and get their support. I continued by comparing them with African slaves, and added that they were unnecessarily carrying the burden of yesteryear's legacies. I questioned how they could be comfortable doing menial jobs in Pune when they could well be with their families like true 'sons-of-the-soil' tilling their agricultural land in their villages. I pointed out that they were in Pune ladling wine down their throats and sending only some income home. I reiterated that their current apathy was of their own doing and that blaming Sampatrao or anyone else for that matter was shameful.

"One of the young men sitting in the corner, broke down agreeing with what I had said and went on to say that the 'bastard' Sampatrao had ruined his family and had taken away his land. Sampatrao's son had even raped his sister. He admitted that it was his cowardice and desire to escape from responsibility that had him sitting pretty in Pune with a small job, small time gambling, some movies, visiting prostitutes and sending small bits of money home. It was easier than tilling the soil in the village. He wept in utter shame. For their family members, especially the mothers, the only hope was that someday their sons would return home to the village and be a part of the family once again. With his head bowed in embarrassment the boy confessed that for the first time in his life he had come across people like us who could guide and support him, and that he was willing to work with us in whatever capacity we asked.

"Mohite and I, we kept mum for a while, expecting response from the others also. The boys obviously needed more time to absorb and digest what we had said to them. They needed time to re-think, probably weigh their options and then arrive at a decision. Realising that, I suggested that we meet again three days later. Subsequently, Mohite and I sat down and discussed another strategy which I thought was our last and only chance."

The professor excused himself for a while. Robert seized the opportunity to talk to Jennifer. "Some grey matter, I tell you. The Indian story is unending, amazing me more and more. You look at Indians today and I wonder how the British managed to rule this incredible country for so many years. I am speechless ..." Janaki leapt to answer the doorbell. It was the delivery boy with dinner boxes that had been ordered. Until then scant thought was given to dinner if at all, since everyone was mesmerised by the professor's story. With the aroma of gastronomical delights filling the air, they became conscious of wanting to break for dinner. They all dashed to the dining room. The professor joined in with, "Hmm...that smells great. Sure makes me feel hungry. I am ready for an interesting Matheran feast. Nayan, spell it out, what's on the menu?"

"Frankly speaking this caterer is pretty talented and innovative so I have trusted his judgment all the way, though I requested him to go easy on the spices. Anyway dinner does not stimulate me when I am with you, Sir. I am very excited to have you continue your story," replied Nayan.

"Oh Nayan! don't be such a bore. Dinner for me is very much 'on'. Delicious Indian food can't be beat," chuckled Shini.

Seeing Nayan momentarily step out of the kitchen, Sathe said, "Shini, these days you seem to like very many Indian things. Tell us about the other Indian stuff you like, that we are not aware of?"

He looked at Janaki for support. Janaki laughed in response. "Well there are so many interesting things here," replied Shini trying to be nonchalant.

"But is there anything or anyone whom you find extra special or interesting?" Sathe was overtly insinuating …

"Sathe, please leave Shini alone. She is such an innocent pet. Why do you hassle her so much?" said Janaki.

"Innocent and she? Preposterous! Have you ever heard of this? A journalist, who trots around half the globe, follows and predicts the next course of the action of the American president and you think she is innocent?" Sathe was unsparing.

The discussion came to an abrupt halt when Nayan re-entered the room. Sathe and Shini exchanged glances; mischief was in her eyes as well.

They enjoyed their dinner, and then scampered back to hear the remainder of the professor's story.

"Three days later we again met at Mohite's residence. It was our last ditch effort to convince the young villagers. All those who had come for the previous meeting had come again and to us that was encouraging. Sheetala and Mohite's wife walked into the meeting room with several other women from the village. Every small detail had been meticulously planned. Seetabai had been briefed regarding the day's meeting and also our agenda. Seeing her and other women from their villages walk into the room, the young men almost jumped out of their seats in utter surprise. Before they could come to terms with their shock, I rubbed it in saying that these women—their mothers, or sisters or wives had come with great hopes and expectations. I then put the ball in their court and appealed to them to declare their decision—either individually or collectively. Gripped with fear and hesitation, the young villagers were completely paralysed and speechless. As per our expectations, our strategy was working. To diffuse the tension, Mohite's wife served tea to everybody, also a deliberate part of our plan. We wanted the men to regroup, rethink and re-examine the ramifications of whatever their decision was to be and how it would shape their future.

"After tea, Mohite initiated the proceedings once again by declaring that the reason they had been called to his residence was the fact that he too, like them, was a son of the same soil, and shared the same emotional bond with the village and the villagers. He then asked them if they knew why we were working for them. We did not have any political agenda; we weren't even seeking publicity. There wasn't even a financial motive. Curious eyes were then focused on Mohite. His face became sombre, and with sadness in his eyes, he first looked at me and then at Seetabai. He then turned to his audience and said that the real reason was the injustice that Seetabai had been subjected to at the hands of people like Sampatrao, and that we had taken it upon ourselves to help her and everyone who had suffered like her.

"Mohite reminded them that they had been given three full days to decide and urged them to declare their decision once and for all before the heroic women present there. He reminded them that these women were looking up to them with great hope. He even compared them to Jijabai, Shivaji's mother. He then leaned backwards and both of us exchanged glances. We allowed two to three minutes to pass. Not a word was uttered. It reminded me of the Mahabharata when Arjuna became speechless on being asked to fight the mighty Kauravas. Brave Arjuna became nervous! It was Krishna who then guided him through the epic battle that followed. A similar situation was unfolding. Our own Krishna was ready in the form of Seetabai.

"I signalled to my wife, Sheetala, who seated next to Seetabai, gave her the cue to start. Seetabai got up, faced the men and began by slandering the men from her village. She categorically said that the village menfolk should be made to wear bangles. They bellowed 'Jai Shivaji'—'Jai Bhavani' only during ceremonies, but had absolutely no fire in their bellies. She berated them for having left, rather fled the villages, leaving their women to tend the soil and the children! She decried their unwillingness to even putting up a fight. She was all fired up and with blazing anger said that the men had no moral right to talk about the heroism of Shivaji. Then, she delivered what we had urged her to say. Her exact words were, 'Saheb, these men are cowards. We should not waste our time and energy trying to convince them. Just like in the past, even in this age, women will decide the children's future. We have arrived at a unanimous decision which is to work on the project of a sugar factory in our village. We cannot predict our success but that will not deter us from trying. Shivaji built his empire against all odds and won his battles. He ruled with justice, compassion and divinity. His kingdom flourished and everybody prospered. Goddess Bhavani had blessed him as fortune only favours the brave. I conclude that Bhavani will bless us too.' Gosh she was awesome! Even today it gives me goose pimples to remember the lady's bravery. Her intelligence was impressive despite there being no academi degrees."

The professor took a sip of water and continued, "Seetabai's words stung the men like bullets, leaving them dumbfounded. They were so ashamed of themselves that they could not even look up and meet her eye. The young man who had spoken during our previous meeting was nervous and edgy. Seeing that, I sensed that he had something to say and I beckoned him to do so. He got up and admitted that he had been mocked at and shunned after their last meeting. His friends had said that the mission was impossible, even suicidal. But the day's proceedings had him convinced that his friends were selfish and cowardly. He declared that he was ready to work on the project with Seetabai and accept her leadership. His name, as I recall, was Tanaji Shinde, and in this way we had our first male warrior.

"The timing was good. Mohite very smartly got up and declared the meeting over, and added his two bit saying that the picture was clear—that the young men did not wish to be a part of the project, and consequently, they would be left alone. He begged them that at least they should not become obstacles and hinder the project at any stage. He requested them to keep the discussions to themselves and not breathe a single word to Sampatrao or any of his men. As we got ready to leave, one man, probably the eldest of the lot, couldn't control his emotions. He began to sob, and in a voice that strained to come out, he saluted Mohite and then choked over his own words. Mohite gave him a glass of water. He took a sip—and what followed next, I will never forget all my life.

"He simply said, 'Saheb, please don't make us feel ashamed of ourselves any further. We have realised our mistake and have understood our purpose in life. If our women can be so courageous, why shouldn't we be? Saheb, we too are ready to work with you on this project.' He then looked at the others for their reaction, then continued, 'Friends, if you agree with me, then stand up and show your willingness. Let us show our solidarity.' The youngsters had been moved completely and everyone stood up. One chap shouted, 'Jai Shivaji' and the others spontaneously followed with 'Jai Bhavani'. I was so thrilled that my eyes were full of tears of joy. If simple people could be made to realise their power, they could move the earth if they wanted to. Obviously they would require good counselling and proper guidance."

Professor Aditya looked at his audience who were completely absorbed in his narrative. He went on. "After this fantastic show of solidarity, Mohite asked everybody to sit down and congratulated them on their brave decision. He cautioned the boys that they were up against the might of crooked politicians and that they needed to be very careful till they reached their goal. He spoke about aggression and alertness, trademarks of Shivaji's rule, and said that they too should be alert and ensure that nothing of the day's discussion and the action plan be allowed to leak out. Otherwise, all the careful planning may not bear fruit. He compared the current situation with events in the Mahabharata when Krishna intervened, and careful planning, coupled with swift, shrewd and courageous execution of his plan helped the Pandavas win their battle against the phenomenal might of the Kauravas."

Robert, who had been listening intently, like the others, could not contain his enthusiasm. He interrupted the professor. "Extremely sorry to interrupt, but I must say I am very much intrigued by so many references to the great epic, the Mahabharata. All I know about this epic is that it is one of the greatest literary works that has ever been written—bigger than anything, either in English, French or Spanish or for that matter even Latin or Greek. I would love to lay my hands on it while I am in India and hopefully will be able to read it. Could a copy be arranged if it is not too much trouble?"

"No, no trouble at all. I shall arrange one by tomorrow," Nayan was quick to answer.

"Great, Nayan! thank you very much." Robert turned to the others, "Let's not keep the professor waiting, let's get on with the story."

"Robert, please do not be so formal. Interruptions are good.

It sure makes me happy to know that I still have my audience's attention and that they are not drifting away into boredom. It gives me great pleasure that you express a desire to read the Mahabharata. However, hopefully, you'll finish reading it during your stay here, and I promise you a discussion on it at the end of our meeting. Will that be okay with you?"

"That would be fantastic! Icing on the cake, I tell you! Thank you professor, you are most generous." Robert was obviously very thrilled.

"Well, to get back to our story, Mohite and I explained to the young group our detailed plan for the sugar factory. Seetabai, who was keenly listening to us, got up and made everyone pledge their undivided support by administering an oath of solidarity, secrecy and total participation. This act of hers amply demonstrated to us her maturity and leadership abilities. We had overcome the first big hurdle. The men were with us, our energy power pack ready to be unleashed. A few formal decisions were made and they were drafted on a piece of paper. This was to be our mandate, our guide. It was signed by everybody present to mark their acceptance.

"The Mohites, Sheetala and I, agreed to be advisors to the governing committee of the project. Seetabai was made the chairman; the pronouncement was unanimously accepted. Two other women were nominated as vice-chairmen. Two men accepted the posts of secretary and treasurer respectively. It was decided that all financial transactions be endorsed by Mohite's wife and no cheque be issued without her signature. All this homework had been done by two of Mohite's colleagues. They had painstakingly studied the Cooperative Societies Act and incorporated their recommendations as applicable to a cooperative sugar factory.

"We met again the following Sunday to work out the minute details. We wanted to build a cohesive group with a single and focused objective. Young men and women were classified into various groups and were given specific tasks to accomplish. Three main challenges were yet to be tackled—the first being the funding of our project, the second regarding the security aspect, and the third was getting competent human resources on board. The third was probably the most difficult as it required the help of knowledgeable agriculturists to run our factory with the assistance of the villagers.

"The first and second hurdles were interlinked, as without adequate security, getting financiers to fund the project would have been very difficult. Mohite and I met a few retired army officers, of whom Major Vikram Singh Bhosle agreed to help our cause. He suggested that we rope in retired police officers. His argument was that people like Sampatrao and the politicians whom we would be up against, may, with the help of their so-called social organisations, engage Seetabai and her colleagues in lawsuits that may become a nuisance. We contacted a few retired police officers, and together with Major Bhosle, called a meeting. Secrecy was top of the agenda and was to be maintained at all costs.

"As things started to fall in place, we realised that our Major Bhosle was also an accomplished technocrat. Safety being his responsibility, information security was his top priority. I knew a few IT guys, who agreed to examine our safety requirement. Their recommendation was to install some sophisticated equipment such as hidden cameras, tape recorders and other useful, but discreet instruments at our meeting venues. Major Bhosle graciously offered his Pune apartment for a year, to be used for our meetings, and that too without payment of any rent. We convened a meeting of our retired executive friends at Major Bhosle's apartment. I opened the meeting by making a simple and frank appeal. I pointed out that the common man was being denied his natural and fundamental rights by the nexus of politicians and the underworld. It was particularly blatant in our villages, where innocent villagers were terrorised and ruthlessly manipulated by the village mafia.

"Following this, we had an in-depth discussion on various aspects of security and a question-answer session, where we answered their questions specific to our project. Every single word of our discussions was recorded. We didn't want any slips or any areas where we could get misquoted. We took care that the information in our discussions was protected and did not get adulterated, as we had been advised by Major Bhosle. After the meeting we took a vote, and were extremely happy that almost ninety per cent of the meeting quorum agreed to join and help us. The remaining ten odd per cent, expressed their moral support but were unable to give any active help due to prior family and professional problems or commitments. We made three groups to tackle the basic security aspect, namely physical security, information security and legal security. Mohite's homework was simply fantastic.

"We decided that around ten ex-army officers, along with their spouses, should move to the five villages that were to be our pilot site. All were obviously Marathi speaking. We educated Seetabai and her four colleagues on the use of surveillance equipment that was to be worn on their person. These were nano instruments in the form of small micro chips fitted to their earrings. Actually, these were listening devices, powerful audio recorders. Seetabai was also to carry a tiny, yet powerful, concealed video camera fitted to her bangle. Only Seetabai, Major Bhosle and we, the project advisors, knew about this instrument. All this preparation was required as our fight was with unfathomable crooked politicians and their bands of thugs."

"Sir, all this is absolutely unbelievable. This is almost like the preparation we journalists make for our sting operations," remarked Sathe.

"I agree with you Sathe. You too should have done this with those nasty bank officers who harassed you for your exposé of the Pride Group. My young friends, there is no substitute for technology. You can successfully wage a war against corrupt politicians, industrialists and bureaucrats, if you are technology savvy," responded the professor.

It was getting late in the night, but nobody was ready to call it a day. In fact, they appealed to the professor to go on with his thrilling narrative. Shini said, "Sir, this has been a huge learning exercise for all of us, and that too in such a short time." She sighed and said, "If only we had recorded the proceedings..."

"For your information, Shini, I am already on it. The entire discussion has been recorded. Professor Aditya is okay with it. In fact, he wanted me to distribute CD copies eventually among us." Nayan's words brought a smile to Shini's face.

The professor continued, "Next item on our 'To-Do' list was to uncover all the facts about available government funding. Mohite pieced together all the information on how we could avail of this facility. We realised that the government funding that could be made available to us would cover only about twenty-five per cent of our requirements. And that too, provided the government cleared our project. I made an appeal to the fraternity of my ex-students working overseas. This was the acid test of how much goodwill I could command. God willing, it happened all right—I succeeded. Around one hundred students agreed to contribute a thousand dollars each, which formed our base capital—money to initiate our project. Not one of them asked me any questions.

"We decided to incorporate a new cooperative society, registered in Maharashtra, with names of each of these contributing individuals. The nominees were family members or close friends. The investment for the seed capital was made through our new society. This entire affair was managed within the available legal framework, all credit to our excellent team of legal and financial experts, who were themselves a competent bunch of retired government executives. Despite this windfall, we were still short of our total requirement. But it was a start—a big booster of faith and confidence.

"We then approached a consortium of four banks. Power-packed presentations were made to the management of this consortium. Our young boys really did an amazing job of making superb presentations in real style. We appealed to the socio-economic obligations of these banks. It worked! The banks agreed, and priority-sector funding and micro-finance was made available to the women members of our society. Making Seetabai the chairman of our sugar factory was our true masterstroke. She accompanied our team for every presentation that we made. Under the banner of 'Empowerment of rural women', we managed to convince all our contributors that they were helping a noble cause.

"Upon clearing the 'funding' hurdle, we turned our efforts to putting together a team that would take charge of operations. We approached three agricultural universities and spoke to sixty young agro graduates. We managed to get ten dynamic chaps on board our team, which already comprised of retired executives from the government's agriculture department. An ex-colleague of Mohite joined us as our COO. He was a kind of 'hands-on' person with in-depth knowledge of running a sugar factory. As such, our venture did not really require so much preparation or sophistication, but we were leaving no stone unturned. We wanted to be one hundred per cent on the dot.

"By now our project report was ready to roll. We had decided to keep politics out and keep our project clean and trouble-free. Therefore, we did not take any help from any political party, not even the Opposition. We steered clear, and to the best of my knowledge, started the only sugar factory set up without political patronage. The first of its kind! We applied to the registrar of cooperative societies and other mandatory competent authorities. Until then, Sampatrao and others hadn't got a whiff of what was happening. Of course, the news of our application finally reached Sampatrao and shocked him beyond belief. He was shaken and stunned! He was obviously furious but managed to conceal his emotions from the public. Some time or the other, we would have had to confront him, and yes, we were up to the challenge—mentally, physically, and technically as well. His hooligans started threatening those villagers whose names were on the application.

"Major Bhosle had cleverly anticipated this and had installed surveillance equipment at their residences. These instruments helped us record audio/video clips of the villagers being threatened by the goons. What can I say? All the goodness of science came to our rescue. Meanwhile, our efforts to get the society registered were on in full swing. The registrar however was delaying the project using one pretext or the other. Some ridiculous administrative reasons were quoted. Eventually, because of our dogged insistence to make our dossier progress, he finally gave in and confessed that he had been instructed to delay the project to the maximum extent possible by the Sampatrao –Salunke clan.

"This delaying tactic was used to test our resolve and possibly even break it. Their thugs continued threatening our activists, but resorting to direct physical violence was not an option because of the security cover provided by Major Bhosle, who had his men smartly positioned in the villages. Sampatrao was clearly helpless, and this itself, was our first victory. He realised that this wasn't a simple case of simple villagers that needed to be dealt with.

"It was then time for us to play the next card. We called a press conference and extended invitation's to select media representatives. Journalists, known to be on the payroll of powerful politicians, were avoided. At the conference, we presented videos of our activists being threatened by Sampatrao's hooligans, and also of our meetings with the cooperative society's registrar. The entire affair had all the makings of a major sting operation. The media was astounded. TV channels, within half-an-hour, aired the 'breaking news', alleging the involvement of Sampatrao and Salunke in this matter. Within a few hours, both the politicians were on TV, denying the charges as expected—that they had never instructed the registrar to reject or delay our application. The registrar was however made a scapegoat and was suspended from duty along with another colleague. Fearing backlash and damage to his political image, Salunke did a volte-face and said that he was all for rural women's empowerment, and that he espoused our cause wholeheartedly. He went to the extent of pledging maximum possible concessions and subsidies for our project. But Salunke was not a man to accept defeat. He was definitely going to play his underhand game and try and sink our project. Crooked politicians do not support empowerment of any sort; they need their vote bank to be poor, illiterate and incapable of independent thought."

"Yes sir! Ministers like Salunke can go to any extent, even for the smallest of gains. A while ago, I wanted to expose two fraudulent charitable trusts run by Salunke in our newspaper *Lok-Vani*. But the editor pointedly refused," said Sathe.

"'Very soon you'll see, the editor will join Salunke's party and get a nomination to the upper house!" Nayan remarked sardonically.

"You are absolutely right. Quite a few 'learned' editors run their newspapers for a few chosen political parties. They write editorials that are completely politically prejudiced. It's all so frustrating," said Janaki furiously shaking her head.

"That unfortunately is the truth we need to repair. However, could we continue with your narration?" Meghnath requested.

"We are talking about Salunke's underhand games. Sensing trouble ahead, we wasted no time in calling for a meeting with our bankers. Seetabai's team and other group-leaders were requested to be present. Caution was the need of the hour. I was apprehensive about the bankers. Money being their only 'mantra', they could easily succumb to pressure from the likes of Salunke. Politicians like him bring in a lot of money for the bank, not people like us. Knowing this, we decided to record our discussion with the bankers."

"I am surprised they didn't object," said Janaki.

"It was done secretly. As you know, I am a strong believer of Krishna *niti*. As long as your heart is pure and your intentions are honourable, how you get to your goal doesn't really matter. One needs to be flexible. If you always go by the book, you cannot oust powerful politicians like Salunke," the professor pronounced with conviction.

Robert was full of admiration for the professor. He spoke spontaneously, "If only India had a few hundred people like you, we British could never have ruled you."

"Guys, let us look ahead. Our problems are the same, wherever we go. It's the solutions that we need to be bothered about. Shall we get back to my story?" asked the professor.

"Please," was the unanimous reply.

"I was right. Salunke used his network and found out all possible details about our project and our people. He realised that 'finance' was the key. He promptly contacted our bankers in an attempt to malign our project. He informed them that the seed capital was provided by a few non-resident Indians, which was against the 'sons-of-soil' ethos. One of the bankers even tried to back out from the project. However, I threatened to expose him with the recording of our prior discussions. Were we to do that, it would have been very damaging and difficult for him and his bank to defend and wriggle out. It was then that the banker acquiesced and said that Salunke was trying to pressurise them. I went to the extent of explaining how one hundred NRIs were supporting this noble cause. He realised his mistake and agreed to go ahead with the funding. So, fortunately, Salunke and his goons failed to sabotage our project.

"Salunke and Sampatrao, both started a campaign to malign us in the eyes of the illiterate farmers, by spreading nasty gossip that I was from the upper class and not a son-of-the soil. We knew they would resort to such lowly tactics, and we were ready for it. We managed to record many of the malicious misinformation about us. In reply, we made a ten point welfare program for the villagers and distributed pamphlets to everyone. Amongst these were transparency in business, change in leadership, assured price of sugarcane, allied businesses, women's empowerment, cooperative banking, cooperative farming, alternate sources of energy, etc. The pamphlets were very effective.

"The success of this prompted Mohite to distribute a second pamphlet detailing the corrupt practices at Sampatrao's factory. That was a little impulsive I thought, as it meant that our battle with Sampatrao was becoming open warfare. He was not going to tolerate such defamation. Sensing trouble, I quickly called a press conference at Seetabai's village. Major Bhosle and his men provided the required security to all attendees. The data that we had put together on Sampatrao's factory was presented by Mrs Mohite.

Besides the journalists, the press conference was also attended by a large number of villagers. It was a raging success.

"That very evening, news about Sampatrao and his factory was telecast on most of the TV channels. The allegations made were supported by video clippings that were supplied by us. Journalists, from as far as Delhi, knocked on Salunke's door demanding explanations. He, of course, avoided the media like the plague. Sampatrao too coiled up in his shell... and their followers went quiet. Our tactics paid off.

"We then trained our guns on the registrar of cooperative societies. We set our media contact to focus on him. Journalists started questioning his efficacy and openly called for his head on TV channels. We also managed to telecast Seetabai's appeal to the government. This all-round approach eventually bore fruit and we got an unconditional permission from the registrar of cooperative societies."

"What an awful lot of mess! And that too for wanting to do some good!" exclaimed Robert.

"Yes Robert. Corrupt and arrogant rulers are quite the same everywhere. Finally, the real work started. Until then, it was all about getting permissions and countering the threats of Sampatrao and company. With the permission granted, we had to work on the formation of the factory, which implied a lot of hard work. All our bureaucrat and ex-defence colleagues were quite upbeat about the project, and they managed to inspire the young boys, villagers and others. Within three days, ninety per cent of the members of Sampatrao's sugar factory resigned and applied for a membership in our factory. All applications needed to be scrutinised carefully by our team at length. Amongst the applicants were a few, known, staunch and faithful followers of Sampatrao! Those were kept pending.

"We were ultra lucky that five of the farmers agreed to make available their otherwise barren land for the factory project. We paid them reasonable compensation. Each and every financial transaction of any significance was recorded. No chances were to be taken because Salunke or Sampatrao, as also others, were waiting for a slip, a blunder on our part. I told Mohite, Bhosle and others not to bother so much about speedy completion of the project. We couldn't afford to take any chances. We cautioned Seetabai against speaking to reporters before checking their credentials, an advice she understood readily. Three young chartered accountants from Pune volunteered to supervise the finances and accounting of our project. To keep everybody involved and abreast of what was happening, we decided to have status review meetings with the villagers on a weekly basis.

"Within nine months we managed to complete ninety per cent of our project. The sugarcane season was nearing. By God's grace and a lot of hard work by our teams, we managed to achieve all our milestones. One fine evening, I got an unexpected phone call from Ramesh Salunke's office. His secretary informed me that Salunke wanted to meet me but he was unaware of the purpose of the visit. I had to humbly decline the request, since the lack of information on the reason was not acceptable. The next day, Sampatrao called and explained Salunke's reason for the meeting. That scoundrel of a chap—shameless guttersnipe—after all the trouble he had given us, wanted to inaugurate our factory! I told him that the definition of a son-of-soil could be a tricky, delicate matter. He didn't seem to understand my statement so I elaborated, 'Mr Sampatrao, your surname being Chavan—in Rajasthan, a Chavan is Chauhan. Similarly, there are examples of Shinde-Sindia, Mohite-Mohta, Salunke-Solanki, Pawar-Powar and so on. So how do we define the origin of these surnames? Hence, how do we decide about an original son-of-the-soil?' He was stunned and of course dashed. He then said, 'Professor, we respect your knowledge. But do you understand our political requirement? Your factory's inauguration is a big event, But it is in our constituency.' Sampatrao pleaded his case by saying that Salunke was, after all, the minister for rural development and was the most eligible candidate to inaugurate the factory, which by then had got nation-wide visibility, thanks to the media glare.

"I agreed with him that the event was indeed in his constituency, the very same constituency that had plundered the poor villagers for so many years. I reminded him that Salunke and he had not only derided our cause, but had tried to hinder it every step of the way. I asked him if Salunke's claim of being a son-of-the-soil was justifiable. However, I assured him that they would be our guests of honour at the function.

"Realising that I was in no mood to give in, he asked me whom we had chosen to inaugurate the factory. I informed him that it had been our unanimous decision to ask Seetabai's mother to inaugurate the function and that the well-known industrialist, Bhadralok, was to preside over the function."

***

Chapter 4

Everyone was pleasantly surprised to hear the professor's proposition for the inauguration of the sugar factory. Janaki's father instantly rose from his seat and cheered in approval. Seeing that, everyone else also stood up and joined in to give the professor a standing ovation. After everyone had settled down, Nayan asked, "Sir, the sugar factory ought to be operational now. But who will guarantee its safety, especially since evil politicians were thwarted in their endeavour?"

"Nayan, you have a valid question. We were all aware that Seetabai and her colleagues would require solid support and a guarantee of safety for the factory to run successfully. We even asked her and her team if they had any solution for this particular problem. Seetabai is wise, though uneducated. She came up with a good proposition. She suggested adopting a tried and tested method used on another occasion. She said that there were thousands of villagers all devoted to Lord Vitthal. These devotees are popularly called Varkaris in the locally spoken Marathi. They very staunchly follow their spiritual discipline. They do not follow any caste or creed, and so they do not discriminate. Quite recently, they had fought the corrupt and mighty politicians, and did not allow a multinational company to put up their plant, which threatened to cause a great deal of environmental damage. We called for a meeting with these Varkaris. Mohite spoke to them and touched their hearts. He urged them to support our cause. A senior Varkari stood up and suggested that all the people working in the factory come together and become Varkaris. This would create a bonding and a sense of brotherhood between them. His idea was well received by everyone and came to be executed within a week. Everyone in the factory turned a Varkari and the entire endeavor then transformed into a sort of sacred project.

"Nayan, the actual motive behind sharing the story of Seetabai with you was to urge you all to think of bringing about a radical change. Such change calls for collective and persistent action, which would need to be executed with absolute dedication and selflessness. I expect you youngsters to take up this challenge actively and bring about this much needed revolution. Actions speak louder than words. Think over all I have said. You alone are capable of bringing about the kind of transformation that is the need of the day," the professor broke off abruptly and left the hall.

Everyone was silent for a few moments. Nayan and his friends seemed to be ruminating over the professor's words. Jennifer said, "Children, the professor is right about everything he's said. I do not see why any of you should feel uncertain about playing an active role in the process of change."

"Mother, we are not at all uncertain. In fact, we're rather ashamed of ourselves for not plainly expressing our desire to work with the good professor. Am I not right?" Shini said looking back at her friends.

"Shini, I feel the same way and am terribly sorry to think I disappointed Professor Aditya." Nayan could not conceal a sense of guilt.

"Nayan my dear, don't say that. You have no reason to be ashamed. The professor was simply projecting his point of view. I think our relationship has matured to a point where we can all be completely frank with each other. Ah! Here comes Aditya. Talk to him Nayan, and be frank," said Sheetala looking at her husband as he returned to the hall.

"Sir, we are all with you. We are sorry we did not express our keenness earlier, but I can promise you that each one of us is very eager to work with you. We give you our word," Sathe said emotionally.

"Guys, I am delighted at your enthusiasm. Fortunately your parents are witness to this conversation," said the professor wryly.

"We aren't going to be mere spectators," cried out Jennifer. "We too shall work along with our children under your guidance."

"That's quite right," said Meghnath. "We too are well aware of the seriousness of global issues. What we need is a clear cut approach to work on them."

"Well," said the professor, "I follow you, and I even understand your apprehensions. Things are difficult, but not impossible. Look at these kids, they're already global citizens. Why else would Shini, for example, be here, in a developing nation, listening to what I have to say? What we need is a global network full of good people ready to help each other. There must be a strong sense of brotherhood to hold it together. We need to awaken the masses worldwide and we can achieve this by employing flexible approaches and the latest in technology."

"Excuse me Professor, but I wish to point out to you that we are just four youngsters out here. We, however, have five other friends who might be keen on joining the team. Do you think we should have a word with them about the network we're building, as also our mission?" asked Nayan.

"Certainly, as I have said before, it is important to build up our ranks. We need to create a big network of good and dedicated people," responded the professor.

"What do you suppose is the most common cause of our global dilemmas?" the professor carefully asked.

"You mean to say there can be just one single cause for so many problems?" asked Mike.

"Qualitatively yes, quantitatively no," replied the professor.

"It is corruption, people! That's the fundamental cause of all our global dilemmas. And I'm not just speaking of financial corruption," he said seriously.

"I think I'm beginning to get your drift, Professor," said Mike.

"There are, in all, seven types of corruption," continued the professor. "These are broadly financial, cultural, political, spiritual, educational, social and ideological. Of these, ideological corruption is the most dangerous and the most complex in nature. It is also the root of all the other six forms of corruption."

"Nayan, so tell me, who are these other friends of yours?" asked the professor turning his attention to Nayan.

"Well Sir, there's Akito from Japan, Manzar from Oman, Sukarno from Indonesia, Hu Mintao from China and Orango from Nigeria. As I'd mentioned earlier, we all met at the international cultural workshop where we heard you the first time..."

"Right, but Nayan, I do think I've made my intention clear to you. We need people ready to act. Are those kids ready to be a part of our network and mission?"

"Well to be honest, I have yet to ask them," replied Nayan truthfully.

"Nayan, you must have a word with your friends and ask them what their objectives are. If they agree with our mission and wish to join us, please do send me their details. Also try to find out if their parents too are willing to participate," said the professor.

Nayan expressed special gratitude to the professor for his time and his guidance. In fact, everybody showed their appreciation and thanked him. Nayan gave him a CD containing photos and brief details of his friends. They then decided to meet again, after about a week, so as to settle upon a final plan of action. The parents too were grateful and said their children were very fortunate to have the professor as their guide. After everybody left, the professor and his wife stayed back and continued their conversation with Nayan, Sathe and Usha.

"Professor, you're aware that my family works for the Pride Group. I'm afraid to think what their reaction might be, if and when, they do come to know about my active involvement in this project. Please professor, tell me how to handle this situation. I'm at a complete loss." Nayan looked tense.

"Don't be anxious," said the Professor comfortingly. "I quite understand your position. I think it's wisest not to talk to your family about your involvement for now. Give it some time; let the plan develop further. In the meantime, continue working for the Pride Group. Who knows, your association with the group may well turn out to be useful to us for our cause."

"But Sir, how shall I put it? I mean you don't understand how disgustingly they'd react when they discover that I am focused on this mission," pleaded Nayan

"They will indeed. And will you be ready to dissociate from your family? You will obviously be obliged to resign from the Pride Group. You might also be denied all the luxuries you have at your disposal right now. Besides, it's likely that you'll have to forget about your share in the family wealth," said the professor bluntly.

"Believe me Sir, I'm already mentally disconnected from the rest of my family. I am well-qualified, so getting a job somewhere wouldn't be difficult. And as far as family wealth goes, I do not have to claim anything. My father has himself deposited a million rupees in my personal account. I also have an apartment in Mumbai which happens to be exclusively in my name. I, as a matter of fact, inherited it from my mother."

"You have an exceptional mindset. You're a real cool guy. Well Nayan, I think things are pretty clear now. I look forward to hearing from you and your other friends. Sheetala and I shall be staying back in Matheran for two more days," he said.

"Why don't you stay at my bungalow itself then?" said Nayan.

"This is your father's bungalow Nayan, not yours."

"Right ho!"

"Anyway, I think it would be great if you could make this bungalow a standard meeting point for our project. There is, of course, no compulsion. I just thought I got good vibes from this place," said the professor.

"That's probably because, here, my mother's soul is among us. She died of a cobra bite right here. My father was unable to her medical treatment in time."

"Well Nayan, that's just fate," said the professor gravely.

A short while later, the Professor and his wife left the bungalow.

Shini, her parents, and her uncle Robert stayed on for a few days in India before they returned to their homeland. Janaki didn't waste any time and left for Delhi with her parents. Sathe resumed his work at *Lok-Vani*, and Nayan too got on working seriously at his job. All in all, everyone had gotten back to their individual routines. After a few days had lapsed, Nayan wrote out detailed letters to his other friends telling them all about his rendezvous with professor Aditya.

It was a pleasant evening in Matheran. The Professor and his wife were enjoying their little holiday. He settled on a comfortable armchair and pored over a few interesting articles. He thought of the Parsis, another great community. Among the ranks of shining Parsi personalities, one name in particular, Bhadralok, stood out. The word 'Bhadra' itself stands for a sacred, great and iconic people, and Bhadralok was, in fact, the perfect representative of all such persons, a true icon. The professor's thoughts were suddenly interrupted by the ringing of his cell phone. He answered it and was pleasantly surprised, for out of some curious coincidence, it was none other than Bhadralok on the line. 'Telepathy', he thought to himself as they spoke. Bhadralok requested an urgent meeting with him. The two men had only met on one occasion before and that was at the inauguration of the factory. They were there barely two hours, and yet, such a short period of time proved to be clearly enough for them to realise that their wavelengths matched. As soon as he hung up, the professor began to make arrangements for his immediate return to the city with his wife. They wondered why, out of the blue, Bhadralok had called for an urgent meeting.

Aditya reached the Bhadralok House well before the projected time. Bhadralok came out to personally receive him. They greeted one another. Presently, the two men entered the private chamber. It was obvious that the matter to be discussed was serious.

"Professor, you must know that I read your articles regularly. The inauguration of the women's sugar factory gave me my first opportunity to make your acquaintance. I have to say that I admire your courage and clarity of thought. I can also see that you are genuinely concerned about the poor people. And professor, odd though it may sound, I stand before you as a simple person," said Bhadralok.

"Come now, Mr Bhadralok, who would ever dare call you a simple man? Why, you're so knowledgeable, not to mention charismatic. Most of us look upon you as a truly great and iconic personality."

"Maybe, but I am nevertheless a simple man. You see, if I wasn't so, my team and I would have successfully countered the dirty games Indrajeet Sankala and all the politicians in his pocket, play."

"Hmm, tell me Mr Bhadralok, what is bothering you? I've always known that the entire Sankala family is jealous of your success. The late Jagjeet tried his best to defame you. His son has been trying to create problems for you in your new projects. He just can't tolerate that you have accomplished so much and are so famous and popular. So what is he up to this time?" asked the professor.

"For nearly a year, he made sure the government wouldn't sanction clearance for any of our ambitious projects. We hoped to build roads and irrigation systems in the rural areas. But our attempts were foiled. To the best of my knowledge, we were the first applicants under the public-private partnership scheme. We had several meetings with all the concerned bureaucrats after having submitted a comprehensive proposal. However, on each occasion, we were told that our dossier was with Ramesh Salunke, the minister for rural development and it wouldn't move a step forward. Only last month, we were informed that Salunke has been delaying the decision. The eminent Madan Joshi from the Nationalist Hindu Party questioned the house as to the status of our project. He cornered Salunke, who somehow managed to wriggle out of the tight spot he was in."

"Right, and let me guess, Joshi and Salunke teamed up the very next day," said the Professor.

"How did you know that?" asked Bhadralok, quite amazed.

"Well," said the professor with a smirk. "I am no simple man. I happen to know both these guys. They're scoundrels, both of them. For wealth and power, these two would go to any extent. They're creating some trouble for you too, aren't they?"

"Yes, that's right. We all thought Joshi would champion our cause in the house. One of my senior colleagues had even met with him and requested his support. He agreed to help us, and so we furnished him with all the details he demanded to know about our project. I, myself, met with him. You must know that under normal circumstances I avoid meeting politicians. You see, I am of the firm opinion that business must be done without political patronage. I believe in merit. But after a year's delay, I began to feel really helpless. I really thought we had found our saviour in Joshi. I was pretty impressed by all the questions he brought up during the house session and how he tried to steer things in our favour. Alas, he built up all our hopes only to deceive us," said Bhadralok gloomily.

"Typical. Tell me, what's the latest status?" asked the Professor.

"Well, a retired senior bureaucrat happens to be the father of one of our young employees. He met with a colleague of mine and told him a few facts. It turns out that the Pride Group, and the Soro Corporation from the United States are planning to submit their own joint proposal for the same project. I don't, however, know if the proposal has been submitted as yet. I'm told the Soro Corporation is known for its aggressive lobbying."

"Indeed, lobbying in the US is nothing but a sophisticated manner of bribing."

"Right you are. There is no better way to describe it. We're talking about a two hundred billion project. Imagine the size and significance of such a project? We were also informed by that same bureaucrat that Salunke and Joshi are working together to clear the Pride Group's joint proposal."

"Well of course they are. The stakes are very high."

"Yes, but they're from two totally different political parties with completely different ideologies. And yet, they're working together towards such a devious end. Is there no honesty left in the world? I just can't believe it."

"Oh! But you have to believe it. This is the reality. The Pride Group and Soro have come together on this project. You must have heard that famous adage that goes, 'Politics is the last resort for the scoundrel'," said the professor.

"Yes I have, but I don't know how it applies really."

"Please excuse me for being candid, but your group has lost several good projects to corrupt competitors. It is because your executives just don't know how to handle the government."

"But professor, the thing I'm trying to stress on is that our group doesn't go by that philosophy. We do not believe in 'handling' the government or managing it, manipulating it, or whatever you wish to call it. It is a corrupt practice. That's all there is to it," said Bhadralok intensely.

"Mr Bhadralok, I am not talking about any corrupt practice here," the professor replied in a calm tone. "It is possible to manage the government without being corrupt."

"How, my dear Aditya, tell me how?"

"It's possible. All you have to do is be innovative, alert, aggressive and flexible. I'm sure you're acquainted with the Indian epics of old. You must know all about the strategies employed by warriors and tacticians like Krishna, Shivaji and Chanakya for instance. These three, in particular, countered the most corrupt and ruthless enemies. What has to be remembered here is that they were extremely innovative in their approaches besides being eternally alert, aggressive but within reason, and flexible in their behaviour," said the professor.

"You said flexibility in behaviour? You know professor, I must have attended quite a few international programs on leadership over the last four decades. I am sixty years old now. I just never thought that behavioural flexibility was quite such a big deal."

"For a while now I've been working on and speaking extensively about my concept of ethical flexibility," said the professor.

"Hold on professor, like I said before, in our model of business excellence there is no scope whatsoever for any ethical flexibility."

"You've got me wrong. Think about it. If you and your executives are so ethical and meritorious, why aren't your projects getting clearance from the government? Perhaps you haven't fully comprehended my definition of ethical flexibility. I believe, that as long as your aim and intent are sacred, you need not worry about the sanctity of the means and methods you employ to achieve your goal. You simply cannot fight the devils out there using ethical approaches. Keep the big picture in mind. You know your final mission, and it is sacred. You also happen to have the purest of intentions. So now, all you have to do is to get rid of the thorns in your path. Fight fire with fire. If people are trying to bring you down using dirty tactics, give them a taste of their own medicine. Bring them down using similar strategies. Remember, that your 'ethical flexibility' is for the betterment of the innocent masses – in their larger interest," said the professor animatedly.

"Now coming back to the hitch with your project, Mr Bhadralok. I'm confident that the dilemma can be resolved. We need to craftily tackle the politicians, bureaucrats and all your nasty, cunning opponents. We are going to have to take a calculated risk. It is far better to do so than to sit back and simply let the project fall in the hands of your corrupt rivals."

"Sounds like a tough task for people like us professor. We've never done such things before."

"Don't worry. As a CEO, you have the privilege of power and authority to bring about changes no matter how radical they are. And personally, I'd be honoured to help you."

"Professor," said Bhadralok with a look of nervous anticipation mixed with excitement, "that would be wonderful. I somehow knew you would be able to allay my apprehensions. In fact, that's precisely why I called you here today."

"Alright, if we are to work on this together, I shall need you to supply me with a team of five or six young and brilliant managers, needless to say, of unquestioned integrity. I may call two or three of my own students to join me in this task," said the professor.

"What's your plan of action then? Will you be able to give me an idea about the nature of the risk we're taking and how big it's going to be? Understand my situation professor. I really can't take any risk that puts the very reputation of the Bhadralok Group at stake."

"I completely understand your anxiety. Give me a week's time. I shall be back with a comprehensive game plan. My only request is that you directly supervise our functioning," said the professor plainly.

"Professor, how can you make such a request?" reacted Bhadralok respectfully. "For one, you are senior to me, and your knowledge and experience are profound. I therefore think that it would be wise for you to supervise me and my team. Besides, I'd be comfortable giving you a direct feedback of the proceedings. You can contact me at anytime. I shall give you my personal number. I really don't know if there's a good enough way to show you my gratitude, Aditya."

"You may thank me once the task is accomplished," said the

professor. "Oh and one more thing, I need you to give me a reasonable amount of liberty to carry out my work. You understand how delicate the situation is."

"Look professor, this is your assignment. You shall be running the show yourself. I can assure you that none of my colleagues shall interfere, no one but Mr Pitushala who has been working with me very closely on this project. He knows all the finer details, and above all, he is a man you can implicitly trust."

"Fair enough, he shall have to furnish us with all those details. You know what—I think it best that he be part of our team itself. What say you?" suggested the professor.

"Agreed," said Bhadralok. "Next week when you brief us about your plan, Pitushala shall be present too."

The two men spoke for a short while about a few other things before Aditya left. It made him happy to think that Bhadralok considered him to be, in a certain way, his mentor, his rescuer. As soon as he returned to his house, he phoned Nayan and Sathe. He arranged to have a meeting with the boys at his residence that very evening. A feeling of excitement consumed both boys as they set out to meet the professor. They could sense that their arrival was eagerly anticipated.

"Lads, sometimes our destinies have great things in store for us. It pleases me to tell you that we have been presented with a great opportunity to test some of our novel approaches, the strength of our little network, and a chance to measure the impact of our calculated efforts. I will in fact venture to say that our mission has, in a way, just begun." This was said with much passion and enthusiasm. Nayan and Sathe were not a little surprised by the professor's zest. They gazed at him amusedly, if not hypnotically. The professor began to narrate the particulars of his conversation with Bhadralok. Once the professor had said it all, it was the boys who now bubbled with enthusiasm. It was a truly challenging task they were faced with.

"Isn't it a gratifying feeling to know that Bhadralok has appointed us to be his rescuers? I probably shouldn't have made such a display of my excitement." The professor laughed heartily and so did the boys.

Nayan was the first to calm down. "Sir," he asked, "how do we go about this assignment? You've a considerable amount of experience handling crooks like Sampatrao and other politicians. But here we're faced with a completely different scenario. I mean we're dealing with virtually all the most powerful, ruthless and cunning people in the circuit, and worse still, they are together as a team."

"Nayan, you raise a valid point. We cannot openly fight these people. We're going to have to create a sort of snare around the enemy. This calls for some carefully calculated moves across the chessboard to checkmate their king. Do you think you could pull out some information about the project through some of your known sources," asked the professor.

"Well let's see. My elder brother Pawan must know a thing or two about it. He is after all a member of Indrajeet's core team," Nayan replied.

"Sathe, how about you? Do you know anyone in the Nationalist Hindu Party in the middle cadre? Anyone frustrated?" asked the professor.

"Well, there are quite a few frustrated people in the NHP. In fact, which political party is free from them? What exactly do you have in mind?" he asked.

The professor went on to explain his comprehensive strategy. He eventually came up with a cohesive plan of action and prepared a detailed presentation for Bhadralok. Nayan and Sathe accompanied the professor. For them, the experience would be invaluable.

Bhadralok introduced five of his brightest and most dynamic managers to the professor. Pitushala too was present. The professor briefed Bhadralok on the plan he had formulated. Bhadralok listened intently and was impressed with the professor's replies to each and every query that came up. Fully satisfied, he approved of the strategy and gave the green signal. He also promised that he would have absolutely anything and everything at his disposal. The meeting was a success. 'Divine' was the name they assigned to the task they were about to undertake, for sacred it was.

Later that evening, the professor informed Janaki and Shini about 'Project Divine'. The girls had never anticipated getting such a wonderful opportunity to work with him. They, along with their parents had a conference call with the professor, so that before long, each person knew perfectly what his or her role was. Every minute detail was looked into. The first and extremely critical step would have to be initiated by Nayan and Sathe.

Sathe went about his work most diligently. He learnt of a Maratha politician by the name of Dhanaji Bhosle in the NHP. This man was a close associate of Madan Joshi. Dhanaji, ambitious as he was, had established his level of authority through the student wing of the party. He was, however, very well aware that the Brahmin lobby would never allow him to grow beyond a certain point. Madan himself saw to it that Dhanaji was never presented with an opportunity to share a big public platform. He was denied every chance to contest a public election and make his way into the lower house. Care had been taken to have him nominated to the upper house with much scheming and manipulation. Dhanaji had a clear picture of what his future in politics would be. His ultimate goal was to get elected to the lower house through a public election because that is where the real power is. Such an election, however, would require the building up of a constituency. He knew that to build up a constituency he'd have to do some major social work, get visibility through the work, and it would have to be publicised as widely as possible. Unfortunately for Dhanaji, joining the Azad party was not an option because it was already dominated by Salunke and his own team of Marathas.

Sathe gave the professor details about Dhanaji. He was convinced that Dhanaji could play an indispensible role in their masterplan. The professor agreed that he would make an ideal pawn. He sent Dhanaji a brief but cleverly worded message through Sathe. It said that a big business group, well known for its ethics and social responsibility, wished to embark on a rural development project in Western Maharashtra. The group was in need of a young politician who would recognise and support their work which would be carried out with the group's official funding of various political parties. It was, in essence, a straightforward and honest donation to political parties, on condition that the funds be spent purely on social work and not a dime would go towards electioneering. The group had concluded that Dhanaji was the most appropriate candidate for their endeavour. They stressed on it being a win-win situation for both.

Dhanaji was delighted to receive the professor's message. He considered the offer to be nothing less than a golden opportunity to further his own scheme. Without any hesitation whatsoever, he agreed to meet Professor Aditya. All the arrangements for the meeting were taken care of by the Divine team. The venue was a classy but not pretentious hotel. Aditya had instructed his young colleagues to plant an audio recorder while he himself carried a micro video camera fitted into a pen. Dhanaji could never have suspected such craftiness on the part of the professor. Politicians tend to think they alone possess all the cunning in the world. The professor wanted the entire session to be properly, and more importantly, secretly recorded for later use.

It seemed like they were having a reasonably productive meeting—the professor and Dhanaji. When Aditya declared that the whole thing was a Bhadralok Group venture, Dhanaji was quite taken aback. The professor however exercised an admirable amount of tact throughout the meeting. After he had made a preliminary speech about the nature of the project, the funding by the Bhadraloks, and Dhanaji's political maturity, he initiated an open discussion.

"Dhanaji Saheb, I can see that you're wondering why it is that a group as huge and reputed as Bhadralok chose you to be a part of their project."

"Yes, it is quite a mystery. I mean I'm neither a minister nor a member of the ruling party."

"Well, you know everyone knows that the Bhadralok group does not believe in political lobbying. But there have been certain major developments and hence drastic changes have been made. Your boss, Madan Joshi, and curiously enough, his archrival, Ramesh Salunke, have teamed up to help the Pride Group against Bhadralok. I suppose you know about Joshi having previously raised questions concerning the rural infra-project proposed by the Bhadralok Group."

"Of course, I know about that. Salunke froze that file and now Joshi has joined him. The Bhadralok Group, as a rule, never spends on politicians unofficially. The Pride Group on the other hand throws money at our feet," said Dhanaji laughing.

"Oh! but the world is changing my friend. India too is changing. It's up to young politicians such as you to lead us through the change. Now I'm no fortune-teller, but I'll tell you this frankly—if you don't act now, chances are, your political career will suffer later on," said the professor bluntly.

"Is that a prophecy or what professor?"

"No, it's simply my analysis. Where will you be five years from now? How do you place yourself in the world of politics? Are you going to be a people's representative? Do you think Joshi will ever permit that? You are already forty-two years old, aren't you?"

"Yes but then what do you suggest?" asked Dhanaji sounding almost exasperated.

"Help Bhadralok and Bhadralok will help you!"

"How's that going to happen?"

"You need to build up your own constituency, don't you? Bhadralok will spend on building social infrastructure for your constituency."

"But tell me, what part will I have to play? How can I be of service to the Bhadraloks?"

"There are two ways as far as I can see. Your party was in power a few years back, so I assume you still have access to some of the old controversial files in connection with Salunke and Joshi. The first thing you can do is to get us copies of those particular records. You can rest assured that we would never get you into any trouble. We have to do what we can to corner those two politicians. If we don't, they'll just go on wreaking havoc."

"I completely agree with you," said Dhanaji nodding vigorously.

"The second thing you could do is give us audio recordings of meetings that Salunke and Joshi have had with Indrajeet on the infrastructure project."

"Oh! That would be very difficult, professor. And besides, it's far too dangerous for me to get into that."

"Dhanaji, you're going to have to take a risk sooner or later. Believe me, your courage will bring you great rewards," said the professor with brazen confidence.

"I don't follow you. What do you mean, professor?"

"Even the most brilliant politicians cannot always cover their tracks, however much they want to. Anyway, let me not mince words and make our proposal clear to you. If you follow the first option and get us copies of the files and documents we need, the Bhadralok Group will finance selected social projects in your constituency. If you manage to procure the audios, the group will set up an industry in your constituency."

"And how would that help me personally? Suppose I were to bring you all the evidence you need, the audios for instance, and the Bhadraloks contribute in a big way towards my constituency—don't you think the association would be plain for all to see? And if Salunke and Joshi were to get wind of such a scheme, God knows they'd ruin me thoroughly. My career in politics would be as good as over."

"Dhanaji," said the professor, "a career in politics calls precisely for such gutsy action. Why are you so afraid of these two men? We are there for you and we shall support you. You must get those files. I'm sure there are a few frustrated bureaucrats who might be of service to you. As a politician, I'm sure you're well acquainted with all these processes, and you'd hardly need my guidance on that."

"Sure, but I've a question professor—how am I going to sustain my political career without adequate finances?"

"Hmm, I think that's a valid question. It is common knowledge that politicians and industrialists invest in each other. This is true all over the world. The Bhadralok Group has a solid reputation and a worldwide presence. In today's fast changing global scenario, a dynamic politician such as you must learn to be business savvy. You must build your own business group. Funding should not be an issue. Investors are always looking for promising projects. You will have a team of experts from the Bhadralok Group who will help you set up your first business corporation. I must say here that a cooperative sugar factory or an educational institution is not the kind of professional venture you should consider. Bhadralok will put up its own industry in your constituency. Take a look at what Salunke has done in his constituency. It's small wonder that he perennially gets his votes from there."

"Of course! But I'm still not confident about being able to get the audio CDs you want," said Dhanaji.

"Come now. Even the high-command in Delhi, which controls the Azad party, wants a formidable candidate to rival Salunke. This, I can see, you know very well. Once you've built up your own constituency, you shall emerge as that candidate. The choice is entirely yours. Like I said, it is a fast world we're living in. If you refuse to take up this challenge, know that we won't be waiting around idle. We have shortlisted a few others from various political parties who we believe are suitable and might be more than willing. Really, which politician would miss an opportunity like this to work with a group as grand as Bhadralok? The best we can do is give you forty-eight hours to think it over. It's really up to you. I'd just like to remind you that if you do agree and decide to work with the Bhadraloks, you will be engaging in 'constructive politics'."

"Professor, may I ask you a kind of personal question?"

"Please do."

"What's in it for you; what's your interest in the project?"

"Ah! I see you're trying to deduce whether or not I have some hidden motive," said the professor derisively.

"Oh no, not at all, professor. It is just a straight and honest question. Your knowledge of politics and experience cannot be disputed. Come to think of it, you ought to have been in active politics yourself."

"I am very much into active politics," said the professor. "What else would you call all of this?"

Dhanaji broke into a nervous laugh and gazed at him in awe. When it was time to leave, the professor once again reminded him that he was free to choose his path. Professor Aditya settled his hotel bill and left for the airport to board a flight to Delhi. It was time to plan his next move. Meanwhile, he had already briefed Bhadralok on the events of the day.

Janaki's father, Meghnath, had indeed been busy. He had pulled some strings and managed to arrange for the professor a meeting with a young communist leader. It so happened that this young man too was striving to shape his career in politics. Professor Aditya met him and spoke at length about the Bhadralok Group's proposal and also about the joint venture between the Pride Group and Soro. He told him that he was going to, in a few days, obtain some explosive inside information about the Pride Group's association with the Salunke-Joshi duo. The house was in session at the time. The communist was expected to raise critical questions about the project based on all the information the Divine team would provide. Janaki too had been playing her part. She'd arranged for the professor to meet with some of her close media associates. Aditya told them about the team's efforts to help the Bhadralok Group. He also requested that they get appropriate media coverage after the questions had been raised in the house. The media in Delhi is known to actively follow the political scene and the professor had every intention of exploiting that fact to the optimum.

It was late in the evening. Dil Bhojani was in his garden, relaxing. Although he lay back quite still on the bench his mind was racing. Bhojani had become quite anxious following the previous month's news that Iran-related projects had been postponed. Salunke was supposed to help Indrajeet get those projects for the rebuilding of Iran, but much to his chagrin, nothing had happened. Fortunately for him, however, he had been presented with yet another opportunity to realise his dream. It was all quite sudden. With Salunke's aid, Indrajeet had managed to get into a completely new infrastructural project. The Bhadralok Group had already submitted a proposal, but Indrajeet was to make a bid at a lower price and to take on a technical partner. Salunke had managed to provide him with a copy of the Bhadralok proposal. Bhojani was very pleased that his own son, Pawan, had been called in to take care of the whole bidding process. Also the Soro Corporation had agreed to partner. Things were looking up. Pawan would make a ton of money by way of project leakages. The project would also expose him to an international network and he would soon have a number of senior political contacts. Salunke and Joshi were both supporting the Pride Group. Big money often forges big rivals to get together!

Nayan spied his father sitting in the garden, lost in thought. The professor had assigned him the duty of obtaining a copy of the Pride Group's project proposal. It was absolutely crucial to get that document. "How hard could it be?" thought Nayan. He was after all just another member of the family. His father and brothers would never suspect his intentions. He could freely walk into any and everybody's room.

He was jolted when he heard his dad, who had just noticed his presence, call out to him in an affectionate tone. He noticed his father looked happy and cheerful, and he could well guess the reason for his happiness. It was the prospect of making money for the Bhojani Empire that had uplifted his father's mood. Nayan thought how utterly contrasting were the personalities of the professor and his father.

"Nayan, come my son. I'm seeing you after a long time. You know my plans for our family. I need not bring them up again. But something great has happened. Providence is once again on our side."

"Yes I can see that in your face dad. There is joy written all over it."

"Oh yes, and you will find that I have every reason to be joyous," said Bhojani grinning.

Father and son spoke for close to an hour. His dad spoke to him in detail about the whole project and about Pawan's part in the whole deal. The project was possibly his dad's last chance to make a lot of money in a short while.

Nayan was up and about early the next day. A feeling of deep spirituality had spread over him. He could feel a major change stirring within. After praying, he walked towards his father's room. Bhojani too was engaged in prayer. Nayan just stood back silently observing his father.

"Nayan my boy, you're up very early today."

"Yes dad, I'm now a confirmed believer in Jagjeet's theory of speed."

"Excellent. But tell me what has prompted this?"

"Well I was thinking about the mega project you were talking about yesterday, and it has gotten me all excited. Besides, I'm even more curious about it because of Pawan *bhaiya's* involvement.

"Yes. Indrajeet has recognised your brother's capability."

"Father, I too want to educate myself about the business and entrepreneurship in general. I think this project might be the best opportunity to do so. Do you think I could, I don't know, maybe study the project proposal or something like that?"

"Yes of course, why ever not? Pawan gave me one copy. You may study it. It's an infrastructure project and so the proposal is pretty complex. Indrajeet very cleverly managed to get a great deal of sensitive information on the Bhadralok proposal."

That last statement particularly caught Nayan's interest. He instantly asked, "Dad but how did he have access to all that sensitive info?"

"The simplest thing ever!" said his dad grinning. "Ramesh Salunke plainly handed over a copy of the Bhadralok proposal to him. Politicians are paid for these small services, you know."

"Indeed! Deshpande uncle did talk to us in quite some detail about political manipulation. So I was wondering dad, could I study both the proposals then—Bhadralok's and Indrajeet's?" asked Nayan feigning innocence.

"Both?" Bhojani broke into a laugh. "Why son, there are no two proposals? There's just one. You see, Pawan simply reworded it while retaining the same original structure, and merely altered the key figures to render our proposal more competitive."

Nayan was appalled by the thought of how money and power could corrupt the human mind. It made him sick to the stomach. But he could not let it show. He had a charade to keep up. "Great, I think it should make for a very interesting study."

Dil Bhojani drew out a leather portfolio from the depths of a drawer in his desk and handed it over to his son. He then stressed on the need for confidentiality and asked Nayan to be very careful while handling the documents. As Nayan held the folder in his hands, he felt a thrill running through him. He quickly returned to his own room where he eagerly extracted all the documents from the leather file. He sat at his desk looking incredulously at the myriad papers. He was outraged by the lack of ethics and blatant manipulation. He looked at all the remarks that had been made by Salunke on the Bhadralok proposal, most of which were addressed to some very senior bureaucrats. He then looked at the proposal that Pawan had drafted for the Pride Group. It was an outright theft. He was enraged at the whole affair and especially at Indrajeet. "Bastard," he cried out involuntarily. But then he remembered that his brother Pawan was equally bad, if not worse. 'And my dad, the father of such a vile creature.' He cringed to think he was a part of the Bhojani family, that it was the same blood that flowed through his veins.

He called up professor Aditya from his room. The professor told him to waste no time and take out two copies of the entire file. It was most important to get a copy of Salunke's remarks. Nayan followed the instructions, and by late afternoon, he had already handed over the documents to the professor, who, on receiving them, gave Bhadralok a call to give him the news. Bhadralok himself was shocked at the low level the Pride Group could stoop to. He mused over how impossible it was for an ethical entrepreneur to make his mark in a country full of scoundrels. He thought about what the professor had said earlier about successfully running an ethical enterprise. Aggression, speed, innovation and flexibility, all were crucial. He was slowly beginning to understand what flexibility actually meant.

The professor's next move was to call Shini. Her job had been to obtain as much information as she could about the Soro Corporation's involvement with the Pride Group. Soro was supposed to be the Pride Group's technical partner. Shini had set out to get details about some of Soro's earlier joint ventures with others in countries like Nigeria, Brazil, Indonesia and Korea. She found, not surprisingly, that they had a long and dirty history of government manipulation everywhere. They spent heavily on bribing the local politicians and bureaucrats. That was their modus operandi. Several top executives of their corporation owned huge properties in most of the big cities like New York, Washington and London. She was able to get her hands on some interesting facts about major bonuses that had been given to the top executives, plus earlier reports published in reputed American newspapers. She organised all the data she collected and sent it across to the professor, and therein was successfully completed yet another important part of the Divine operation.

The following evening, the professor got a call from Dhanaji Bhosle. He spoke optimistically and said that he had managed to get copies of three files that had been cleared by Salunke and one that Joshi had cleared. Each of these dealt with government contracts allotted to unmeritorious private companies. 'Strike three,' thought the professor. Dhanaji had, however, been unable to get any audio recordings of conversations between Salunke and Joshi. But the professor was nevertheless happy with his efforts. It was obvious that Dhanaji did not wish to risk displeasing Salunke and Joshi overtly. Basically, politicians develop this dreadful habit of not even trusting their own parents. Having played his part and fulfilled his side of the bargain, Dhanaji requested a meeting with Bhadralok. It was now up to Bhadralok to return the favour and help the politician as he had promised. Aditya arranged a meeting for him at the Bhadralok office where Dhanaji finally handed over the four files.

As he structured all the information he had obtained from his team, Professor Aditya was convinced that there was sufficient ammunition for litigation. Well connected as he was, he sought the counsel of two retired high court judges whom he knew personally. He wanted a professional evaluation of the worthiness of all the documents and evidence he had accumulated. He wished to ascertain if there was a valid case of civil and criminal offence. The severity or the degree of the offence had to be ascertained. It was nevertheless presumed enough to threaten Salunke, Joshi and Indrajeet. The professor knew that if the three crooks were cornered they would do just about anything to save themselves. Indrajeet was an influential man and could well afford the best lawyers in the country. Also, there was always the option of bribery. Salunke would most likely deny any relationship with the Pride Group. Madan Joshi, too, would somehow use his political clout to save his neck. While the professor's primary intention was to safeguard the interests of the Bhadralok Group, he also had every intention of making Indrajeet and his two goons perceive him as a very real threat. He believed that the whole affair would serve to educate the common man about the truly fraudulent nature of their political idols.

Bhadralok, along with the professor and the Divine team, came together to carefully plan out the next move. Shini arranged to have a press release about the Pride Group's theft of the Bhadralok proposal. She also made mention of Salunke's and Joshi's involvement, and references to their numerous manipulations in the past as well. The disclosure of the Soro Corporation's involvement was of course what made the biggest impact. The news was aired on virtually all American news channels, and before long, it was all over the Indian media. The whole issue created a huge uproar in the house. The young communist politician, whom the professor had met, declared that he would be able to provide some valuable evidence in the house the following day.

As was expected, Madan Joshi denied having any interest in the project and praised the Bhadralok Group. Salunke, on the other hand, had a tough time trying to salvage the situation. The entire nation saw him in a disgusting light. Indrajeet's PR officer too made a statement to the press insisting that the Pride Group would never resort to any fraudulent means to get any government project. It was the scandal of the century. The news was aired round the clock on all channels and radio stations. All the exposure put Salunke's political career in absolute jeopardy. He was now burdened with the huge task of eliminating all other chances of information leakages. He seemed to be in a state of total torment. In his desperation, he began negotiating with several senior communist leaders and appealed to them to stop any further exposure. The professor knew that the larger part of Salunke's wrath would be directed at their young communist comrade. A few security agents were deployed to protect him. He had been temporarily lodged at an inconspicuous hotel in Delhi.

The following day was to mark a new chapter in the history of Indian industry. It was the first time that an ethical group such as the Bhadralok was expected to triumph over its corrupt and disreputable rival. Indrajeet had a team of private detectives all working round the clock to prevent further discredit of the group. But his associates and he were shooting in the dark. It was possibly the first time he had felt things spiral out of control. He might have even remembered the tactics of his late father, Jagjeet. Ironically for Salunke, a number of his associates from his own party were secretly enjoying his plight.

The next day when the stock market opened, not surprisingly, the Pride Group's shares had plummeted. On the other hand, the Bhadralok's share prices had soared. Stock markets abroad too reflected a similar reaction. In the house, Joshi and Salunke were seen sitting well apart showing nervous agitation. A lobby that regularly sponsored the Pride Group was unaccountably very inactive.

The young communist produced a copy of the project proposal bearing Salunke's remarks, and another copy of the Pride Group's cloned version. The members reacted with shock and revulsion. Salunke and Joshi had nowhere to hide. The chaos that erupted made it necessary to postpone the session. The episode even managed to get international coverage at lightning speed. The media mercilessly commented on the dubious backgrounds of both corporations. Some of the news channels even showed documentary evidence of some of the old files that had been fraudulently cleared by Salunke and Joshi.

It had been a miserable day for Indrajeet and it was just as bad for the Bhojanis. Pawan was so affected by the recent events that he suffered a fainting spell, caused by drop in blood pressure. His father, Dil Bhojani, who was a long term patient of hypertension, suffered an acute attack, serious enough to merit a visit to the hospital. Indrajeet received a call from Salunke that evening. Salunke was furious. He had set his people working day and night to find the culprit who had exposed them. He was convinced that the project file that contained all his remarks had been stolen from Indrajeet's office. Indrajeet too set out with a vengeance to pin the culprit down. He seemed quite certain that the leak had taken place from the Bhojani residence. Things got really ugly. Old man Bhojani felt a twinge in his heart at the thought of his youngest son Nayan. It had obviously been a fatal blunder to have trusted him with the copy of the proposal. He was distraught by the nature of the betrayal. He was, after all, their own flesh and blood. But then another thought struck him. Nayan could never have managed any of this all by himself. There had to be somebody else running the show, and Bhojani had a gut feeling that that somebody was in fact, professor Aditya.

Dinner at the Bhojani's that evening was a solemn affair. One might have thought there had been a death in the family. Nayan sat before his father and brothers. No words were exchanged until Pawan broke the silence and declared gravely that Nayan had ruined his life and career, possibly permanently. Charan looked quite frightened too. He knew that Indrajeet would never spare them. Old man Bhojani looked like he had aged a great deal in the last few days. He beckoned Nayan up to his room, and with a heavy heart, commanded him to pack his bags and leave the house without delay. It was probably the only thing he could do, in some small way, to abate Indrajeet's wrath. Nayan had foreseen such an eventuality. He offered no arguments but quietly packed his things and left the house. He would be putting up with Sathe for a while.

Within two days, the Bhadralok Group was awarded the project. It was a palpable victory—a fitting finale to a disgusting corrupt plot. A globalised business environment compelled the government to act fast, rather appropriately. An enquiry committee had been appointed to investigate the whole episode. Ramesh Salunke had refused to resign his post as minister. His team was working ceaselessly to find out how the documents and files pertaining to his previous projects had been stolen from the government offices. It had already occurred to Salunke that it was probably professor Aditya who had masterminded the entire operation. He could not, however, be sure of the nature and extent of Bhadralok's involvement. Out of sheer frustration, Salunke finally decided to call up the professor directly. The recent episode with Seetabai and the sugar factory was still fresh in his memory. He resentfully remembered that the professor had meddled in that particular affair too. The growth of the professor's network meant a very serious threat to ambitious politicians like him. He dialled the professor and waited for an answer. He was, he had decided, going to speak as civilly and calmly as he could, and hide his inner turmoil.

"Professor, hats off to you. I am amazed at your intelligence, your networking skills, and above all, your courage. I daresay you'd make a fine politician."

"I disagree, Mr Salunke. You see, I firmly believe that a lot can be achieved without having to resort to politics," said the professor coldly.

"Perhaps you're right. But we both know that politics presents you with the ideal platform to execute your plans, and it is the fastest and more legitimate way to reach the masses."

"Maybe so, but I think politics today is unproductive. People no longer respect politicians. You may think the people in your constituency admire you, but you are deluded. If you examined their true sentiments, you'd find that your people do not have any respect for you."

"Hang on you haggard hawk of a professor. I find it curious that you're slandering politics. Did you not just use the crafty tricks of the trade yourself to help the Bhadralok Group?"

"I see what you're doing here Salunke, but let me tell you, your sly words do not provoke me."

Salunke sniggered. "Old fellow, your intelligence amuses me. But if I were you I would exercise more caution in its employ. You could not even dare to conceive what I can come up with."

"Oh but you're wrong. I can see right through you. You reveal your strength when you salute the Azad in Delhi."

That last statement was more than Salunke could digest. He erupted in rage and roared out like a crazed animal. "You damned rascal. You son-of-a-bitch, don't you dare talk about my strength! You'd do well to worry about your safety and that of your family. You motherfucker, don't mess with the devil himself," he threatened.

"Ah, there you are. You're now revealing your true colours. By the way, this conversation has been fully recorded, thank you. I salute technology."

Salunke instantly disconnected. 'That went well', thought the professor. He gave himself a pat on the back and promptly called up Bhadralok to give him the news.

The trouble began a week later. It was all over the news. A gang of hooligans had tried to assault Aditya and his wife. Luckily, their attack was foiled by the private security guards who had been stationed outside their residence. The assailants were armed with traditional weapons, and the assault, had it been successful, would probably have proved to be fatal. Unfortunately, none of the thugs had been caught. It, however, wouldn't have taken a genius to figure out that Ramesh Salunke had had a part to play in the whole sordid affair. Even without evidence, people were certain he had planned the attack. As soon as Shini learnt about it, she spoke to her dad. Mike, being a senior and well respected lawyer, proved to be most resourceful. He suggested the professor's security should be managed professionally, especially when he was travelling. He was quite a staunch Jew. In fact he was so proud of his Israelite heritage that he even had friends in the Mossad. It so happened that one of his close friends was an ex-Mossad officer, who was glad to help, and chalk out a security plan. It was for the Bhadralok Group to execute it.

Nayan and Sathe sat discussing their next course of action, now that Operation Divine had been successfully executed. Shini and Janaki too, like the boys, rejoiced. Bhadralok had arranged a small reception at his residence to express his gratitude to the professor and his team. He inquired about the current occupation of both Nayan and Sathe. He had a plan in mind and was upset that poor Nayan had been obliged to leave his home. Nayan had sacrificed so much for the Bhadralok Group. He admired his courage the most. As a gesture of appreciation, he declared that Nayan would work with his group as an officer on 'special duty', knowing very well that Prof Aditya wanted Nayan for a bigger assignment. He also provided a special budget for the future projects that Aditya and his team would undertake.

Sathe, however, was to continue working with the *Lok Vani*. He was pleasantly surprised when Bhadralok offered to pay up his debts and settle all the loans his family had taken. He also arranged for Nayan's and Sathe's security. The biggest surprise of the evening was that Bhadralok had decided to make Janaki's father, Meghnath, his political advisor. Janaki's dad would bring the group the much needed political maturity.

It was a cloudy Saturday morning. Nayan and Sathe were chatting together when Nayan received a message on his mobile from his father. Curious and anxious, he read the message. His father was in Matheran and he wanted to meet him as soon as possible. Nayan didn't know what to make of it. It was such a sudden and unexpected development. He thought it wise to call his father first. The voice he heard on the line was remorseful and for a moment he even thought he heard his father cry. "Please son, come to Matheran. Come soon," were the only words Nayan could distinguish, and they pierced his heart. He quickly packed a small travel bag and was all set to leave. But Sathe wouldn't hear of him going alone. He insisted on accompanying him. The two boys reached Matheran late afternoon.

They were shocked to find Bhojani lying motionless in bed, with no one but Deshpande by his side. "Come Nayan," he beckoned, "Your father has been anxiously awaiting your arrival."

"Father, what happened? You look sick."

"My son, you are right. You were always right. I have been mistaken all along. I'm only sorry that the realisation came too late. It is all over now."

"But dad, what do you mean by that? What has happened? Talk to me," cried out Nayan frantically. He looked at Deshpande and asked, "What's wrong uncle? Please, what is happening?"

"Perhaps I should let your father speak to you himself. All I can say is that he is very ill," Deshpande said gravely.

"Nayan, my son," Bhojani said weakly, his voice a little above a whisper. "Barely forty-eight hours after I asked you to leave, your brothers demanded that I too leave the house. They even threatened to physically kick me out if I refused. I was shocked out of my wits.

I didn't understand at first, but then Pawan made it all too clear. He bluntly said that if he were to continue working with the Pride Group, it was imperative that we completely dissociate ourselves from each other. Charan was of the same opinion. So you see, to my sons and to Indrajeet I am of no use anymore."

Nayan read in his father's eyes a plea for mercy and forgiveness. He couldn't hold back the tears. He did not know how he could console his father. He tried to speak, but could say nothing. It was as though his throat was frozen. His father was undergoing the very painful process of self realisation. Although late in life, he was beginning to understand the importance of love, emotions and interpersonal relationships.

"Nayan, time is running out for me. I feel it. I must rewrite my will. Pawan and Charan are wealthy enough. You, my son, have not been given enough, and I am worried about your wellbeing."

"No father, you have given me enough. A flat in Mumbai and money in the bank—what more could I possibly need? I don't want to hear of you changing your will. Pawan and Charan have big dreams. Their need for your wealth is far greater."

"Nayan, I want to ask you something. Do you think I could perhaps have a word with your professor?" Bhojani asked.

"I will connect you to him right away," said Nayan and dialled the professor immediately.

Dil Bhojani spoke to the professor briefly and expressed his gratitude. He then passed the phone over to Nayan. The professor, not wanting to lose focus of their objective, asked Nayan to try and get audio recordings of any confessions by his father, of the crimes that he and Jagjeet had together committed. This would, of course, be a tricky task, considering the condition old Bhojani was in. But the evidence would be extremely damaging to the Pride Group and the Sankala family. The recordings would confirm Sankala's unethical partnerships and associations with different politicians, bureaucrats and other persons in high positions. Nayan saw reason in the professor's request but nevertheless needed time to gather his thoughts. He said he would call the professor later that evening.

He spent the whole day by the side of his ill father. When it was dusk, Sathe decided he should leave. Deshpande, however, elected to stay back. The Bhojani family physician had come all the way from Mumbai to check on him. He examined him thoroughly but could not settle on a final organic diagnosis. He insisted that the illness was primarily psychological. He did give him a few medicines, but he knew that to treat the case successfully, no medicine was needed, just the right psychological reassurances. Such was most often the case with his rich clients.

Later that evening, Bhojani got out of his bed and stepped out for a walk with Nayan. He once again broached the topic of his will. Nayan looked at his father gently and held his hand. He told him that the wealth his father wanted to leave him was not important. He said that he would much rather his father shared the wealth of information he possessed about the Pride Group's frauds and scams. Bhojani was shocked at his son's appeal. He pleaded with him to quit his fight against the Pride Group and gave good reasons why it was necessary to stop. The first was that the Sankala family was just too powerful. If at any point they chose to, they could easily have Nayan killed. Secondly, Nayan's brothers, Pawan and Charan, both depended on the Pride Group. If the Group's wellbeing was threatened, they would be too. The third was that if Bhojani were to bring down the Sankala family he would go down with them too. All his ill-gotten wealth would then have to be surrendered to the government. Bhojani would rather that the wealth go to Nayan, who would use it for genuine philanthropic causes. That last proposition left Nayan completely confounded.

Later that evening Nayan had a long telephonic exchange with the professor who maintained that Nayan's priority at that point was to get as much info about the Pride Group as possible. He had yet another piece of advice for Nayan. He told him that it was essential to have Bhojani's assets, both legally and illegally obtained, assessed by a competent chartered accountant and a lawyer. The purpose was to have the wealth split between the brothers in such a way that Nayan was given all that was legal while his two brothers would be left with all the vast illegal wealth. The idea was brilliant and he was confident that Dil Bhojani would find it acceptable especially after his two other sons had heartlessly kicked him out. The whole affair however had to be carried out with care. The professor reminded Nayan to take good care since he was playing with fire.

It was after dinner that Nayan sat with his father and Deshpande. He decided it was finally time to himself bring up the topic of his father's will. He also wanted his father to confess to him about all the Pride Group's indiscretions. Bhojani, not surprisingly, was easily convinced that Nayan should be conferred the legal part of his wealth. He was, however, not well disposed to the second part of the idea. It was difficult to get him to open up about the Pride Group. The very next day a team of professionals came to the Bhojani bungalow in Matheran to scrutinise the old man's assets. They were able to successfully divide his wealth into what was legal and what was not. The bungalow in Matheran and Nayan's flat were both legal. The Bhojani residence in the city was however not quite legal. The team very carefully and thoroughly examined Bhojani's shares, his bank and corporate deposits, bonds, jewellery, heirlooms and the other six flats in his possession. Nayan got a large chunk of all that was legal. Thus it was that Bhojani's will was completely altered and duly registered in the few days that followed.

Nayan stayed on with his father for a few more days. But the very day he was to leave Bhojani received a phone call from Pawan's wife. She was sobbing on the phone. She told him that Indrajeet had moved Pawan from the corporate office and placed him in one of the subsidiaries as a director. It was the equivalent of falling down several steps in one's career. They believed that Indrajeet had made his decision based on the appeals made by the other members of his coterie. They held Pawan and his family directly responsible for the loss of the huge project, and in their opinion, he and his family should suffer the consequences. Pawan's competitors obviously insisted that he be relieved of all his important duties. Under no circumstances could the Pride Group afford sabotage again. Pawan could not cope with this humiliation and had taken to drinking. He spent every evening in a state of complete inebriation. Not even his brother Charan could knock any sense into him.

In desperation, Pawan's wife decided to call Dil Bhojani and ask him to return to the house and fix things. Bhojani tried not to be unfeeling and consoled her as best he could though he doubted the veracity of her story. He did not assure her that he'd return. He did not trust Pawan anymore and suspected that he might have instructed his wife to talk to him and act as a mediator between the two. Besides, there was always the twisted possibility that Indrajeet might have told Pawan and Charan to place their father under house arrest. The Pride Group had obviously got an idea of the professor and his network's strength. They had begun to see professor Aditya as a very real threat. It was therefore of prime importance to keep Bhojani from interacting with him. Fortunately, Bhojani was no fool and knew a trap when he saw one. He told Nayan that it was likely that Indrajeet would not give up easily, and would most certainly try another trick to get at Bhojani if he didn't go back. On the other hand, the whole story about Pawan's demotion could also be true. He didn't put it past Indrajeet to do something so drastic. There was no way of ascertaining the truth behind this whole matter.

The next morning Bhojani awoke earlier than usual feeling stronger and more positive. He had a quick shower and prayed. After his little prayer he felt even more relaxed and happy. Nayan was glad to see his father in good spirits after such a long time.

"You look well today, father," he said happily.

"Yes indeed my son, I am happy because I feel that all my anxieties have been quelled. I cannot really describe the feeling but I suppose it is something like the freedom a bird feels as it flies in the open sky. Yes that's it! I feel like my soul has left my body and is wandering freely about the universe. What joy it is, to call the universe your home. I can hear the words of Lord Krishna beckoning me, calling me to join him."

The happiness on Nayan's face faded when he heard that. He suddenly felt anxious for his father. "Father, don't say that. Don't tell me you hear the lord calling you. It can't be true. For the first time in so many years dad, I feel close to you. I feel like I have only just found my father who was hitherto lost to the wickedness of the world."

"Oh but Nayan, I'm not leaving you at all. I'm not going back to your brothers either. I cannot help it. I am convinced that the lord is calling out to me," said Bhojani.

"Dad, I can see that this must be a great spiritual feeling for you. But I don't understand why you feel it. Have you made up your mind about something? I've never seen you quite so joyful before."

"You're right. I have in fact made up my mind about something. I am ready to share with you every detail about the misdeeds of the

Pride Group and the Sankala family, who have flourished thanks to horrendous parasites like me. I shall also share with you the very sensitive sources of confidential data related to Indrajeet's present activities."

Nayan asked his dad if he could take an audio recording of all the confessions. Bhojani agreed.

The following day, Sathe came to Matheran and brought along with him a state-of-the-art voice recorder. The boys recorded everything Bhojani said with small intervals every now and then. The whole process took two days, but in the end what they had was priceless. A few things between Deshpande's narrations and Bhojani's submissions were common. Dil Bhojani revealed many shocking details about Jagjeet, Indrajeet and their close associates. It was after having collected all the information that the real daunting task would begin. Nayan's friends would now have to collate all the appropriate evidence to support Bhojani's confessions.

Bhojani was mentally exhausted. The two days of talking and confessing had taken their toll on him. On the second night he had an early dinner and retired early to bed. He awoke the next morning early at four o'clock. Sleep eluded him so he sat on a bench just outside the bungalow. He was enjoying the solitude and freshness of the morning. His expression was calm and serene—and he sat very still. And then it happened. Two bullets pierced the flesh of his neck. Dil Bhojani died on the spot. The marksman was obviously an expert and the shots had been silenced. There had been no noise and the skillful shooter simply disappeared into the morning mist. It was six o'clock when the milkman came to the house. He saw Dil Bhojani slumped over on the bench, blood drenching his collar and shirt. He was at first paralysed by the sight, but after a few moments he pulled himself together and shouted out to Nayan. Nayan hurried out to his father, but the old man had long been dead. No one could possibly survive two shots in the neck. He fell to his knees and cried hopelessly. It now made sense to him. His father had been right about having heard God's call. But why did his departure have to be so unceremonious, so cruel? He tried to console himself while the milkman called the police. He tried to calm down and called their local family doctor.

Sathe and Deshpande reached in time for the funerary rituals.

Later that evening Nayan called the professor. He could not hold back his tears and broke down over the phone. He said he was now an orphan with nobody to love him. The professor listened to him and tried to console him.

"Come now Nayan, there is no need for you to feel forsaken. We are all with you. I know it is difficult having to deal with the loss of both your parents, but you have us. Please do not despair."

Nayan started crying again. Sathe stood beside him. He too was hurting for his dear friend's loss. He gently patted Nayan on the back in an attempt to comfort him. He knew exactly what Nayan was going through. After all, both the boys had lost their respective fathers to the villainy of the Pride Group. It had been the Sankalas who had killed them.

"Nayan, it is possible that Indrajeet had Salunke's men kill your father. I think it would be wise for you to exercise a little caution yourself. You must tell Sathe to be careful too. Salunke already tried to get even with me too. Fortunately for me, his plan failed. But I very much doubt they're going to sit quiet now. They're likely to attack us again. We have to be ready for an assault. You had better leave Matheran as soon as you can. It would be better and safer for you if you stayed at your flat in Mumbai. The Bhadraloks would be in a position to provide better security cover in the city," the professor advised.

"Sir, I leave for Mumbai tomorrow. Sathe and I have to coordinate the next phase of our assignment. I had a word with Shini and Janaki today. We are going to need a little more time to execute our plans," said Nayan.

"Yes, but don't work yourself up too much. Don't forget that we've just had a major victory. Our plan to get the Bhadralok Group the project was after all a great success. It has of course come at a heavy cost. I'm so sorry for your poor father."

"Please professor, I'd rather not think about it. I know the Sankalas. Even if they hadn't killed dad this morning, I'm sure they would have done away with him at some point later. But with dad gone, I'm now beginning to worry about uncle Deshpande's safety. I've already told him to keep his association with us absolutely secret."

"Good. I think he should be alright as long as we don't directly use any of the information he has given us. We cannot risk having our enemies learn about our allies. Be sure to warn your friends not to use Deshpande's references without consulting me first. We need to be discreet."

"Right then, my team and I shall get down to work and we'll keep you posted at regular intervals."

"Sounds good Nayan; I wish you the best of luck."

The following day, Nayan and Sathe reached Mumbai and Nayan moved into his flat.

***

Chapter 5

Dear Professor Aditya,

My colleagues and I have been reading about you in the news and watching you on television for quite a while now. Your fight against Ramesh Salunke and the Pride Group has truly inspired us in our own efforts against corruption. Our politicians, our bureaucratic system, corrupt industrial houses etc are beyond repair. We have to destroy the malfunctioning system to create room for good people to be able to come forward and lead our nation. We know very well your penchant for mythology. You will find that the elimination of devils and scoundrels was perfectly acceptable and justified in our great epics. All of our great gods and goddesses simply killed the scum that walked our planet defiling its beauty and virginity. My colleagues and I firmly believe in, and engage in such purposeful destruction.

Our organisation goes by the name 'Radical Reform Group' or simply 'RRG'. To give you an exact account of the work the group has done over the last three years, please take a look at the table given below. It lists all the successful assassinations of corrupt individuals under different categories.

Category of devil	Number
Senior politicians	4
Junior politicians	10
Bureaucrats	21
Industrialists	2
Educationalists	3
Police officers	11
Lawyers	10
Agents in various fields	30
Culprits other	39
Total	**130**

Our modus-operandi is extremely unique and tech-savvy. No investigative techniques or machinery has ever managed to uncover any evidence that points to us. Besides, the hundred and thirty killings have created a very strong and definite impact in the specific localities where they were executed.

Our intention is to instill terror in the minds of all those corrupt 'worms' in our society, and our primary focus is the government machinery. We are of the opinion that this is the only road to radical reform and we hope to expand and have a real nationwide influence.

Our group, as of today, has twelve hundred activists. We are all professionals in different fields, employed at different places, executing different tasks. It would perhaps please you to know that about two hundred of our activists are women.

Now that I have given you a basic idea of our group I shall come to the main purpose of this letter. I would very much like to meet with you. If you wish to bring in reform in our nation's systems, our modus-operandi alone can help.

I have instructed one of my colleagues to drop this letter off at your residence. He shall act as my messenger until such time as we meet. He shall visit you once again this Sunday afternoon at two o'clock. Sir, as per Indian philosophy, a messenger is neither arrested nor killed. Please uphold that principle and do not let any untoward incident mar the heights that we can take our relationship to.

I eagerly await your reply.

With best regards,

Yours truly,

Ranjan Rishi

Aditya read the letter twice and slipped into deep reflection. It was alarming that the youth in the country was fed up enough with the corruption in the system to fight the problem in such a destructive, barbaric way. And in all his youthful vigour and over-enthusiasm Rishi imagined that his idea was radical, attractive, even effective. The truth was that assassinations of corrupt individuals was not an answer to the problem. It was neither a foolproof solution, nor a legal exercise, nor a spiritually acceptable one. Ranjan Rishi had to be stopped, the professor decided. He needed to be carefully and tactfully convinced that he was mistaken about what he imagined to be his path to salvation. The RRG must channel its energy in the direction of righteousness. The professor decided he should meet him and try to persuade him to follow the correct path.

Rishi's envoy met with Aditya at exactly two o'clock in the afternoon on Sunday. Aditya told him that he wished to have a meeting with Rishi himself on the coming Thursday. He also offered to have the meeting at his own house. The messenger very politely requested the professor not to attempt to record the discussions. Aditya consented. The next Thursday, Rishi came over to the professor's house. He was accompanied by two of his young associates. Both Aditya and his wife received them courteously.

Rishi was an electronics engineer by profession working with a multinational corporation. His two young associates were both bankers with two different reputed banking firms. Rishi was born in a middle class family in Patna, the capital city of Bihar. His grandfather was a Sanskrit scholar, and his father, worked in the state government's irrigation department. The father was a man with a genuine conscience who refused to take anything in the form of bribes and kickbacks, so was a misfit among his corrupt colleagues and superiors who harassed him no end for his resoluteness. One day, the old man decided that he could no longer tolerate the persecution, and in a moment of utter weakness, he committed suicide leaving behind a wife and a young son. This incident obviously affected Rishi profoundly and he decided to devote his life in retaliation against the same system that killed his father. He began to get in touch with other youngsters like himself, who had suffered at the hands of the authorities. Like his grandfather, Rishi was excellent at communication. His arguments were always very persuasive and forceful. He soon built a large network of like-minded youths.

The RRG, as they called it, worked with very simple and transparent rules. There was a test for both entry into and exit from the group. Exit for a genuine reason was always allowed. Rishi's philosophy was that any member of the RRG, even after his voluntary exit from the group, continued to be a member emotionally. He continued to share the same beliefs and aspirations and maintained a good rapport with Rishi. All operations of the RRG were carried out with the money given by the members. The group had no godfathers and no donations. Key decisions were taken by a governing committee. Each assassination carried out was well-planned. Even the minutest details were taken care of. For each assignment, a 'master plan' was created drawing upon the different technical experience and expertise of the members, and then it was executed ruthlessly. The secret of the success lay in their ideology. Being a shrewd observer, Rishi quickly learnt that a young mind can be easily mesmerised by the use of a powerful ideology. He was careful not to approach persons aged forty or above. The RRG's members were most active in the states of Bihar, Uttar Pradesh, West Bengal, and more recently in Maharashtra and Karnataka too.

Professor Aditya elected to initiate a clear and straightforward dialogue with Ranjan and his associates.

"Ranjan, your people have done away with a hundred and thirty rogues in the last three years at an average of forty-three per annum. Now you claim that these killings have created a definite impact in specific areas. But tell me, has it really reduced the corruption in the system? What about all the corruption outside our government? What about those elements that corrupt our system?" the professor asked.

"I follow your questions, professor. If you don't mind I'd like to make my case here. Our killings have, I admit, not reduced corruption substantially. They have, however, created a limited impact in certain areas. But unfortunately, the impact hasn't lasted beyond a year in most cases."

"You must have had to kill off even the scoundrels who simply replaced the original ones. Am I right?"

"Yes, on quite a few occasions actually. You see the fear and the impact brought about by our actions lasted for a little over a year, but after that began to diminish. We have also killed a number of corrupt rogues outside the system—a few crooked entrepreneurs and educationalists too."

"But aren't they too a part of the same system we speak of?"

"Well yes, in a way. But when we talk about the system, my people and I, we refer to the governmental system."

"Friend, the government is just one part of a much larger system that operates far and wide, unchallenged," said the professor with the air of one in command.

"A system much larger, operating far and wide," asked Ranjan, with a look of incomprehension. "What do you mean?"

"Well for you to really grasp what I mean, I need you to understand something else. Now listen carefully, there are different types of corruption. You, I believe, have been focusing on only one type—financial corruption, to give it a name. But there exist six other forms of corruption—cultural, social, spiritual, educational, political and ideological. Yes, even something as fundamental as an ideology is corruptible. And I suppose I don't need to tell you that it is by far the worst kind and the most difficult to tackle. What I think you need to know is that killing is no solution here. The purging of ideologically corrupt individuals everywhere will not rid us of the twisted ideologies that have crept into our society."

"Do you mind explaining exactly what do you mean by ideological corruption professor?"

"Take the terrorists for instance – they proliferate like pests. You kill a few of them, and some new groups spring up as if from nowhere. Where are our women? Suffering under the burden of social corruption, unable to express themselves. How do you propose to eradicate this sort of corruption which denies a woman her rights? Will you go about murdering every socially corrupt person out there? To do that would be to wipe off a good fifty per cent of our population."

"I suppose you're right. We do predominantly target financial corruption and overlook the other types. But why shouldn't we? What's wrong with specialisation? It is the order of the day isn't it?"

"You, my friend, by killing corrupt individuals, are taking far too many systemic, behavioural, legal and operational risks. I am sorry but I am just not in agreement with your methods."

"Risks? What risks are you speaking of professor? What do you mean?"

"All your ex-RRG members—the ones who resigned—aren't you worried that they might leak out vital information about your organisation? You may not always be able to carry out your plans successfully. One tiny little mistake could expose you. What service to society do you hope to render from within a prison cell?"

The professor looked straight into Ranjan's eyes.

"So what are you saying Professor Aditya? Do we simply shut down RRG operations?"

"All I am saying is, your process is too dangerous. Stop killing people! There are other, better things you can do. Join our 'global reform mission'. We share the same purpose after all, and our methods are clean. We engage in the positive sort of networking. We even use the most advanced technology. I'm sure you've heard about the dreadful political games Ramesh Salunke plays. We have no intention of killing him for his misdeeds. But what we are doing is something far more effective. We are trying to render him powerless and bring about his political death. We favour mind over muscle. You surely know of the Pride Group? Indrajeet's grand design is to build a great industrial empire both in and outside India. His ambitions harm our nation. So if we crush his purpose, we crush him."

"You may be right, but I am still not convinced. I do not think it is possible for us to do away with corruption that is so widespread and hopelessly festering."

"Your organisation boasts of a number of smart and intelligent members. If you associate with us, the execution of our mission will be more effective, with your gamut of skills obtained in fieldwork and past operations."

"Sir, my associates and I consider it a privilege to have shared our thoughts with you. But before I give you my final answer, I need to consult my core team. We have always worked by consensus."

"Undoubtedly! When, may I ask, would you be in a position to let me know of your decision?"

"Give me a week. The meeting for us has been quite an eye-opener." Ranjan and his associates rose to their feet, saluted Professor Aditya and his wife Sheetala, and left.

Aditya and Sheetala spent the evening unwinding with old popular Hindi film melodies and strains of Rafi and Kishore.

The professor received a phone call from his friend, John Knight, a Swiss banker. It was a well known fact that many Indians had stashed away their ill-gotten, corrupt 'black' wealth in Swiss banks. John expressed his opinion that the only way this money could be brought back to India was by applying social and political pressure on the Swiss banks which were protected by international agreements and local banking laws. Switzerland was heading for parliamentary elections, and according to John, this presented a great opportunity to pressurise the Swiss politicians into disclosing or releasing the funds held by Indians. Professor Aditya couldn't agree more. John was requested to fly down to India to formulate a detailed plan of action. He flew down to India on the next available flight.

The professor invited all his young friends to meet him. The night before the meeting, he wrestled with various ideas on how to get the funds back into India. As per John's estimate, around 37 per cent of the Swiss deposits were of Indian origin. The sum in question was around a staggering 1456 billion dollars. Exact figures were almost impossible to ascertain as Swiss bankers, bound by their own secrecy laws, were not obliged to divulge information.

Professor Aditya said, "We will appeal to the conscience of the Swiss people and through them get to the bankers. We shall tell them that forty per cent of our population still lives in abject poverty without even basic needs fulfilled. We will present to their youth the real 'Slum Dog' that exists in India. We will approach all social, cultural, academic, economic organisations—even the chambers of commerce and other allied outfits. The bankers have to be made aware of the fact that by allowing such deposits they are helping the culprits who are exploiting the poor and amassing wealth."

A few youngsters were not convinced by the professor's argument. They wondered why the Swiss would actually want to help Indians. The professor said, "Ours will be an emotional plea. We will aim at their hearts. For those who are practical, we can probably show a commercial angle as well. We could tell them that by returning the money to India, the Swiss would help to uplift our economy and the entire world would benefit from such a move. Switzerland too could benefit as India prospers. See friends, there is no harm in taking this route. The only hurdle is that of financing this venture. There will be costs that will have to be incurred and we will need funds for that. We shall request the Bhadralok Group to help us."

"That would be splendid. The Bhadralok group is held in high esteem in my country. I am sure with them in the picture we could attract some of the well known and high profile public figures in Switzerland, and with them on the scene, our presentations will reach a larger audience," responded John.

The discussion had an electrifying effect and every participant was charged with excitement. Sathe took up the responsibility of making the necessary presentations and a concise documentary showing the pathetic living conditions of the four hundred million Indians living below poverty line. The professor agreed to attend to the more important presentation to be made to the chambers of commerce in Switzerland. It was understood that the project was to be under wraps until it was ready to be rolled out. One small leak and the Indian politicians would be breathing down their necks.

Next morning, Professor Aditya and his young colleagues called on Bhadralok to discuss the critical issue of security. With each passing day, this problem was getting worse. Through the good offices of the Bhadralok group, licensed weapons were arranged for the professor and his group. It was agreed that the professor be accompanied by his colleagues wherever he went. In addition, help of an international security agency was to be taken, as and when required. The professor contacted Mike, Shini's father, as he had connections with some Israeli security agencies. He called up his contacts and a security cover was arranged for the professor.

Nayan got a phone call from the professor inviting him over for a meeting. Obviously it meant that something urgent had cropped up. Nayan dashed off to the professor's house and was glad to be greeted by the happy, smiling faces of the professor and his wife. The professor commented, "So your hard work is starting to pay off now, isn't it?"

Baffled, Nayan asked, "What hard work are you referring to sir?"

"Don't try and act so innocent Nayan. A strategist like you must have quite a few things up his sleeve to win the game this way!" Sheetala joked.

Nayan's confusion turned to trepidation and he hesitatingly asked, "Aunty, am I missing something? What game are we speaking of . . .?"

"Nayan, Mike called up last night and was asking about you," said the professor. At the mention of Mike's name, Nayan's heart fluttered. What was it? Was it something that he had done to displease the Herels and Shini?

"Young man, don't look so innocent—we know what you have been up to?" said Sheetala.

Nervously Nayan dared to ask, "Sir, for god's sake, will you tell what is going on? Are you folks pulling my leg or something? Why on earth would Mike be asking about me?"

"Because Shini loves you, silly! And please don't tell us some stupid thing like you didn't know that!"

"So Nayan! Are you in love with Shini?" Sheetala insisted on having it from the horse's mouth.

"Stop embarrassing him, Sheetala. If he was in love with Shini, he would have surely told me about it... after all he is my best disciple," the professor said impishly. He then went over to Nayan, held his hands and said, "Congratulations Nayan. The Herels would like to know if you would accept their daughter's hand in marriage. They would love to know how you feel about this."

"Aditya, look at him. Does he need to spell it out? Of course he is in love with Shini. It was clear as crystal from the day I saw them together."

"But Sheetala, let him say so. After all it is his decision."

Nayan did not know what to say. He got up, gave the professor a hug and said, "Thank you sir! Thank you both. Yes, I do love Shini and ... oh gosh I would love to marry her."

"In that case, I am going to ask you two questions and I want honest answers. You lost both your parents recently. You have two elder brothers. Will they take the lead and arrange the marriage? Also would they insist on Hindu rituals and get you to marry the traditional way?"

"Sir, you already know that my relations with my brothers are strained. I have a better idea. Can I make a request?"

"Yes, go ahead."

"I would like it very much if you two took the lead in my marriage. For me you are like my parents now. I will definitely invite my brothers but I doubt if they will even bother to attend."

The professor was indeed very touched. "It will be an honour for us."

Sheetala couldn't hold back her tears. She hugged Nayan and said, "It will give us great pleasure. After our daughter's death, we had forgotten what it was to be a parent. Today you have brought back those fond memories. We would be more than proud to be your parents."

"Sir, we can have a Christian as well as a Hindu wedding. We can have the best of both," Nayan said enthusiastically.

"Both? Actually three kinds of weddings Nayan. Your father-in-law to be is a Jew. We can begin with the Christian ceremonial exchange of vows followed by Hindu Vedic rituals, and later have a Jewish mitzvah party. That would be perfect for you as global citizens. It would be the ultimate declaration of religious harmony."

There was no time to waste. Professor Aditya picked up the phone and called Mike. To call at that late hour was nothing short of bad manners, but this time around ... Mike was going to be a very happy man. Shini too came on the phone and thanked the professor. She insisted that she was utterly indebted to her 'Guru'.

The date for the engagement was set and the Herels agreed to come to Mumbai for the ceremony. Sathe took over the arrangements. Janaki too came down for the engagement. Of course, as expected, Nayan's brothers did not turn up. The only family present was Nayan's maternal uncle who came from Pune to attend the function. A few Vedic rituals were performed and the two young lovers were engaged.

Work on the presentations to be made to the Swiss were started in earnest. Bhadralok's Swiss offices arranged for the professor's presentation before six social organisations and five chambers of commerce. It was arranged for the professor to be showcased as the ambassador of 'Progressive India'. Three major cities—Basel, Bern and Zurich were targeted for the presentations.

Sathe took care of the minutest detail. A powerful, heart wrenching documentary stressed the complete plunder of the underprivileged at the hands of a few unscrupulous Indians who were amassing wealth by exploiting the poor and then stashing it away in Swiss banks, giving rise to the painful disparity between the rich and the poor. The very first presentation, at the central hall of the 'City University of Switzerland', was attended by over three hundred students and social activists. The emotional appeal was followed by a standing ovation for the Professor. Aditya graciously accepted the praise and asked whether the beautiful people of Switzerland wished to continue allowing the loot, the blood money of the Indian poor, to come into their country and run their economy? Did they not want to build a safer, stronger, and a sacred world where all living beings could exist with some dignity? Would they not halt this unfair practice and beg their leaders to amend the Swiss banking laws, at least as far as funds from India were concerned?

The response by the Swiss youth was overwhelming. That evening the presentation organised by a Swiss NGO evoked similar response.

As the professor and his team reached their hotel in the evening, they were thronged by several journalists. The professor spoke his mind at length and tried to educate the media regarding the necessary changes to be made in the Swiss banking methods. Of course, all this was extensively reported in the leading newspapers and TV news networks. Aditya's purpose was served. His appeal was aired. "It may be legally right for Swiss banks to bring in Indian funds, but is it morally admissible? Does it feel good to promote an entire economy by encouraging tax evaders from India at the expense of the poor people there?"

The euphoria generated over the statements compelled a few Swiss politicians and thinkers to react. They came out in support and publicly echoed the professor's views. Perhaps a few did it to get political mileage, but it definitely served the pupose. These politicians started questioning Swiss banking laws on public platforms. Subsequent presentations were made to the chambers of commerce, associations of intellectuals, and bodies of retired Swiss bureaucrats and judges. The issue of Indian funds was all over the Swiss media. The Indian media was quick to follow suit, and the professor was 'hot news'. In America and Europe too the media gave him wide coverage.

The publicity generated by his Indo-Swiss activities, as expected, enraged certain sections of Indian politicians and industry. What right had professor Aditya and his activists got to represent and champion the cause of 'Indian Poverty'? The professor started receiving threats of defamation and libel suits but the Indian media was quick to react and crushed the allegations as baseless and prejudiced. The very same politicians and industrialists, who had tried threatening the professor, backtracked when they realised that their strategy of maligning him was becoming counter-productive. He had, by then, become a hero in the eyes of the Indian youth who openly supported his cause.

With every passing day, the pressure on Swiss politicians kept mounting. Indian youth residing in Switzerland staged protest marches. With the elections round the corner, the NGOs started demanding the government declare its stand on the issue. In retaliation, a few Swiss banks claimed that funds available with them were being used solely for the development of the Swiss economy, and that the repatriation of these funds would have a disastrous effect on the Swiss economy. NGOs and other social organisations put up banners all over Switzerland saying, "Swiss prosperity – yes! But definitely not at the expense of the Indian poor."

Ten days prior to the elections, aggressive campaigning went on all across Switzerland. Top on the agenda was the Swiss accounts of Indians. It was the hot topic on hoardings, billboards, clips on TV and in cinema halls, banners, etc. The Bhadralok Group financed the entire initiative. The impact was phenomenal. A few independent candidates contesting the elections declared support in favour of the campaign, and vowed, if elected, to do everything within their power to compel their banks to return the Indian deposits. The Swiss political parties were thrown out of gear. The Opposition decided to make the most of the opportunity and declared that, if elected to power, it would force the banks to return the 'Indian money'. All this sent shock waves through India, as many of these depositors were prominent people in the public eye in India. Indian NGOs jumped at this opportunity and demanded the government take the initiative to bring back these funds.

The Swiss government, reeling under the pressure, called a Senate meeting and a resolution was passed to have the Swiss banking law amended, and to return the money of the Indian depositors within two months after the elections. It was a huge success for all Indians. To cash in on the hype generated by the announcement, Professor

Aditya immediately called a press conference. The conference was attended by hundreds of excited journalists from all over India, given the magnitude of the news. One journalist asked the professor if he would contest the forthcoming elections in India. He said that good, honest Indians like the professor should actively participate in politics. Another journalist asked if the Swiss banks would release the names of their Indian depositors whose money they were to repatriate. The professor agreed that there was a dearth of honest, sincere politicians. He also indicated that if not himself, a very close associate of his would definitely contest the elections. As to the names of Indian depositors, he very emphatically said that the Swiss banks could be persuaded to reveal the identities of their account holders.

As the professor started getting more and more visibility on the national and international front, the risk to his well-being also increased. His security advisor warned him of the risks and suggested that the security cover be beefed up. The possibility of the Indian mafia making him a target was very real. Obvious names that came up on the list were of Ramesh Salunke and Indrajeet. The professor received threatening calls. Bhadralok immediately had the professor and his family moved to a safer house with better security. When all this was happening, Sheetala's health became a cause of concern for the professor. Ever since the death of their daughter, she had developed high blood pressure and become anxious and nervous.

A few days later, John Knight called up Professor Aditya from Switzerland to give him the good news that the Swiss government was going to release the list of the Indian depositors. The declaration was to be made immediately following the Swiss elections. News channels, especially in Switzerland and in India, were thrown into a frenzy, and speculation as to the names of these supposedly illegitimate holders started everywhere. Indian politicians, supported by a few industrialists, immediately, started a campaign against the Swiss banking system, international financial speculators and foreign intelligence agencies. An interesting game of self preservation was played out by them alleging that it was a ploy to malign Indian politicians and industrialists.

Soon after the elections, the new Swiss government kept its promise. Twenty-four names of Indian depositors were made public. These accounts had unreasonably large holdings and the sources of funds could not be ascertained. Not surprisingly, the name of Ramesh Salunke was on that list. Since he was a cabinet minister handling a very important portfolio, his rivals, both inside and outside of his party, started targeting him as 'anti-national'. The media too went into a tizzy. Salunke's camp witnessed frenzied activity as it prepared their boss' defense. A press conference was called and it was declared that Salunke had never had any transactions with any Swiss bank, either directly or indirectly. The camp's pitch was that a true patriot like him would never indulge in such illegal activities. His supporters claimed that it was an international political conspiracy to ruin his career and to damage his party's image. They claimed that some western countries with vested interests were scared of his meteoric rise in Indian politics.

Salunke hired a PR agency to hit back at his critics and to do some image building. The Indians were not fooled by this, and instead of it working in his favour, it backfired, as the public now started suspecting his involvement in the Swiss imbroglio even more. As a face-saving measure, the Indian government promised publicly that it would investigate his alleged involvement and take action if he were found guilty. As elections were round the corner, senior party leaders started distancing themselves from him as they did not want to be seen associated with a man whose image had been tarnished in such an explosive scandal. His earlier involvement in the fake government securities scam amounting to over a billion rupees was perhaps also on their minds. Salunke had then managed to get off the hook by making scapegoats of two of his close political colleagues. He was a ruthless man, known to go to any extent to safeguard his interests. Jagjeet and he were cunning, unscrupulous, merciless men, who with each other's help and the mafia that they had nurtured, crushed anything and anyone who dared to come in their way. But the present situation seemed way beyond Salunke's control. His partymen, now apprehensive of the party's performance under his leadership, convinced him to step down and asked him to battle it out on his own. His party workers suggested to him to take legal recourse in the matter. He was cornered.

Professor Aditya called a meeting of his close associates. Bhadralok was requested to chair the meeting. The agenda was Salunke's Swiss holdings. Deshpande too was requested to join as his political experience and understanding was vital. In the meeting, Deshpande suggested that they should file a case against Salunke, with the government as a respondent. This would make both answerable in the court of law. Otherwise, he feared that the ruling party, of which Salunke was a member, would conceal the important facts, and play for time, thereby making sure that the issue of Swiss funds fizzled out on its own. It was also possible for the government to use all its clout with the Swiss authorities and postpone the proceedings.

Bhadralok was in agreement with Deshpande's views, and he suggested that they use the services of Rusi Wadia, a well-known jurist, to file the case. Rusi was also known for his professional expertise and outstanding work ethics. His grit, determination and fighting spirit were unmatched in the court of law. He had an impressive track record of having successfully fought six public litigation cases against high profile politicians and industrialists. Professor Aditya was of the opinion that John Knight, with his in-depth knowledge of the Swiss banking system, would be an important asset in the case.

A week later, they filed a public litigation case against Ramesh Salunke. As decided, the government was made a respondent. John flew down from Switzerland to help Rusi Wadia in his case preparations. The Salunke camp too geared up for the fight. They put up Prem Mansukhani, a well-known, astute criminal lawyer, against Rusi Wadia, as the defense counsel. Mansukhani, besides being a brilliant lawyer, was also known to be a lobbyist with exceptional networking skills. His understanding of loopholes in the legal system was profound and he cleverly exploited them to the maximum advantage. He knew all the tricks of the game, and had managed to get quite a few branded criminals off the hook. He was quick at spotting a chink in his opposition's armour, and when he did so, he would ruthlessly move in for the kill and finish off any challenge. 'Social responsibility' and 'moral accountability' were terms tantamount to 'cowardice' in Mansukhani's vocabulary.

Bhadralok was not too happy with Mansukhani's appointment as the defense attorney for Salunke. He had represented a few unethical business establishments in cases against the Bhadralok group. So he suggested to the Professor that Mansukhani should step down and not take up Salunke's case. Aditya was in complete agreement. He called Nayan and Sathe to his residence to discuss the latest predicament. He always welcomed ideas from young fresh minds. Sathe was quick to react and suggested that they contact a few NGOs and convince them to conduct demonstrations outside Mansukhani's office and residence. The idea was to harass the lawyer and have him socially boycotted. And if that wasn't enough, he further suggested that they contact Sonare of the 'Shoor Party' and ask him to threaten

Mansukhani, an opportunity he wouldn't miss knowing his enmity with Salunke. He was certain that Sonare would be more than willing to take this up and hit at his arch rival.

Sathe's suggestion, though it seemed correct, wasn't exactly viable. Mansukhani wasn't a guy to bow down to threats or demonstrations or social boycotts. The other suggestion—asking Sonare to threaten Mansukhani wasn't feasible as although Salunke and Sonare were adversaries in politics, when it came to money, they were known to help each other using various fronts for their mutual benefit. Nayan suggested that the professor use his powers of persuasion to steer Mansukhani away from the unethical path.

Bhadralok offered to accompany the professor for his meeting with Mansukhani. The sheer presence of an eminent personality like Bhadralok would obviously put a lot of pressure on the lawyer. However, they decided against such a move for two reasons. The first that the megalomaniac Mansukhani might insult Bhadralok. The second and the more important one being the fact that such an open involvement of Bhadralok would directly link him with the professor. A common friend managed to get an appointment for the professor to meet Mansukhani along with the faithful duo of Nayan and Sathe. Fifteen minutes was all that was sought of the lawyer's time, although he would have given more. Aditya decided that anything beyond fifteen minutes with that devious man may prove to be counter-productive.

The meeting was scheduled for a Saturday evening at the business centre of a posh hotel. Avoiding any of the standard courtesies, the professor came to the point directly. "Please sir, we are here to humbly request you to step down and not represent Salunke. We all know that he is not innocent and your stepping down would serve our nation well."

"Professor, I agreed to meet you as I respect your intelligence. A man is innocent unless proven guilty. Don't you think that my client deserves a fair opportunity to prove his innocence? Who are we to decide the right from wrong? Remember attorneys are mere facilitators who represent their clients in the name of justice." Mansukhani tried justifying his stand.

"I have to agree with you on that. Your professional stand is correct and also logical. But as a human being, what about your social responsibility and moral obligations? You have been brilliant all through your professional life, and have earned respect, name and fame. Isn't it time you did something for your nation?"

"Nation's cause is a relative concept. I am a professional lawyer and my primary duty is to my client. Does a doctor deny treating a wounded criminal? For the doctor, a patient has to be treated, criminal or not. Likewise, Salunke is my client, and I am bound by my code to give him the best defense. Let the courts decide who is right or wrong. As for you, why don't you just ask your lawyer to prepare well for the case? For you Salunke may be a culprit. For me he is but a client."

"Mr Mansukhani, shall we dispense with all this legal talk? I came here to appeal to your soul and not to your brain. With your talents, I am sure you can distinguish between what is true and what is not. Someday, you will regret your choice when your inner self stops listening to your reason. Only then will you realise the real meaning of the 'ultimate goal of life'. Let me tell you, the Swiss holdings of Ramesh Salunke are not only illegitimate but are also illegal."

"Professor, the legality is yet to be decided. And a better place for that is the court of law."

"Let that be decided in the court. But are the fund holdings legitimate? Don't these funds belong to the millions of Indian poor?

I am sure you agree with me!"

"Professor, for the sake of this argument, I shall agree with you that these funds do belong to the Indian poor. But can you say for sure that Salunke robbed them of their money, and also managed to deposit it in Swiss banks?" Mansukhani was beginning to get impatient and annoyed.

"My learned friend, you know very well that crooks like Salunke do not leave any trace behind. They are very adept at covering their tracks."

"Precisely my point; let your lawyer bring all his evidence to the table and prove Salunke to be an offender."

Professor Aditya, Nayan and Sathe were floored by this deliberate provocation. To meet aggression with aggression, Aditya countered, "I must say I am disappointed. A person of your calibre shouldn't have to resort to such gimmicks. The less said the better. God forbid, but if someday you are cornered, no amount of evidence or arguments will protect you. Just your inner voice will keep on haunting you about your lack of social and moral credits in the balance sheet of your life! This is not a dose of philosophy. Wake up to what is morally and legitimately correct for the poor Indian. That should be the fodder for your mind, and to ungraciously quote you … leave the legalities to the court of law!" retorted professor Aditya.

"You have crossed the line. I'll see you in court," Mansukhani was red in the face as he stormed out of the room in a huff.

Rusi Wadia and John Knight started preparing their case. Mansukhani was a formidable opponent and underestimating him would be folly. Besides, Mansukhani had Salunke's network and Indrajeet's almost limitless resources entirely at his disposal. It was an uneven fight, just like the epic fight between the Pandavas and the mighty Kauravas. Yet, the war was won by the 'righteous'. The world had seen many such uneven wars. Rusi Wadia, on the other hand, was helped by Bhadralok's resources, some Swiss NGOs and a small team of retired judges.

The case was fought hard with both lawyers giving their inspired best. Their arguments were aggressive and effective. Mansukhani laid bare the weaknesses in the Swiss banking system. He called the case and everything associated with it a politically motivated ploy to crush his client's career. He alleged that the Swiss and the Americans had conspired to trounce his client's hope of contesting for India's next prime ministership. Obviously, Wadia anticipated and managed to tackle all such arguments. Finally Mansukhani played his ace. He denied that his client had deposited any money in Swiss banks, and argued that if at all there was any money there in his name, then it had to be someone else bearing the same name as his client. He alleged that institutions like the American CIA could well have deposited funds in his client's name to see him charged for treachery.

On judgment day, the honourable court pronounced its much awaited verdict. Ramesh Salunke could not be proved guilty of having deposited funds in Swiss banks. However, the court ordered the government, who was a respondent in the case, to initiate an enquiry into the deposit process of specific Indian account holders in order to trace the source of their funds. It gave the government fifteen days to complete its inquiry.

After the judgment, Mansukhani egged Aditya, "You'd better ask Rusi Wadia to be better prepared next time." To that the professor coolly replied, "Mansukhani, take it easy, where's the rush? The battle may just be over but the war is yet to conclude!"

The following day, Bhadralok, Aditya, John, Rusi Wadia and a few other colleagues met to chalk out the next course of action. Wadia came up with a very valid suggestion "See, we do not have any doubt about Salunke's guilt. The court however accepts only evidence. That is fine. I know for sure that some of the very close associates of Salunke must have deposited the funds on his behalf. No politician would dare to indulge in such a risky act in person."

"Okay, so ...?" asked the professor.

"Ask some of your colleagues to go visit Salunke's hometown and make them stay there for a fortnight. I suspect he will definitely try to destroy the evidence of his close associate's involvement. After all, he has to protect and shield his stooges from being caught, and also because they comprise his close coterie. No seasoned politician would want to displease his coterie. And Salunke still has a long political career ahead..."

The team's mood surged since after the adverse judgment the morale was down. Sushil Mohite was unanimously selected as the man to keep a watch on Salunke and his movements. Mohite, and a few of his trusted associates, moved to Mulapur, Salunke's hometown, and constituency for many years. His winning margins from Mulapur had only increased with every election as he had managed to keep his vote bank happy by ensuring adequate amount of progress there. Mulapur was a well-developed town with reasonable infrastructure in terms of roads, power and water. At least one member of every household, if not more, was employed by the various small business enterprises, run directly or indirectly by Salunke, such as sugar factories, banks, schools, etc. He made sure that big projects never made it to his constituency, as they would bring in people from outside thereby exposing his 'simple' voters to the external world. His motto was very simple: to keep the people happy as well as completely dependent on him. He alone must be their leader, their sole master. He had ruthlessly crushed all attempts at leadership by others in his constituency. In a way, he was like Jagjeet, absolutely merciless and exceedingly self-seeking.

Salunke moved to Mulapur, probably to put his house in order as Wadia had correctly anticipated. Mohite and his colleagues kept constant, invisible vigil. Rumours were agog about Salunke's continuous presence in his hometown. Was he there to distance himself from his colleagues or to get rid of them and obliterate any connection he had had with them? The route to the Swiss money had to be broken and fast. The first few days saw hectic activity at the Salunke residence. A week later, a group of young lawyers were seen working late at his guest house. Mohite and his men were not able to find out the exact nature of the work being conducted. Nevertheless, a daily report was sent to Aditya to keep him abreast of all the activities in Mulapur.

Two days prior to the court hearing on the inquiry, the Swiss banks gave out the names of two individuals who handled transactions related to the Salunke account. The names sent shock waves all round as they were of Hambir Kadam, Salunke's trusted aide for over forty years, and of Balram Chaudhari, Salunke's treasurer. The media became obsessed and these men hogged notoriety. All of a sudden, Salunke and his family left Mulapur and returned to Mumbai, and convened a press conference where Salunke denied any knowledge whatsoever of the transactions done in his name by Kadam and Chaudhari. He admitted that the two men were his close associates, and that he had been terribly saddened by the fact that his two trusted aides had done things behind his back and used his name to deal with the Swiss banks. He declared that he had no knowledge from where the funds came and how they were sent over to Switzerland. This denial from Salunke sent another series of shock waves throughout the country, especially in Mulapur. It was absolutely inconceivable that Kadam and Chaudhari could have managed to conduct these transactions without his knowledge and approval. No one was surprised. It was common knowledge that he would crush anybody who even remotely threatened his political hold. The story of his son having left him while his daughter-in-law stayed back to assist him in his political affairs was well known. Such was the man's character.

His categorical refusal to accept the blame by passing it to his associates stunned his followers. They had not expected that he would ditch them so brutally. For Kadam and Chaudhari, the pressure was immense especially with the media coverage; they just couldn't handle it and they both committed suicide. It was a dark day for Mulapur! As expected, news reporters started hounding Mulapur though Salunke's men tried their best to keep them out. The families of Kadam and Chaudhari were under a lot of stress and decided to leave town to get away from the media glare, at least for a while. Before they could do so, Mohite managed an in-camera interview with both the families at their respective houses. Expecting to be stopped by Salunke's supporters, Mohite, through his network of bureaucrats, had sought police protection prior to these interviews. Salunke, knowing that he could not afford another public scandal did not put up much of a fight and let Mohite and his men conduct these interviews. He did not want to upset the people of Mulapur as this was the only constituency from where he could hope to get re-elected in the forthcoming elections.

The interviews with the families of Kadam and Chaudhari weren't of much use. Statements made during the interview were vague and without any substance. Salunke had obviously either threatened them with dire consequences or had assured them of enough financial assistance, with promises to take care of the family members. While all this was happening, media representatives were having a field day. People of Mulapur, silently, helplessly, and sadly had to cope with all the scandal their little town was facing.

The court ordered the Central Investigative Agency to carry out a full inquiry into the suicides of Kadam and Chaudhary. In all this Salunke's name had been badly tarnished and he urgently needed to do some damage control and re-consolidate his position. The show had to go on, especially with the elections round the corner. Professor Aditya knew that it was a good time to exploit the situation. He approached Avdhut Deshpande for advice on a suitable strategy. Deshpande came up with two suggestions. The first was to file another application in the court of law, requesting for the funds held in the name of Salunke to be returned to India and deposited in the national treasury. It was Indian money after all! Salunke had denied any knowledge of its existence and the two people who had transacted the funds were no more. Hence, in the absence of any heir or claimants, the best recourse was to get the money back into India for the state to take control over it. The court accepted this viewpoint and ordered the government to start the process immediately. The Swiss banks were quick to respond and confirmed that the funds would be repatriated immediately.

Deshpande's second suggestion was quite dynamic. Hoardings, placards, banners etc. were to be put up in every lane, on public walls and across roadside poles of Mulapur splashing the following message – "Kadam and Chaudhari were used yesterday! Could it be your turn tomorrow!" Within forty-eight hours, the small town was ringing with these words. Salunke's followers tried tearing down these banners but were stopped by groups of young boys posted by Mohite. These boys belonged to Ranjan Rishi's group of black belts and were up for a fight. Salunke's followers were even beaten up by them at certain vantage places in the town. The police, normally at Salunke's beck and call, decided to stay away and turn a blind eye. It was as if destiny was finally catching up with Salunke. Mohite's idea of using Rishi's men served also to test them before the bigger assignment that was in its nascent planning phase. The people of Mulapur were in awe of these young boys for what they had done to Salunke's supporters. Discussions regarding him and his 'reign of terror' started surfacing at many street corners; the people and their town were finally shedding their fears and were ready to speak their minds.

The insurgency brewing against him started gaining momentum. In the sugar factory elections that followed the episode, Salunke's group lost heavily for the first time ever. In the past, the group had registered landslide victories. This loss was cause for serious alarm. Salunke rushed to Mulapur, where he was scheduled to address a large gathering. The word had been spread, and there was a lot of expectation amongst the people, who wanted to know how their leader would refute all the allegations that had been made against him. Professor Aditya and Mohite were not going to let this meeting be a success. The professor again reached out to Deshpande, who by then had become a sort of a 'political guide' for him. The experience gained with the Pride Group had indeed been enriching. Once again, Deshpande came up with an excellent idea. Working on it, Mohite rounded up all the unemployed youth of Mulapur. Spreading a message by way of gossip, or rumour, or word-of-mouth is a known, effective tool to create public awareness. Salunke had used this tactic for election purposes earlier. Now it was time to use the same tactic against him. These young boys were given a target of fifty to seventy families each. Their job was to approach each family and appeal to them to boycott the gathering. Obviously, they were to be paid for their efforts. Mulapur needed to show its anger and frustration against the man who had let them down so badly. A change in leadership was called for.

To give a semblance of legitimacy to the entire operation, it was decided and arranged to have identity cards of a recognised NGO issued to these youngsters. Salunke's camp chose to ignore the operation, as they were arrogant and confident that the simple and cowardly people of the town would disregard the boycott plea and rush in large numbers to listen to their very own '*neta*'. But they were mistaken. Mohite's home-to-home propaganda was extremely successful and the gathering was a big flop. There was hardly twenty per cent of the normal turnout, and those who attended were Salunke's own followers and his business associates. Salunke felt terribly insulted and he left that very night. It was a rude shock for him that his own people had stayed away and not attended his public address.

After the humiliation in his hometown, he directed his attention to his network in Mumbai. He wanted a detailed update on Professor Aditya and his activities. He was informed that Sushil Mohite, who had caused him embarrassment in Mulapur, was actually working under the guidance of the professor. The fact that the professor and his wife were no more staying at their original residence was also found out. Apart from these two minor details, nothing much was known about the professor and his team. Salunke was worried at the professionalism, almost Mossad-like manner in which Aditya was managing all the activities. He was sure that Bhadralok Group was supporting the professor. Since his entire focus was the forthcoming elections, he knew he needed some drastic measures to retain his constituency. His political rivals in Delhi and Maharashtra were already capitalising on the Mulapur fiasco. A few well-wishers even suggested that he find another constituency which would be safer for him. He was indeed extremely irritated and frustrated at his current predicament. His political career was at stake, for the first time in forty years. The predator had become the prey and his nemesis was Professor Aditya.

Salunke used his connections within the Home Ministry and found out all the minutest details about Professor Aditya's relatives and friends. The professor's mother-in-law was residing alone in Delhi after the death of his father-in-law. An old lady, living all by herself was a 'soft target'. Getting a hired killer, for a paltry sum such as a few thousands was extremely easy. Young men from other poverty stricken states were always available for such jobs. They would execute the job and then disappear into obscurity, and tracing them proved to be a nightmare for the police and investigative agencies alike. The mafias in Delhi and Mumbai were increasingly making use of these fellows to do their 'hits'. One fateful afternoon, Salunke had one such shooter hired, and had the professor's mother-in-law killed in cold blood. In the evening, the professor got a call from Delhi.

The unknown assailant said over the phone, "Professor you idiot, you better note that you cannot touch our boss. Stop your nonsense immediately and praise our leader of future India, Ramesh Salunke – *Jai Hind*! You are good in cultural reforms—don't step into politics if you want to stay in one piece. If you act smart, like your mother-in-law, your wife will be chopped and cut, and you also. So shut up you bastard…" The caller paused, as if he was waiting for the professor's reaction.

The sudden news about the killing of his mother-in-law stunned the professor. His face turned ashen and he was at a loss for words. Not wanting to buckle down in the face of adversity, he said, "You coward, you rascal, you have killed an old innocent lady. Why don't you shameless people have the guts to fight your equals? That butcher Salunke will rot in hell with blood on his hands and loads of crimes to call his own. Tell that swine that he may have won the battle but he has awoken a giant and the war has started. That rascal can hurt us and bleed us but we will not give up—tell that to the demon …" Aditya's voice trembled with anger and helplessness. Unable to exercise control over his voice, he disconnected the phone.

He took a deep breath, had a glass of water, and went into his prayer room. With the picture of Shiva, the destroyer of all evils, in front of him, he began to meditate. Meditation always soothed his nerves and had a calming effect on him. He decided to wait until the morning to tell his wife about her mother's killing. The entire night, he kept making notes. He was noting down every thought that came to his mind. He knew he had to bounce back from this tragedy and move on. The Ravana in Ramesh Salunke had to be destroyed. It had to be an example for all young Indians. Killing the man was an easy job. That was not what the professor wanted; the man had to be finished on the personal, political, financial—all possible fronts. It had to be a complete destruction.

In the morning, the professor told his wife about her mother's death. She was terribly shocked and inconsolable. He tried his best, but she was completely devastated, especially knowing that her mother had met a violent brutal end. Aditya called up Nayan and Sathe and informed them of the heinous crime hoping the youngsters would be able to comfort his wife. After all, Nayan was like a son to them. A psychiatrist, a good friend of the professor was requested to check Sheetala's condition. She was hypertensive and the professor was advised to be by her side for at least a week. Of course, Aditya suspended all work to be with his wife.

As his mother-in-law's death was a murder, the crime branch took over the body for post mortem and other forensic formalities. It was decided that after two or three days, when all formalities were over, the body would be returned and flown over to Mumbai for the funeral. Janaki and her father Meghnath arranged for all the assistance that the police and other authorities required. In Mumbai, the professor's wife seemed to be coming to terms with her mother's death and her health too started recovering. The professor was taking good care of his wife, right from making her cup of coffee in the morning to serving her dinner. On the third morning, the professor made a hot cup of coffee as usual and called out to his wife. As there was no response from her, he called out again and again, till he felt uneasy. He rushed to her room only to discover the worst. His wife lay quiet, her body motionless with eyes open wide, staring blankly at the ceiling. She was gone. Frightened, confused and nauseated with panic, he called Nayan, the doctor and whoever could help him from reeling and collapsing himself. Nayan and Sathe reached as the doctor pronounced her dead. She had succumbed to a massive cardiac arrest. Overcome with distress and grief Aditya stood speechless, gazing out of the window, possibly reaching out to the Lord with his question—Why? Why me? Was this the price to pay for seeking justice? Was this the cost for attaining honesty, discipline and equality for a society which is condemned by scavenging politicians? Was it a demonic repayment for the good—the global good that his lovely Sheetala and he were striving to bring forth? There was more blood on the hands of Ramesh Salunke. The price for Aditya was the death of two family members … and counting?

Sheetala was cremated with full Hindu rites that were observed for three days. The media had been busy connecting both deaths. The police started its customary investigation, but knowing the depth of Salunke's reach, Aditya did not even try to take stock of the goings-on. He knew who had ordered the murder and brought misery to his family. Nayan, Sathe and the others sensed the intensity of the storm brewing in their guru's mind. He became obsessive with his work and started pushing all the projects as if deadlines were to be met. Nayan asked the professor if he should arrange for a condolence meeting for his wife and mother-in-law. But the professor did not even answer. He shut the 'family' chapter completely out of his mind, and instead asked Nayan to arrange a meeting of the core members of the team. The meeting was expected to be long as he hoped to firm the next set of actions.

In the evening, John called up from Switzerland. He first offered his condolences and then went on to give the good news that the Swiss government was returning Salunke's money to India. This was the first piece of good news since the double tragedy for the professor. It was indeed a huge success. Hearing the news, Aditya felt vindicated. He called Mansukhani and said, "Mr Mansukhani, the country has got back its funds. You may have saved Salunke from the clutches of the law, but his ill-gotten gains will not prosper. Don't forget, it is payback time! For starters, his own people have punished him. Smart criminal lawyers like you never win because you harbour felons. I suggest that with whatever is left of your status and standing, please go and serve the cause of your nation. You have earned enough name and wealth. Now perhaps it's time to give back."

"Professor Aditya, thanks for the advice but save it for someone who needs it. For me, my practice is all that matters to me and I do not need a philosopher riding on my back. I worship my profession and I fight my courtroom battles very passionately. I love to fight cases and win them."

Early next morning, Nayan called on the professor at his residence. After the loss of his wife, the professor had become quite aloof and impassionate, a state of affairs that Nayan wasn't comfortable with. He decided he had to speak to him to get some insight into his current state of mind and perhaps help him in some way. He reached the professor's residence only to find him meditating in front of a photograph of Lord Shiva. Nayan decided to wait until the professor had finished.

Coming out of his meditation, the professor saw the contemplative look on Nayan's face. Anticipating the question, he himself offered an explanation, "Yes Nayan, it is Lord Shiva I am praying to." Nayan raised his eyebrows.

"You know Shiva is the destroyer of all evil. Today our world is threatened by a few individuals and institutions that are damaging our life ruthlessly and mercilessly. That needs to be stopped before it gains momentum. Shiva is beckoning me to think on those lines. Destruction need not always be physical; it can be strategic or ideological. We must destroy this evil before it destroys everything that human beings have stood for. In doing so, we will have to be ruthless ourselves and not let our emotions cloud our logic. Why Shiva alone? Krishna too was known for his cunning! We need to target the very source from where scoundrels like Salunke derive their energy and strength. His fuel comes from the Pride Group. Apart from taking the project away from the Pride Group and getting it re-awarded to the Bhadralok Group, we haven't done much to thwart the evil designs of the Pride Group. Don't you agree?" Nayan nodded in agreement.

The professor and Nayan had a man to man talk. The newest weapon in the arsenal of Aditya was 'constructive destruction'. At the behest of the professor, Nayan organised a two-day seminar at Matheran, where Shini, her parents, Robert and many others from their 'outer' team too were to figure. The thought that the 'global friends' were all to meet was so welcome in the midst of all the hard work and exhaustion. Deshpande, Mohite and Ranjan Rishi met the professor to discuss the agenda for the meeting and to finalise the security arrangements for the participants. The meeting was convened to discuss the next milestone for the entire team.

One of the biggest challenges for the team was to eradicate the corrupt influence wielded by some notorious, so-called religious gurus in India. These dangerous, powerful people rode upon the financial muscle provided by a few corrupt industrialists and equally corrupt politicians. Indrajeet of the Pride Group was known to sponsor two such gurus—Dakshin Baba and Bada Bapu. The ashrams of these gurus were regularly used for clandestine business meetings and political negotiations. What was alarming was the fact that decisions concerning national security also were taken in these 'ashrams', a fact that was proudly publicised. Quite a few influential foreigners, bureaucrats, local and international mafia bosses were known to visit these ashrams for their 'spiritual exercises'. Bada Bapu, popularly known as 'BB' was the most notorious. He had huge properties and other financial holdings in a total of twenty-eight countries. He was often referred to as the 'King Maker'.

There were times when BB and Dakshin Baba would be on a collision path—both being power centers, competition was but natural. Their blind, innocent followers were exploited in the bargain. The networks of the gurus were huge, horrible and outright sinful. Earlier attempts by some Indian and foreign journalists to uncover them were stamped out systematically; in most cases by their tragic accidental deaths. Professor Aditya knew about this enormous power, and also knew it would take a herculean effort to bring down these monsters, if ever. Quite recently, the two gurus had played the vital role of unofficial arbitrators to help resolve the dispute between two warring factions in the Indian corporate sector. Even in that dispute, in the background was a game of 'power exchange' played by the two gurus; the two corporates being pawns in their game.

The Matheran meeting was a total success; management by Nayan and his team was absolutely spot-on. An unexpected visitor to the meeting was Seetabai who was included by the professor at the last minute. She and her women associates were running the sugar factory very well, and hence the professor thought that her presence would be a great source of inspiration to his group. The meeting was attended by over seventy delegates and many important issues were discussed threadbare. The two day meeting was chaired by Avdhut Deshpande, who requested the entire congregation to stand in silence for two minutes and offer condolence to the professor for the loss of his wife and mother-in-law.

The professor took the podium and said, "Friends, the deaths of my dear wife and my mother-in-law are indeed a big personal loss for me. But I believe many sitting here have suffered similar or even worse strokes of providence in their battles against corruption. Seetabai lost her husband, Nayan lost his mother, Sathe lost his father, and the list goes on. But all of them are standing tall and confident today. Let us remind ourselves, that as long as our soul remains unconquered, our war against the evils of our society will go on. We may lose a few battles along the way, but the ultimate victory will be ours. Our triumph with the Indian funds in Swiss banks is absolutely unprecedented. Who would have thought that the Swiss would actually repatriate the funds? The Swiss achievement, Seetabai's sugar factory, and the awarding of the business project to the Bhadralok group are our sources of perpetual energy and enlightenment. With these successes behind us, we can only look forward and move ahead. We are here for the next two days. Let us come up with a detailed and pragmatic agenda and make this world of ours a better place to live in."

Two teams were formed to handle two major projects. The

first team was headed by Sushil Mohite and was to prepare for the forthcoming elections against Salunke. Deshpande, Seetabai and Ranjan Rishi were to assist him. The other team comprised of Modi, Mike, Robert, Deepali, Janaki, Sathe and Shini, and was to work on exposing Indrajeet and his Pride Group. The group was to work under the professor's close and constant supervision. Nayan was given the job of facilitating things between these two teams. Coordination was extremely vital. As Salunke and Indrajeet were closely connected, simultaneous destruction of both had to be carried out; taking on one of them without the other was not advisable, perhaps not even possible.

***

Chapter 6

Mike's office in New York was the venue for the first meeting of the group. Present at the meeting were Robert, Modi, Shini, Janaki, Deepali, Sathe and Mike himself. The brainstorming lasted several hours, at the end of which they all concurred on a definite road map for their mission. They gave it a code name – 'Pride Group Assignment' or simply the PGA. The first task was to collect maximum possible data about the Pride Group's companies, either directly held or joint ventures, listed on the New York, Mumbai and London stock markets. A mutual fund dealing in currencies and commodities, operating mainly in a few European cities, Hong Kong and New York, was also promoted by the group.

Shini, Janaki and Sathe, set about collecting all the written text on Pride Group available in all print media. They also decided to analyse past TV interviews of Jagjeet and Indrajeet. Mike, with help from the 'Friends of Israel', decided to gather information on the

Group's offer letters to various investment funds in the US. They even decided to tap the speculative brokers operating at the various stock markets around the world.

Work started in earnest, but soon, in a matter of two weeks, the PGA team members realised they weren't making much headway in the analysis of the complex and voluminous data. They decided to get the assistance of financial experts who were specialists dealing in capital markets, metal and currency markets, mining, petroleum and infrastructure; all core areas of the Pride Group operations. As access to such expertise was beyond the means of the PGA, the team decided to consult Professor Aditya and Bhadralok, whose group's finance arm was a potential source for such specialists.

As expected, Bhadralok agreed to provide the required experts from his business group. A simple psycho-analytical test was administered to each of them, and ten professionals were selected by Professor Aditya. The professor then conducted a couple of induction sessions for them, where the nature and importance of the PGA was impressed upon them. Bhadralok also assured them appropriate recognition and rewards once the PGA operation was successfully completed. The induction was followed by a long, detailed training session, where senior bureaucrats, technical and financial auditors of international repute, and senior lawyers were invited to explain to these specialists, various types of techno-commercial manipulations. Two of Mike's friends were specially called from New York to Mumbai to conduct a few sessions on international business collaborations and related manipulations. The last session was conducted by Anatoli Guschchev, Robert's friend, who explained to them how the nexus between industrial houses, mafias, politicians and bureaucrats worked, and also about the involvement of bogus NGOs and religious trusts that were in reality private money-spinning business ventures.

All the sessions were conducted 'in-camera'. Bhadralok later suggested that the sessions be dubbed in a few Indian languages; Marathi and Hindi being top priority. This was necessary as the fight against Salunke was now very imminent, and these trainings would come in handy even there.

Meanwhile, the group of finance specialists moved to a house on the outskirts of Mumbai. The house was well equipped with advanced electronic equipment, and conferencing and data storage facilities. Sathe returned to Mumbai to be with the team and monitor its progress. Security arrangements were made by the Bhadralok group. The Pride Group was active in three major areas – mining, infrastructure and petroleum. Its entry into petroleum was the latest. Overseas, the Group was active in a few countries in the Middle East and Africa, USA and Europe, and the smaller countries of the Asia-Pacific region. The PGA team managed to put together thousands of pages of information on Indrajeet, his close associates and the Pride Group. A few details on the late Jagjeet, that were perhaps not available in the public domain, were filled in by Deshpande.

The PGA team worked furiously for close to six months and put together a huge amount of incriminating information but they were not able to crack the investment fund that dealt in metals and currencies. It was headquartered in Hong Kong and was named 'Hyper Wealth'. It's modus operandi was quite a mystery. Robert, through some of his very affluent and influential friends, got to know that the fund was popular with rulers of a few Middle Eastern states, international mafias, high profile bureaucrats and corrupt politicians from around the world. It was closely managed by an elite group of brilliant professionals, and it was almost next to impossible to get any information on the fund or its functioning. Their efforts were leading nowhere, so Mike, Robert and Nayan decided to consult professor

Aditya. It was quite obvious that some out-of-box strategy needed to be adopted to tackle the issue of 'Hyper Wealth'. The professor was convinced that it was absolutely vital to reach the core of this fund, if they were ever to get to Indrajeet.

Many astonishing facts came to light. There were such blatant legal violations, that one could file at least fifty criminal cases and two hundred civil cases against the group and its promoters. The challenge was in safeguarding all this evidence and then fighting these cases to the end, which knowing the delays in the Indian legal system, and the might and reach of the Pride Group, seemed an uphill task. But it had to be done nevertheless. Pride's foray into mining had been very dubious, with Jagjeet procuring many mining licenses illegally. Thousands of acres of land belonging to innocent farmers had been seized either by using bogus papers or by using force and coercion. Funds for the acquisition had been managed through a few corrupt banks and had been taken in the names of several bogus companies. The master of this 'land grab' had been Ramesh Salunke.

When Indrajeet took over from his father, he continued the dirty work, the only difference being the sophistication with which he executed all the illegitimate processes. He upped the scale several times higher by unscrupulously getting the basic laws and regulations amended or new ones framed in favour of his Group. His contracts for building roads, airports and waterways were all designed to give him enormous advantage. Ministers and bureaucrats in key government positions, enrolled on his payroll, were his accomplices. Indrajeet also managed to bag power projects across many states with inconceivable concessions and subsidies. The entire power costing and pricing was done in his favour, leaving absolutely no room for any public scrutiny. Most of the project related investments made were inflated by almost 100 to 200 per cent.

The Pride Group's international joint ventures were never put under any scrutiny, and all audits—financial or otherwise, were a farce. Its recent SEZ projects were huge opportunities for politicians like Salunke to invest their illegal funds. Some of the foreign loans taken were moved around through bogus companies registered in countries close to Indian shores. 'Hawala' rackets were regularly used to send black money overseas, which would then be brought back as white capital through companies primarily incorporated in the Middle East.

The Pride Group routinely used two international mafia gangs to silence or to get rid of its business rivals, nosey journalists, honest bureaucrats and NGOs—anyone or any institution that posed a threat of any kind. Even terrorism threats were countered by these gangs. The group kept going from strength to strength by regularly financing most political parties in India, whether it was the Rightists, the Leftists, the Secularists or regional parties. It didn't matter what the political leanings were, power was the sole thing of importance. Such was the might of the Pride Group that exposing its promoters and caretakers entailed a huge amount of risk.

Aditya, Nayan, Modi, and Rusi Wadia met Bhadralok at his residence. They agreed that a long drawn out legal battle in India was not going to serve their cause as success could not be taken for granted. Nailing the group in India was going to be extremely difficult as the police and the investigative agencies were corrupted by the likes of Indrajeet and Salunke. Rusi Wadia came up with the idea that they should take their battle overseas where the Pride Group's influence would be limited. He suggested the group's business affairs abroad be thoroughly investigated, and cases be filed against it in foreign courts. Everybody agreed with him. A few cases, where there were gross violations of law and human rights, were to be filed in India as well. It would serve to create awareness amongst the Indian people about the malpractices of the group. Besides, it would keep the group busy fighting in India as well as overseas.

Modi and Mike started work on the group's foreign affairs and at the same time in India. Public litigation cases against the group were filed by five different NGOs. This was a first for the Indian corporate sector. No other corporate had been so systematically challenged in India's corporate history. The Pride Group was quick to react and deny all the allegations. Not only did it refute everything said against it, it also lobbied hard, as a result of which, a powerful newspaper in India conferred the 'Best Corporate Award' on it. A TV channel even selected the group for 'Best Corporate Governance'. Following these announcements, Indrajeet and some of his close associates were seen on many TV channels, saying that the awards were a result of their transparent and ethical business processes.

Meanwhile, Mike and Shini, with support from the Bhadralok Group, called six press conferences in the US and presented their cases against the group. This set off a panic wave among the US shareholders and business partners who demanded a detailed inquiry into the group's operations. The stage was set for the PGA to make its next attack. As things were beginning to heat up, Modi and some of his American-European friends offered to stay for a month in New York and assist Mike. Rusi Wadia too offered to stay for up to three weeks. Mike and he set about meticulously examining the Group's foreign transactions for any incriminating information that could be used against them. They also made a public appeal in countries where the group had business interests, for the people to come forward and share any and all information against it.

The appeal was quite a success. Three hundred responses were received, mostly from the group's vendors, distributors, ex-business partners, ex-representatives, a few bureaucrats in the government, and business rivals. Another hundred were received from shareholders and financers. Even a few banks, worried about their huge investments in the group's ventures, offered to share details about their dealings with the Pride Group. With all the bad publicity, the group swung into damage control mode and hired the services of the best PR agents in the US. Money not being an issue, they paid exorbitant fees to set the image right. The agency arranged for Indrajeet to appear on American TV, and also managed to get a few articles printed in some of the important national newspapers. The agency made a strong pitch for the social work that the Pride Group had done, and by making references to the corporate awards that the group had recently won, attempted to portray the group as a business entity built on strict moral and ethical values.

The PGA pushed the pedal even more by stepping up its attack. Mike and Wadia made several presentations to a host of audiences and raised many critical issues against the group, such as illegal land acquisitions in India, inflated project costs, bogus bank accounts, bogus companies, government concessions that defied all reasonable logic, etc. Prima facie evidence was presented to support all allegations made, as a result of which, shareholders in the US and Europe became jittery and filed legal cases against the group. Indrajeet and the Pride Group were neck deep in trouble, now having to fight lawsuits overseas in addition to the ongoing ones in India.

As had become his daily morning ritual, the professor was meditating, when a feeling overcame him that Lord Shiva was communicating with him, and suggesting to him a different strategy to deal with Indrajeet.

Beaming with excitement, the professor wasted no time and immediately called up Bhadralok and relayed his spiritual experience.

They decided to meet and discuss the new approach, as both agreed that although it sounded extremely good, execution was going to be very difficult. They decided to mull over it for a week and then take a firm decision. Professor Aditya was convinced that Indrajeet and the Pride Group would be completely exposed and proved guilty if the new line of attack was employed. Bhadralok, after a week's deliberation, agreed that the new strategy was definitely worth a shot. Both of them decided to visit the US and discuss this new line of thinking with Mike and other members of the PGA.

Professor Aditya requested Bhadralok to defer the trip by two weeks, as he wanted to give his undivided time to the other team engaged in the battle against Salunke. The Swiss bank scandal was looming large over Salunke and he was still bleeding from the loss of his public image. With the elections now imminent, the picture was very bleak for the politician. Aditya knew that it was the right time to move in for the kill and finish him and his political career once and for all. Although considerably weakened, Salunke was still a very formidable opponent, and hence a lot of work, coupled with a fair amount of meticulous planning was the need of the hour. He wanted to be with his team for these two weeks and set the wheels in motion to steer them on a winning course.

The plan, as presented by the professor, required fifty colleagues of Ranjan Rishi to stay with fifty families, identified by Seetabai and Mohite, in Salunke's constituency. Initially they were to be trained in the different aspects of handling general elections. Avdhut was to become their coach and mentor, with the assistance of three senior retired executives from the central investigation agency. These were to move around the constituency keeping a watch on Salunke and his associates. All activity in the enemy camp was to be reported to Seetabai and Mohite.

While these men were secretly monitoring Salunke's movements, a 'door to door campaign' was started, under the supervision of Seetabai. A group trained in public speaking started addressing small groups of villagers, telling them about Salunke's misdeeds, showing how he was exploiting them for his personal gain, and more importantly offered answers to the problems they were facing. Things, at times, even turned violent. Seetabai, now an ace at the job, was prepared for such a reaction and arranged to record some of the aggression resorted to by Salunke's followers. These recordings were sent to prominent TV channels, who had earlier branded Salunke as an anti-national in the Swiss bank fiasco. The channels were only too eager to telecast these recordings damaging Salunke's image even further. Realising the damage this new publicity was doing to his election efforts, Salunke immediately ordered all violence to be stopped, and to start a counter 'smear' campaign against Seetabai and her group. The countermove met with little success and his party workers became restless, arrogant, and openly hostile. Having been ignored after the previous general elections, the people weren't in a mood to listen to anything. Salunke's paid hooligans were no match for Seetabai's motivated and determined activists.

Rishi's commandos were entrusted with the responsibility of providing security to everyone. Salunke and his followers were reduced to being mere bystanders, haplessly watching their constituency slip away from them. Salunke had made the cardinal error of underestimating his 'urban' opponents. He decided to play his last card, that of bringing in his daughter-in-law to campaign for him. He hoped that this would win the villagers over to his side. That ploy too did not work. Deshpande, familiar with such tricks played by politicians, was already in discussion with Salunke's estranged son who lived in Mumbai. He requested him to go over to Mulapur and campaign against his own father. The son immediately came and made twenty public appearances in one week. He appealed to the villagers not to vote for his 'villain' of a father.

Salunke was shocked when he got to know about his son's presence in the constituency. Not knowing whom to turn to, he contacted Indrajeet, being confident of his friend's help in these difficult times. Indrajeet's response was lukewarm, realising that Salunke was no more a potent force in the political circles. Salunke had been marginalised in his constituency, and was not even sure of a victory. Obviously, his hold in Delhi would subsequently be feeble, which in turn would seriously affect his negotiating power at the center. A politician without any power, even if he were to win from his constituency, would be of no use to Indrajeet, who was already in talks with Salunke's political rivals. Indrajeet had no political ideology or following; for him politicians were pawns to be used for gaining power. Not to break off the contact completely, he offered Salunke money for his election efforts. Salunke, however, knew that money was not going to help him win this election.

Another ritual that the professor followed daily was to have his morning cup of coffee while watching the international news on television. One day, his attendant announced the arrival of a gentleman named Naidu who was seeking the professor's audience. As the name did not ring a bell, the professor went out to see who his early morning caller was. He was in for a pleasant surprise. Standing in front of him was his college mate whom he hadn't seen in the last three decades. Naidu had been an excellent sportsman, a badminton champion in their college days. Being a sportsman affected his studies and he would invariably seek Aditya's help in preparing for the college exams. Naidu's father was a businessman who traded in commodities required by many government organisations. He had hoped that his son would take over his business, but Naidu, being very ambitious, had other ideas. He was a natural entrepreneur as was evident from his skills in successfully managing many college events. Naidu's interest was in shipbuilding. Even back in college days he had visited Goa and Mangalore, two big ship building hubs in the country, and had developed some very important contacts.

After college, Naidu moved to Goa and started a small workshop making barges required for transporting iron ore. Within a short time, his business flourished and he managed to get a few important international contracts. With the help of a Muslim friend who had businesses in Singapore and Malaysia, he set up a business branch in Singapore. Business from the Singapore branch picked up very fast and Naidu shifted the headquarters of his company to Singapore. Despite all the success and the riches that came along, he was far from happy on the personal front. Although nothing was apparently wrong with either him or his wife, as per all medical investigations and interventions, they couldn't have a child. Frustrated, he turned to spiritual help.

Naidu's spiritual quest led him to Bada Bapu. His relative took him to attend a religious discourse of the guru in Chennai. There was a huge crowd of over fifty thousand devotees waiting for the proceedings to begin. Bada Bapu sat on a tall, ornate dais; his long white beard made him look very imposing, almost majestic. After recitation of a few religious hymns, he went on to give a one-hour discourse on Bhagavad Gita's 'Bhakti Yoga'. His command over his subject and his overall demeanor exuded extreme spirituality. The entire audience was spellbound. Naidu too was overwhelmed and he decided to approach Bapu with his problem, feeling reassured that the guru had all the answers. Reaching Bapu in that crowd was next to impossible, hence Naidu's relative decided to request Bapu for a personal appointment. He approached one of his executives and asked if they could get an appointment. The executive very politely told him that he would need to send an email, detailing the reason for the appointment, along with the resume of the person seeking the audience. He said that Bapu's staff would sift through all such requests, and based on the merit of the request, an appointment was granted. The number of requests being enormous, it was physically impossible for the guru to meet each and every disciple.

Being a successful businessman with ventures overseas and a large turnover, getting an appointment with the big guru turned out to be rather easy. On the appointed day, Naidu visited BB's office in Chennai, which was also his residence, perhaps one of his many residences worldwide. A huge campus housed the guru's residence. Naidu was astonished at the obvious opulence and was quite bowled over to see some very impressive photographs of the guru with major celebrities that included very influential political leaders, industrialists and other dignitaries. The whole atmosphere was so imposing that he began to feel extremely anxious. He was escorted by a secretary into the guru's chambers, while his relative was asked to wait outside.

Naidu's meeting with BB lasted for twenty minutes. He was in raptures as he was completely mesmerised by the exhilarating experience. At the end of their meeting, BB gave him two chains, one with dark stones meant for him and the other for his wife. He asked Naidu if they could meet again the following week. Naidu accepted willingly without any hesitation. He felt so indebted and blessed, that he bent over and touched BB's feet twice, as if in complete surrender. He was in seventh heaven; he hadn't been this happy for a long time. Finally his prayers had been answered, he reassured himself. For the next meeting, he took his wife along. The couple was in for a pleasant surprise when BB offered them an apartment on the campus to stay. After several such visits, the couple started regularly attending the on-campus activities of the guru. On one such occasion, BB suggested to Naidu and his wife that he would like to visit Singapore, stay with them and deliver a few discourses in the city. For Naidu it was a great honour that his guru had thought it fit to stay with him. When BB came over, Naidu went to great lengths to make sure he was absolutely comfortable and that his visit was a complete success. Naidu was already a known figure in Singapore, but the visit of the great guru enhanced his social and spiritual status phenomenally.

A few months later, BB invited Naidu to attend a meeting of his 'core' group. A presentation covering the group's new projects was made by a secretary, during which he made an appeal to the participants. One of BB's charitable trusts required two hundred acres of land. Naidu was so impressed with the presentation that he spontaneously offered the fifty acres he owned close to Hyderabad. BB stood up, walked over to Naidu and embraced him. He then said, "My son, the trust and I are forever indebted to you for spontaneously contributing to our cause." Naidu's joy could not be contained.

The guru's office was quick to react, and a fat, voluminous agreement was put together for the land that Naidu donated. Naidu did not think it necessary to read the agreement in detail. Blinded by his faith, he signed the document at all the required places and handed it over to the trust. As if to show appreciation, BB felicitated Naidu in the subsequent spiritual gathering in Mumbai. Naidu couldn't have asked for more. His journey with BB until then had been a fantastic experience.

The following summer when Naidu, along with his wife, visited Hyderabad for his father's death anniversary, they were shocked to learn that the land they had donated to the trust wasn't being used for any spiritual cause, but was instead being developed for a SEZ project of the Pride Group. They visited the site and were stunned to see big boards of 'Pride Group SEZ,' and a lot of construction activity going on. They couldn't believe their eyes; both were terribly upset and also very sad. Although the betrayal was staring at them, Naidu decided to get the facts and then make a judgment. Perhaps this may be a case of encroachment by the Pride Group. There had to be a logical answer. He was still convinced that BB wouldn't let them down so badly. The great guru wouldn't indulge in such a dastardly act. Something had gone terribly wrong!

He decided to make inquiries at the local administrative office of the village sarpanch. He went there incognito, not to arouse any kind of suspicion, and inquired about the transfer of the land by the BB Trust to the Pride Group. Naidu had to bribe the sarpanch and he was shown all the papers related to the land transfer. It had been a blatant commercial transaction, details of which would be available with the district office, the sarpanch informed Naidu. It took two days and more bribe money to know the exact details of the transaction. The land had been sold by the Trust to the Pride Group for a staggering one hundred million rupees. He had been horribly deceived by his own guru, a fact that took Naidu almost a week to reconcile with.

He and his wife consulted their solicitor friend only to be told that all the paperwork was legal and that it had been a bad mistake to have signed the agreement blindly. A lawsuit wasn't advisable, especially since the Pride Group was also involved in the transaction. Having no recourse, Naidu was almost giving up, when he accidently came across a news item on Professor Aditya. He had to contact his old college chum. He was confident that his friend would help him this time as well.

Naidu narrated the entire episode to Aditya and also showed him all the agreement papers. The agreement was indeed official and terribly one-sided. Clearly, the document indicated a total transfer of ownership, and the BB Trust had every right to deal with the land, the way it deemed fit. Besides, there was no specific mention that the land had been donated for a spiritual cause. The entire agreement was legitimate and even the sale transaction by the Trust was perfectly lawful. Even if a lawsuit were to be filed, the defense would get away by declaring that the land was sold to raise funds for a spiritual cause, and there would be no challenging such a declaration.

Naidu and the professor discussed several strategies to confront the BB Trust. One thing they were certain of was that, like Naidu, there were many other gullibe, trusting fools who had been ensnared by the Trust and fighting it was going to be a monumental task.

Professor Aditya asked Naidu to come after four days. Meanwhile he set about doing his homework on the guru. BB had four big campuses in India and three overseas. Although he was politically well connected, his clout was not as big as that of the other two gurus in India. He was desperate to become the 'numero uno' by increasing his follower base. This was the chink in his armour. Professor Aditya suggested to Naidu that if they were to beat BB, he first needed to become his inside man. The way to get close to the man was to take up the challenge of promoting him and propelling him to the number one position.

Aditya had his plan neatly chalked out for his next meeting with Naidu. As per his plan, Naidu was to get close to BB and gain his confidence. He would need to take over the task of promoting the guru himself. Aditya suggested that he organise a couple of national campaigns and get promotional material such as photographs, posters, banners, pendants, calendars, etc. made, all at his own expense. All this would then be sold to the devotees and the profits would be shared with the BB Trust. That would give them an opportunity to get evidence against the guru, highly necessary to nail him eventually. Aditya warned Naidu that patience was the key if the assignment was to be a success.

Naidu mulled over the professor's suggestion for a week and then decided to go ahead. Aditya promised him the support of his colleagues in the execution of the assignment. He gave him an unlisted number for all further contact and asked him to resort only to phone conversations and avoid any personal contact. The enemy could not be underestimated; hence care and secrecy were primary.

For Naidu, this would be his all-important mission for the next few months. If it were accomplished successfully, it would awaken millions of innocent Indians who were trapped by such bogus gurus across the country.

The date of the general elections was declared. Like most politicians, Salunke swung got into action Because of the anti-propaganda that had been done by Aditya's team, it was a 'make or break' situation for him. Some of his true well-wishers suggested he contest elections from another constituency, which would be a safer bet than Mulapur. This hurt Salunke's pride. The constituency that he had nurtured for so many years, from where he had never lost an election until then, was suddenly unsafe for him. That was an insult. He felt violated; destiny was playing a cruel joke on him. He didn't want to take any chances. He increased his presence in the constituency. He shed all his arrogance and became humble with everyone in a bid to salvage his reputation but the people were too smart to get hoodwinked by this. He started taking keen interest in the minutest details of his election campaign. Alas! it was a little too late. His followers were not enthusiastic about his election. The damage done to his image and credibility by the professor, the bank and other scandals was quite irreversible. Besides Seetabai, Deshpande, Mohite and Ranjan Rishi were working furiously towards their agenda—the downfall of Ramesh Salunke.

The crusade against him was on track, and it was time to put up a candidate against him. Choosing an auspicious day, Aditya announced the candidature of Sushil Mohite. The two adversaries, being 'sons of the soil' from the same constituency guaranteed a 'battle royale'. Like Salunke, Mohite too had been busy conducting various awareness programs and had become a known name, a familiar face in Mulapur. Having served as a government employee, he had his 'inside' contacts and was able to put together a fair amount of sensitive and damaging data on Salunke's affairs in the constituency. There were gross misappropriations of several government subsidies and funds, in the name of bogus charitable trusts, that made their way into the pockets of Salunke's close relatives and friends. He approached a few local newspapers, and through them, made public all the misuse of government machinery and funds. Every day he would throw a question at Salunke through these newspapers. Soon his jabs became the talk of the town, and billboards displaying the same questions started appearing at street corners. Salunke's followers found it increasingly difficult to maintain any dialogue with the people as they started pushing for answers. They were ridiculed and mocked at openly. The once submissive people of Mulapur were now coming out of their closets and confronting them head-on.

With morale ebbing and support dwindling, Salunke decided to address the people of his constituency, and announced the date of his election rally. It was to be a mega event, a show of might, a reality check for him. He wanted to assess the mood of his people and take stock of his standing. Budget not being a constraint, his followers resumed their campaign with new found vigour; it presented an opportunity to make some quick big bucks. The people of Mulapur, now wary of Salunke's every move, dismissed it as yet another election gimmick on his part.

The professor's men were not to be left behind; they too picked up their campaign efforts. Rishi and his men, Avdhut Deshpande, the three executives from the intelligence agency supervising proceedings, Mohite, and the professor himself, all started working furiously towards Mohite's campaign and for the 'big blow' they were to deliver to Salunke as he inched towards his public rally. One day prior to the public meeting, TV channels went wild 'breaking news' of the phenomenal unlawful wealth Salunke had amassed. Six of his close associates, who handled all his 'black money' transactions, were put through all sorts of sophisticated interrogation techniques. They collectively admitted that Salunke's unaccounted wealth was to the tune of a staggering one and a half billion US dollars.

The wealth included land, buildings in various cities, gold, partnerships in eleven companies run either by family members or close friends, shares of blue-chip companies, investments in the Pride Group, and more than two hundred fifty million US dollars stashed away in Malaysian and Thai banks. Most of the land owned by him was grabbed from the farmers either by cheating them or by exploiting their poverty. Besides this, he ran a drug racket involving several hundred agents and around fifty strong men for money collection and recovery. He was directly or indirectly involved in the murder of sixty people including journalists, political rivals, industrialists and writers. He patronised Bada Bapu,

The interrogation of his associates also revealed his lust for the fairer sex. Businessmen and a few industrialists were known to provide him with women, at times even their family members, to curry favours in return. Quite a few girls from his constituency and also from other neighbouring villages were sexually exploited by Salunke and his associates. TV channels repeatedly kept airing snippets of the interrogations, damaging his image further. The villagers of his constituency were shocked beyond belief. He appeared on TV, but his attempts at defending himself were far from convincing. He had been let down; let down badly by his own men, his own trusted and otherwise competent associates had been literally torn apart by some very smart interrogators.

The government was left with little choice but to take into custody Salunke's associates, who seemed relieved at being arrested rather than having to face the wrath of their leader. Salunke, who was then residing in Mumbai, tried his best to prevent these arrests, but the news was too big for the government to ignore. In a spontaneous outburst of public anger, villagers of Mulapur attacked his palatial residence and completely destroyed it. The man they had worshipped for so many years, whom they had repeatedly elected as their leader, who held a demi-God status, turned out to be the devil incarnate. The attack on the house became national news and further added to his frustration and humiliation. The party high command in New Delhi suspended him 'until he could prove his innocence'. The suspension was the last straw; it was as if the carpet had been completely whisked off from under his feet. He suffered a minor heart attack. So lousy was his reputation that even playing the sympathy card was impossible. In fact, his illness was assumed to be another trick. He was ruled unfit to travel, his campaign went bust, political career was doomed and his personal life hit its lowest.

Everything was as per schedule; the planning, the execution and the timing had been perfect. Ranjan Rishi and his men, stationed in Mulapur for over three months, had worked very hard to reach this stage. The use of technology had paid rich dividends. Now the fight was entering the final round, and as decided, four of his senior associates, privy to all of his wealth, accounts and illicit businesses, were kidnapped and taken in for interrogation. Professor Aditya had arranged for a team of Mossad operatives to come over and take part in their grilling. Israel was only too happy to cooperate, as the cartel operated by Salunke was known to fund terrorist organisations in exchange for drugs.

The ex-Mossad interrogators conducted all the questioning very skilfully using the vast array of technology at their disposal. It was imperative that the examinations reveal damaging and incriminating evidence that could be used in the Indian as well as international courts. The contemptible man was like a huge octopus with limbs and tentacles reaching far and wide. His reach was immense; exposing him was extremely risky. Aditya and his friends were well aware of the peril but were ready for the consequences if anything should go against the plan. People like him had to be destroyed so as to restore the faith of the common man in the goodness of life.

Salunke was a desperate man. He wanted the best lawyer to defend him and get him out of the current mess. He decided to appoint Mansukhani as his counsel once again. His idea was to slap a defamation suit against Aditya with the intention of appealing to his gullible voters stressing his innocence. He approached the lawyer only to be refused, much to his horror and frustration. Mansukhani had been following developments—the interrogation of Salunke's six associates and their subsequent arrest. Word had also reached him about the kidnapping of the other four and their interrogation by the professor and his friends. He knew Aditya to be a very meticulous man and was sure that the evidence piled up against Salunke would be very difficult to fight in any court of law, and he was not one to take up a losing proposition. He politely declined to represent him, which made Salunke extremely angry. That very night some thugs attacked Mansukhani's apartment and in the process also beat him up injuring him very badly.

An obviously shaken Mansukhani reached for his phone, dialled Aditya's number, and in a weak, humble voice said, "Professor, you were damn right. I may have won our first battle, but the ultimate victory is yours." Realising that something was amiss, Aditya, in an equally unassuming voice replied, "No, Mr Mansukhani, I have yet to win the war. Victory will be mine when the last man supporting the evil son-of-a-gun, Salunke, turns away from him and comes over to our side."

"Professor, I speak to you as a man who has been literally crushed by Salunke's men and whose home has been brutally vandalised. If it weren't for me, he would never have come out of the Swiss Bank scandal and look at his audacity now."

"Mansukhani, my dear man, remember the old adage, 'As you sow, so shall you reap'? It's Karma—the law governing cause and effect. Why blame Salunke? All my efforts of persuasion went down the drain when you had a chance to pull yourself away from the evil. You could have avoided helping that rascal escape but you continued on the wrong path."

"Yes professor, no denying that. Your karma theory is a solid one, albeit striking me late in the day. I have amassed wealth at the cost of my peace of mind! Here I am confessing, so please don't abandon me."

"Mansukhani, with your phenomenal learning and experience to back you, who, just who am I to extend help to you?"

"No professor, please don't say that, I beg of you. Yes, I have won many a lawsuit in my time, but there's more to life than winning cases. My inner voice is challenging me about my real achievements, and unfortunately, I cannot find a suitable answer. At my age I have nothing to show, nothing to boast of, except for the cases that I have won, resorting to manipulation of situations, people, evidence... oh it's a lousy story to tell!"

"Hey man, you are obviously hurting now. This 'inner voice' that you speak of, I suspect may be just a passing phase. With the passage of time your hurt will ease and you will be go back to your manipulative ways. If not Salunke, there will someone else. I am sorry but I find your so-called transformation implausible, and the regrets that you express are a result of wounded pride."

"Sir, I don't blame you. I would have felt pretty much the same were I in your place. But let me tell you, this entire episode has been an eye-opener. I do want to tread the righteous path. Please just believe me. I do not know how I can convince you, but my inner voice is definitely calling."

"Mr Mansukhani, give it a month. If you feel the same even after that, we shall talk again. People do change; I am a firm believer as I have seen it happen to Avdhut Deshpande and Ranjan Rishi. Both these gentlemen were on the wrong path for the better part of their lives, but now they are committed to undoing all the wrongs they have done. They are devoted members of our Global Reform Group and dedicated to the service of humanity."

"Fine professor, it's a month from now! I shall, till then, assess my life's mission. Many thanks for your patience. You are a compassionate man without any vengeance in you. You are one of a kind. Thank you for giving me a second chance. I know I shall rediscover myself for good this time."

Professor Aditya felt inclined to believe him. He thought him to be genuine and his repentance real. But could such a manipulative mind change so suddenly? He was not sure. But he was willing to wait.

Meanwhile Ramesh Salunke, without wasting any further time got himself another noted lawyer from Mumbai. He upped his campaign by putting up large hoardings in his constituency explaining his version of the 'ultimate truth' or that's what he called it. He hired the services of leading Bollywood stars, cricketers and even television stars to campaign for him. He had the belief that his simple voters, who for so many years had believed him and his appeals, would now believe again, especially if the appeals were made by celebrity idols. Mohite too, ably supported by Seetabai and Ranjan Rishi, stepped up his efforts and reached out to the villagers on a one-on-one basis. Recordings of the interrogations done of Salunke's wealth managers and other associates were shown at vantage places. The villagers of Mulapur would turn up for these recordings in large numbers.

Professor Aditya was certain that Salunke would employ every trick he could—distribute huge sums to the poor illiterate villagers, attack, capture and indulge in bogus voting, fuel riots in the constituency on election day thereby scaring the voters away from casting their vote, tamper with the voting machines, etc. Even the possibility of the local administration colluding with Salunke, having fed off him for so many years, was very real. This last phase of their fight against him was extremely critical. Till then, Salunke had met with little success with his election efforts. The professor and his colleagues had effectively combated him on all fronts. They decided that it was absolutely imperative to bring in more technology and provide man-to-man protection to the working committee through this entire final stage.

Mike and Shini flew from the US and brought with them a few American journalists. The entire team moved to Mulapur with the intention of mounting pressure on the local administration and police, prompting them to stay away from the Salunke campaign.

Rishi and his men were entrusted with the responsibility of protecting the voting booths and the voters. Seetabai, and a few of her women colleagues from the sugar factory, were to keep vigil at all important places in the constituency.

The move of getting foreign journalists into Mulapur proved to be very strategic as the central government was then obliged to send a special team of election supervisors to monitor the voting. This spelt trouble for Salunke as his chances of manipulating the votes diminished considerably. As an alternative, within forty-eight hours, he put up new hoardings all over the constituency with a fresh emotional appeal. Seetabai and her colleagues rushed to Professor Aditya with this news. No chances could be taken as one could never know when the mood of the voters could swing. Out of pity and confusion, they could forgive him and give him a fresh lease, it being his last stint. Deshpande came up with an equally emotional counter-attack. Within twenty-four hours huge hoardings were put up all over. They carried hard hitting, yet very emotional slogans and photographs of the many farmers cheated by the Salunke camp. The rendition in Marathi was quite poetic, with a rural touch, almost like folklore.

The Salunke camp had not expected such a swift and effective counter-attack. With the election date fast approaching, Salunke, in a last ditch effort, tried inviting party leaders at the state and national levels to campaign for him but he was trounced there too. Two days to D-day, their started a 'whisper movement' in Mulapur, a last attempt to gain voter sympathy. Activists spread the word that 'their own Salunke Saheb' had been taken seriously ill. Victory in the elections was the only cure for his illness. Deshpande smartly projected the minister in his customary good health, enjoying food in a gluttonous orgy. The day of the elections saw the old and religiously disposed folks giving a mythological parallel. 'Rama did not forgive Ravana. Krishna did not exonerate Kansa. Why should you pardon this devil called Salunke? Isn't it time to weed out the bad and bring in the good and make the future of your children safe? You have been given the opportunity to throw out corruption and that you must. Exercise your franchise today and make your present and your future safe—and let honesty prevail!'

Mulapur witnessed a record turnout at the elections. The media was thrown into a frenzy; journalists—local and foreign—thronged the booths. In all the excitement, Ramesh Salunke was nowhere to be seen. He had perhaps absconded accepting his defeat.

As expected, he lost the election by a huge margin and there was a landslide victory for Mohite. Good had prevailed over evil, truth over untruth. The streets of Mulapur witnessed spontaneous celebrations.

Salunke committed suicide in his private apartment in Mumbai. The entire country was buzz with the news. Deshpande, Professor Aditya, and Mohite attended the funeral and even consoled his son. Though stark enemies in their lifetime, Aditya and team did what was politically and humanly correct.

The victory against Salunke was only the tip of the iceberg. The bigger challenge of global reform lay ahead. A lot more needed to be done. The next step was to seize his ill-gotten wealth and return it by way of compensation to all those who had suffered on account of his evil designs. The remaining part of the haul could be deployed in two ways: to build necessary civil infrastructure in the constituency and to fill the depleted government treasury. Professor Aditya used the presence of the international media to pressurise the government to establish a fast-track court for expeditious legal and operational proceedings required to deal with Salunke's wealth.

The government, within a fortnight, appointed a special court to scrutinise the ill-gotten booty. A committee headed by Professor Aditya along with Bhadralok, Modi, Mohite and Seetabai was initiated to assist the court in its execution. Deshpande was appointed the honorary secretary, a position he promptly agreed to take up. It was decided that the government appoint an independent auditor to ensure perfect transparency. Time-frames and deadlines were set so that the daily proceedings could be telecast on local TV channels. The people of Mulapur deserved an assurance that the wealth that Salunke had amassed at their expense would be returned to them and used for the well being of their constituency.

The committee completed its job in a record two months, ably supported by the government and other related agencies. Sathe made an effective case-study presentation covering all aspects of the battle against Salunke. The presentation was dubbed in fifteen Indian languages. Bhadralok took it upon himself to personally finance the creation of this presentation and later to make ten thousand copies for distribution. This 'educative' presentation was then sent to various social working groups, schools, colleges, government offices, youth clubs, newspapers and other media organisations, foreign consulates, non-resident Indian groups, women's self-help groups, religious and cultural organisations, philanthropic institutions—the list was enormous.

***

Chapter 7

Aditya got a call from Mansukhani in the early hours of a fine Sunday morning. "These last several weeks, I have been introspecting over my life's misdeeds and have had frank discussions with all my family members. My inner voice is now compelling me to join your Global Reform Group and follow the righteous path. My son-in-law, who works with me, does not like the idea one bit. In fact he is vehemently opposed to it. He is right in his own way, as my joining you would certainly not go down well with all the notorious clients that I have represented as a practising criminal lawyer. We have been privy to all their nefarious activities, and obviously it would upset them very much if I were to take such a step. Not only my son-in-law, but my daughter and my wife are also opposed to my decision. For the first time in my life I am faced with a dilemma that I am not able to resolve myself and hence I seek your help. I sincerely want to work with you; perhaps my heart is seeking retribution for the crimes that I have helped go unpunished by getting all the crooked politicians, industrialists, mafia members off the hook." He waited for the professor's response.

"Mr Mansukhani, I understand and sympathise with you. You wish to absolve yourself of your past sins, but let me caution you that such purification of the soul comes at a price and with a fair amount of risk—risk to you and to your family members. They have so far enjoyed all the material comforts that you have provided, thanks to the dishonest crooks you have had as clients. I suggest you take time out to think clearly, say a week more, before you announce your decision. Meanwhile, I could perhaps suggest to you a via-media."

"Please professor, that would be real kind of you," Mansukhani said.

"Well, we are currently working on a very important project and you could start by contributing towards it. The project is very ambitious. Obviously your involvement will be kept confidential."

"May I ask about the project?"

"Not right now and certainly not on the phone. We still have to assess the genuineness of your desire to work for us. After all, you have been a very seasoned criminal lawyer. I am sure you can appreciate my apprehension."

"Absolutely professor, I understand."

"Fine, in that case I shall convey to you the date and time of our next meeting. If you would like a week to think over our discussion, we could catch up next week."

"Oh no professor, I cannot wait that long. It's already killing me, this predicament. Please, let me know the date and time of our meeting. I wouldn't miss it for the world." Mansukhani was sounding very anxious indeed.

"Great, we shall be talking very soon."

Within an hour, Mansukhani got an sms from an unlisted number giving him the details of his meeting with Professor Aditya. The venue was a small hotel on the city outskirts. After a thorough body check, the lawyer was lead into a simple, moderately furnished room, that was obviously fitted with sophisticated recording equipment, as his experienced eyes were quick to notice. While being frisked, he was aware that his body prints were also taken. The professor was a meticulous man; Mansukhani had no objection to all of that.

Nayan was also present at the meeting, The professor started by saying, "Mr Mansukhani, you already know a lot about our mission, our ideology, our work processes and about our associates. We have no secrets here, none whatsoever. As regards your wish to join us, we are not sure about your reasons, but we intend to find out. If you don't mind, you will be subjected to a credibility test, only then we can proceed with our meeting. I shall ask you three questions, and I want straight, honest answers. Am I clear, and do I proceed?"

"Please do," responded Mansukhani.

"What and how much do you know about Indrajeet and his Pride Group? Would you share with us all those bank account numbers where you have deposited all the money you have earned, white or black, while working for your criminal clients? Will you hand over all the confidential papers of the criminal cases you and your son-in-law have handled of the current home minister? You must answer these questions truthfully before you can expect to work with us."

Mansukhani was visibly upset. He looked at the professor and said, "Now I understand the reason behind your success. I have to say that you are a phenomenal exponent of Krishna *niti*."

"Please do not speak of Krishna *niti* without a good understanding of what it really means. Obviously you do not, because if you did, you wouldn't have helped scoundrels like Salunke! Krishna *niti* or not, are you willing to answer my questions?" The professor wanted to come to the point.

"Answering these questions is as good as me writing my own obituary, isn't it?"

"Absolutely not! Your information and the papers will be kept in strict confidence until we are convinced about the genuineness of your intentions. But on the other hand, if you betray our confidence, we shall most certainly turn them over to the appropriate authorities. Think it over."

Mansukhani's mind was made up. He knew he had to do what was right. For him nothing was going to be more sacred than joining the professor and serving his cause. He agreed to the three conditions, and the next date was set when he would bring all the relevant information and hand it over.

For the next meeting, Mansukhani got all details of his bank accounts, and the original case papers of the criminal case that he was representing the home minister in. His account of the Pride Group's illegal activities checked out to the last detail. Nayan and Professor Aditya were now convinced that Mansukhani indeed espoused their cause and was ready to join them. He was straightaway assigned to the Pride Group Project or the PGP that they were readying for. Taking on Indrajeet was going to be a different ball game altogether. Salunke had been dealt with rather easily; his arrogance and recklessness were his undoing. Indrajeet, on the other hand, was a very shrewd man with a well-knit network of politicians, mafias bureaucrats, bogus NGOs and the so-called religious leaders. Breaking into this nexus and exposing the man was as difficult as breaking the 'chakra vyooh' of Mahabharata and defeating the Kauravas. Lord Rama too had to put faith in a well-meaning member of the enemy camp Vibhishana, to kill the demon king Ravana. Here, Professor Aditya had taken the calculated risk of allowing Mansukhani to join them in exchange for valuable information.

Later in the day, Nayan got an unexpected call from his brother Pawan who asked to see him urgently. Nayan realised the reason for the call as three of the criminal cases filed by the GRG against the Pride Group, directly involved and implicated Pawan. Although Indrajeet had started preparing his defense by eliminating some of the evidence, he was making no attempt to protect Pawan's interests. On the contrary, he was perhaps preparing to let Pawan take the fall, by making him a scapegoat in the criminal cases filed against the Pride Group. Pawan was running scared and was miserably insecure. Besides the possibility of him being criminally charged and convicted, he also feared for his life and the lives of his wife and children. The modus operandi would be to point all the evidence in the direction of the scapegoat, and just when the case would be ready for hearing, arrange an accidental, untimely death of the fall guy. Out of sheer fear, Pawan had just arranged for his family to move to a friend's house in Haryana, but wasn't sure if he or they were safe there.

Nayan insisted on meeting Pawan only in the presence of Professor Aditya. Having no choice or say in the matter, Pawan agreed. The tables had turned; the hunter had become the hunted. As agreed upon, Pawan met Nayan and professor who proposed to him that if he would cooperate the police might in return reduce the jail term. He initially insisted that he be spared a jail sentence. But considering the magnitude of the crimes, conviction was not avoidable. He also wanted to assess the possibility of Indrajeet getting away, considering his connections and reach within the entire judicial system and the government bureaucracy. If Indrajeet managed to come clean, Pawan's days would certainly be numbered. Aditya made it clear to him that giving him guarantee of anything but his safety was beyond him. He assured Pawan that he would help him to the extent possible, but guarantees of any sort were not offered. Pawan was left with two choices – join Aditya and the side with 'truth and morality' or become Indrajeet's scapegoat. Aditya asked him to give it some thought for a few days and then revert back to them.

A week later, Pawan agreed to go along with the professor and his proposal. The professor asked him to transfer all files and documents to his team working on the Pride Group Project. This was not easy as Indrajeet had put Pawan on a perpetual watch. The smallest hint that he could be working with the professor would be fatal. The entire issue was to be handled with utmost care. Deshpande and Modi came up with a workable solution. A religious function was arranged at Pawan's residence where friends and relatives were invited. His wife and children also attended the function, to make it look natural. Amongst the relatives who attended the function were Modi's four female assistants. They arrived at Pawan's home with a suitcase as if to stay for a couple of days. The following day, after the function, the four women collected all the important files, papers and CDs and packed them in their suitcases. They left along with Pawan's wife and children, who were escorted back to Haryana.

Mike flew down from New York with two of his trusted assistants to help with the PGP work. Meanwhile, Rusi Wadia and Mansukhani got busy verifying all the papers and documents. Some of the papers were extremely incriminating as they directly established the involvement of the Pride Group in blatantly illegal business transactions. The evidence was enough to book the top executives of the group, including Pawan, for a good ten to fifteen years, with hefty penalties. But in Mansukhani's opinion, the evidence collected until then wasn't good enough to pin the crimes on Indrajeet, as his direct involvement in any of these transactions could not be ascertained.

Indrajeet had shrewdly empowered all the top executives to take key decisions independently. Hence, although the executives could be held responsible for the actions of the Pride Group companies, direct involvement of Indrajeet, and thereby getting a conviction against him was going to be a formidable task.

Professor Aditya called Pawan for a meeting to keep him abreast of the developments. He informed him that they hadn't yet got anything against Indrajeet substantial enough to have him convicted on a criminal charge. Even if that was the case, submitting all the new evidence to the court was absolutely important. Damaging the reputation of the Pride Group would hurt Indrajeet very badly and would weaken him and make him vulnerable for their next attack. Mansukhani assured Pawan that he would manage a jail sentence of a maximum of three years if Pawan surrendered to the authorities. Obviously, his ill-gotten wealth would also have to be forsaken. Pawan spoke to his wife and then decided that surrendering was the only 'real' option for him.

Professor Aditya asked him to go through a comprehensive interrogation by the PGP before surrendering to the police. He agreed, and Mike, with the help of his two assistants, put Pawan through an exhaustive question and answer session. The entire interrogation was recorded and released to American and European media, which wasted no time in telecasting it on major TV news channels. Indian TV channels followed suit creating chaos in the Indian business circles. The Pride Group fraud had the distinction of being the biggest fraud in Indian corporate history. All these events took Indrajeet completely by surprise and didn't leave him any time to do any damage control. Pawan's interrogation revealed names of very powerful and prominent politicians from the ruling as well as the Opposition parties. It shook the entire 'corridor of political power'.

The government was left with no option but to appoint a high power committee of two retired judges, three senior bureaucrats and two senior political representatives, to conduct an independent and speedy inquiry into the allegations made. The media retaliated by objecting to the presence of the political representatives in the committee, and instead, demanded the appointment of two respected members of the society as their replacement. The government, already red faced, accepted the demand.

The media frenzy that followed covered different stories about the Pride Group. It dug out many details about the late Jagjeet and his fraudulent corporate methods. Indian farmers, especially those whose lands were usurped by the Pride Group, joined in. The politicians who were implicated by Pawan's interrogation, started targeting Indrajeet and his associates.

Indrajeet's army of lawyers and solicitors swung into frantic action building his defense. He spent millions on showcasing his good side, his family and the Pride Group on all media platforms. A few benefactors of the group's philanthropy were interviewed repeatedly by some TV channels. Advertisers, corrupt journalists, 'so-called' NGOs—almost everybody who could make a fast buck cashed in. Indrajeet appeared on several TV channels with his clichéd explanation. "This entire charade against me is a conspiracy staged by a few multinational corporations. Even some foreign governments are scared of India's fast rising economic prosperity and do not want India to become a global economic power. Our rivals in those countries do not want us to enter their markets. … They fear our competition and therefore wish to block us.…In a way, this can be viewed not only as a war waged against the Pride Group but as an open economic war against our beloved country."

Rusi Wadia and Mike were quick to react, and vehemently

objected to Indrajeet making it out to be a 'national' matter and got a court injunction against it. The court pronounced its warning to Indrajeet. His going to the media and making such inflammatory statements only served to damage the reputation of the Pride Group even further as the media made capital of this court 'warning'.

The committee completed its inquiry and submitted its report to the court within three months. The court subsequently engaged a couple of investigative agencies to assess the authenticity of the report. Meanwhile, the Central Investigative Agency, running a parallel investigation, also tabled its findings. The government, bereft of a choice, had to expel the politicians who were implicated—from the cabinet and from the ruling party, until the court could arrive at a verdict. A month later, the court pronounced its judgment. Three executive directors, seven vice-presidents, and eighty-one senior managers of the Pride Group were found guilty of criminal charges. They were sentenced to varying years of imprisonment based on their respective levels of crime. Their personal wealth was seized and attached by the court. Pawan, having already surrendered himself and his wealth, got away with a four-year jail term. Indrajeet's lawyers, as anticipated, managed to convince the court, that, as the chairman of the group, he was not directly responsible for the activities of the group's companies, and hence was not aware of all the misappropriations that had been happening without his knowledge. They pleaded 'not guilty' for Indrajeet and insisted that the court penalise the 'Pride Corporation' as a legal entity instead.

The court penalised the 'Pride Corporation' to the tune of seven billion rupees, the highest fine levied. Enraged shareholders staged demonstrations outside the group's headquarters. Four foreign investor groups, too, filed cases in their home countries seeking compensation. They demanded that the penalties be paid out of

Indrajeet's personal wealth and not from the Pride Corporation's account, which would indirectly affect the investors. In the aftermath to the judgement, Indrajeet was faced with criminal cases in India as well as overseas.

A meeting was convened at the Professor's residence. The agenda for the meeting was to the review the progress of the GRG. The professor gave an overview of the latest projects and their status. He congratulated Seetabai, Mohite, Deshpande, Sathe and Rishi for their courageous work on the Salunke case. He then skirted the issue of Bada Bapu. In the post lunch session, the main topic was the Pride Group Project. Although they had tasted some success in the opening rounds, Indrajeet was still a free man and far from destroyed. They had a brainstorming session on how to bring about a total collapse of this business empire. Bhadralok said, "The next attack should be our final assault. The Pride Group's rout should be total and complete. Let us not leave any stone unturned."

"I agree entirely with Mr Bhadralok. If we don't get Indrajeet this time, we may never get him. We obviously need to deploy an altogether different approach to tackle him, something out of the box. We must employ a new line of attack; expenses and risks associated should not be a constraint. It has to be a telling, decisive blow that will finish the man once and for all," said Aditya.

Mansukhani agreed. "You are correct, professor. And I may just have the strategy that can do the job. But it is risky and we may have to incur heavy expenses. I am not sure it would fit your ideology but given the current state of affairs and the man we are dealing with, this may be the only option."

"Mr Mansukhani, you are an accomplished lawyer and your association with Indrajeet and Salunke puts you in the best position to assess the need of the hour. Please explain your plan."

"To the best of my knowledge, Indrajeet and his coterie run a mutual fund called 'Hyper Wealth', operated out of Hong King, and which deals in metals and currencies. The investor portfolio consists of very high networth individuals. Some of the powerful and wealthy Sultans and Sheikhs of the oil producing countries have invested in this fund. The fund itself is a closely guarded secret."

"Isn't it solely owned and run by the Pride Group? If not, getting information on the activities of the fund would be next to impossible," Nayan interrupted.

"No Nayan, the fund has a partner in a Muslim country. Getting information on the fund will be difficult and risky as well."

"But risk is what we have agreed to take. We understand, that to have to deal with Indrajeet, we will have to confront risk at all times," Bhadralok said.

"As we already know, this fund is even used by criminal organisations and terrorists to park their funds. The Sultans and Sheikhs who have invested in the fund probably even finance their illegal actions through it. My gut feel is that even the Pride Group, using the mafia connections, funds some of the terrorist organisations to do their dirty work internationally," Mansukhani continued.

"But why would Indrajeet involve himself in such a risky proposition? After all, he is a very astute businessman!" asked Deepali.

Mansukhani turned to Deshpande and said, "Perhaps Mr Deshpande here would like to elaborate on that. I only handled the criminal cases of the group as their lawyer while Mr Deshpande was actively involved in its core functioning."

All heads turned to Deshpande. Colour drained from his face; he was clearly uncomfortable but he managed to keep his composure and said, "What Mr Mansukhani has indicated is only a half truth. Although we formed the core of the group, we were never privy to any of the group's transactions that involved big money and big risks. Jagjeet, in his days, and later, Indrajeet, both kept us out of the loop when it came to the big fish! During my time with the group, I did handle payments to local mafia outfits. To answer Deepali's question, let me say that this is conjecture on my part as I do not have proof of what I am about to say—the Pride Group often recruited the services of criminals to eliminate business rivals, pesky journalists, and at times, even some interfering politicians and social workers. How else were they to get business licenses in countries where it wouldn't have been possible otherwise? And what of the security of its own people and business interests in countries that challenged the Pride Group's establishments there? At times, the group has even terrorised politicians to change their stance or to bring about some procedural change to directly benefit its financial ventures. I would even go to the extent of saying that the group has been directly instrumental for the collapse of certain governments in India and overseas."

There was a momentary silence. Although it was acknowledged that there was a nexus between the Pride Group, the mafia, and the terrorist organisations, the story coming straight from the horse's mouth had quite a different impact. "Well now we know what risks we will face should we make 'Hyper Wealth' our target to bring down Indrajeet," said Aditya resignedly.

"Oh yes! Even we will get our hands dirty if we are to take this route. It would need us to connect with some of the mafia organisations, a task horrendously expensive and terribly risky. With such contemptible crass and scum of the society there is always the danger of being double crossed and finding oneself in an abyss. Also, I believe it would tarnish the reputation of the GRG, and furthermore, let me warn you—if Indrajeet gets a whiff of this, he will go for the jugular and surviving that would require a miracle. He has media connections all over the world and he will stop at anything until he has branded us as an outfit with ties to the underworld. We will lose all credibility and that is something we cannot afford."

"Absolutely correct, Mr Mansukhani! These are dangerous grounds. We will most certainly have to think of the most watertight strategy there is," Professor Aditya said.

"Friends, personally speaking, I am ready to take this risk myself. I have been party to many crimes committed by Salunke and Indrajeet. Perhaps God is beckoning me to pay back for the crimes that I helped commit. I am quite familiar with these mafia networks, and hence, it would be apt for me to do the initial spadework. Once we get the basic direction we are looking for, it will be easier for you all to get involved."

"Mr Mansukhani, we very much appreciate your sentiments. I am sure you are aware that you will pay with your life, should things not work out," reacted the professor.

"Professor, I have been most ardently watching your lecture CDs these last four weeks. They have helped me choose my path. You've said repeatedly that the purity of the soul remains unconquered even though the body may perish. Well then, Indrajeet may cause me to die but he will not conquer my soul. I am not bothered about my life as long as my soul is free; my spirit is free." Tears rolled down his cheeks. Aditya walked up to him and put a comforting arm around his back. They decided to take a small break and reconvene later.

Everyone agreed that Mansukhani would shoulder the responsibility of doing all the necessary ground work. His involvement was to be kept strictly confidential. The discussion then moved to the next item on the agenda—Bada Bapu. A unanimous decision was taken to enlist the services of the young cadres of the Hindu Samiti to expose religious frauds like him. Modi and Naidu were given charge of the BB Project and were assigned a small young team of enthusiastic workers. An overall plan was decided and some major milestones were identified. On that note, the meeting concluded with specific roles and responsibilities assigned to every team member.

The very next day, Modi met Naidu and discussed the first three major targets of the project. Naidu, with two of his associates in disguise, met Bada Bapu on the pretext of sharing with him the presentation of the 'Strategic Propaganda Movement' that the so called learned man himself had prepared. Bada Bapu was immensely impressed especially when Naidu declared that he was willing to personally finance the entire movement. Under the garb of making a strong pitch for the movement, Naidu requested the guru for details of his spiritual powers, the social work conducted by him and his wide network of devotees. Being obsessed with the sole ambition of becoming India's top spiritual guru, Bapu agreed immediately.

Naidu was aware of Bapu's mistress, Chanda Devi. Bapu's empire had two leading ladies, two pillars—one was his mistress, and the other his wife, fondly called Guru Mata. Both these women wielded enormous power themselves; it was as if there were two parallel power centers within the empire. Guru Mata, along with their grownup son Vishwas Raje, controlled three India-based centers, while the rest were under Chanda Devi's control. Among the two, the mistress was the more influential, with a lot of political clout. She was BB's spokesperson especially in the political circles. Many members of the BB Trust owed their allegiance to her and she would regularly oblige them using her political leverage. So much so, that even BB himself was somewhat wary of her power. She was endowed with beauty and grace but had an equal dose of cunning in her character to match.

Crafty Naidu planned to exploit the rift between these two women to eventually bring about the downfall of Bapu. He wormed himself into the good graces of Chanda Devi and Vishwas Raje. He ensured that his dealings with both were tactful and did not overlap. Having achieved enormous power and wealth, Chanda Devi sought fame which had eluded her until then, by virtue of being the 'other' woman. Naidu had spotted this weakness and promised her a share of name and fame that was due to her.

He then started instigating Vishwas. Twice he took him to Singapore and arranged his so-called discourses, presenting him as 'Junior BB', whose sole aim was to be in absolute control of his father's empire. Naidu advised him to attack Chanda Devi's weaknesses. He gathered details on her financial frauds and political networking and set Vishwas to exploit the situation. Naidu then penetrated Chanda Devi's camp, befriended her, then started tripping and tricking her. She trusted him more and more and he started attending some of her important meetings involving political transactions. Within six months, he convinced BB that he was in a position to draw a truce between the two warring groups. The guru was elated and believed he had found his man. He started giving Naidu considerable access to his private records and personal accounts.

Naidu arranged for wide distribution of the promotional material on him, which included tapes, CDs, flyers, newspaper advertisements, etc. Keeping his involvement confidential, he arranged for a similar promotional exercise for Chanda Devi as well, which helped him gain her full trust and access to all her confidential records. Making most of the opportunity, Naidu's team dug into the data available and managed to create individual dossiers on the guru, his son and Chanda Devi. Meanwhile, Chanda Devi who had begun to rely on Naidu even more, started seeking his advice on her personal investments. Likewise, BB too started involving him in all his new business dealings. With access to all the information, all the three dossiers were updated with authentic documents and incriminating evidence, enough to nail the guru in any court of law. An innocuous looking 'techie', assigned from the Bhadralok technology division, joined in. He, while remaining invisible, was to hack into BB's corporate systems and help in getting more data.

It was time to go for the kill. Nayan called up Naidu and asked for a meeting.They both met at a nondescript restaurant where Nayan asked Naidu if he could persuade Chanda Devi to give details of her intimacy with BB. Naidu was to convince her that these details were required to project her as BB's real life partner and confidante, and in the process denounce Guru Mata as the 'other' woman. She would be hailed as the real Guru Mata which would increase her popularity and bring her the fame she craved. Completely taken in by his persuasion, Chanda Devi even parted with a few of her personal photographs taken with BB, and also some of his love letters to her.

Naidu put together a huge amount of explosive evidence, which included land transactions with the mafia, money stashes in various foreign banks, investments in the Pride Group, favours sought from politicians for illegal constructions of his several centers, commissions accepted from industrialists for fixing their transactions with ministers, exploitation of several unsuspecting devotees such as Naidu by making them dole out money for use by the BB Trust—the list was endless. Modi, Wadia, Mansukhani and other experts got busy scrutinising, sifting and sorting the evidence such that several criminal cases could be filed against BB.

Just before breaking the scandal, Naidu and his family returned to Singapore where their security would be assured. The media, of course, lies in wait for some misery, disgrace or *tamaasha* to report and lapped up everything against BB, Chanda Devi and Vishwas Raje. The entire nation was abuzz with the exploits of the so-called 'spiritual guru'. Thousands of devotees were completely devastated to see their guru embroiled in such dishonour. In the turmoil that followed, all three started blaming and framing each other for their ills and predicament. Politicians, industrialists including Indrajeet, and other prominent people caught in the scandal denied any connection with the guru. The Pride Group defended its land acquisition from the BB Trust and also its investments in the group by claiming both to be nothing other than perfectly legal business transactions.

The second attack included releasing some of BB's intimate photographs with Chanda Devi, labelling it as a clandestine affair of the guru. Devotees all across India were shaken to the core by this revelation, especially as their guru always advocated fidelity in many of his discourses. Vishwas was quick to brand her as a home breaker trapping his father into moral deterioration and ignominy. Guru Mata too openly blamed her. While accusations and allegations were flying around, BB surprisingly remained calm and silent. When the entire affair started getting ugly, he eventually gave his clichéd reaction. "All allegations are baseless; nothing but a pack of lies. Chanda Devi has been an ardent follower and a great pillar of strength, and my relationship with her has never been anything other than platonic. Our great Indian mythology is full of such examples, and I see nothing wrong in what I have done. As to my financial transactions, they are perfectly legal and transparent. If there have been any misappropriations, they have been done without my knowledge. This entire affair is a conspiracy waged by my spiritual rivals to malign me. I have nothing to fear or defend. The truth will out in due course."

BB's statement was rejected by his core team and Chanda Devi as it indirectly accused them of having perpetrated those 'financial frauds'. His comment about the platonic love he had for her also didn't go down well. She was hurt and angry enough to approach representatives of the GRG on her own. Meanwhile, the GRG made capital of the BB fiasco with the media. Chanda Devi bore the brunt of it all which only infuriated her more. She submitted documentary evidence on the guru's involvement in certain crimes. The disclosure of Salunke assisting the guru in the horrific killing of some Indian and foreign journalists working to expose him shook the nation.

Naidu and Modi presented all the evidence collected to the GRG advisory team. Although, prima facie, the evidence was good enough to book BB in criminal cases, they were not confidant of having him get convicted, since it is unfortunately not uncommon to hear of sabotage by the corrupt Indian investigative agencies and the fraudulent judiciary system. Hence, the team decided to focus their attention overseas and then march into India with the attack. They started at the grassroots – that of contacting the family members of the journalists murdered by the guru, to rekindle the gory issue and then ask the next-of-kin of the slain journalists to file criminal cases in their respective home countries. On similar lines, efforts were made to foment enough hate and anger among several foreign and NRI devotees duped by BB, so that they would want to file criminal cases against the conman whom they believed to be their spiritual guru.

Within a couple of weeks, quite a few criminal cases were filed against BB and his trust in different countries, which in turn, moved the Indian media to follow suit. In the midst of the pandemonium that followed, another piece of news made waves. Chanda Devi, it was learnt, committed suicide, though the media and investigators suspected it to be homicide, considering the fact that it was this lady who had revealed to the world the nexus of politicians, industrialists and mafia outfits that were connected with BB. As usual, the government directed the central investigative agency to look into the

Chanda Devi case. The foreign media started demanding the Indian government arrest him so that justice could be done to all the families of the journalists that he had eliminated. Eventually, the government, albeit reluctantly, apprehended him and remanded him to judicial custody until the inquiry reached its conclusion. Till such time his Trust was to be handed over to an official liquidator and the various campuses were to be sealed and attached to the court.

A month later, BB's lawyers arranged for bail and had him released. Two politicians, amongst those who had been named by Chanda Devi, helped him so that he wouldn't implicate them in the court of law. They also arranged for the best legal counsel for his defense. The entire scandal had taken a huge toll on BB who became physically and mentally very weak. He was shifted to a small but well-guarded farmhouse on the outskirts of Delhi, away from his disciples and devotees. One fateful night, an angry mob of more than hundred disillusioned devotees attacked the farmhouse. The security guards could not handle the rampage, and they fled leaving the mob to set ablaze the house with BB inside. By the time the local police managed to arrive, the frenzied mob had dispersed and all that the police could find was cinders and the charred remains of the house and its evil inhabitant who was identifiable thanks to his 'spiritual' rings and chains. As for the GRG, yet another chapter on fraud was closed.

Professor Aditya called for a special meeting at his residence to felicitate the BB project team. He acknowledged the brave and heroic efforts of Naidu in exposing Bada Bapu and his deadly network. The professor said, "It is my opinion that our young colleagues have gained enough experience of working on our projects. It is my wish that Nayan take charge of our next attempt to expose the Pride Group.

I know that this is extremely critical for us all, but from now on all our initiatives should be shouldered by youngsters like him, Sathe and others. I shall be very happy to guide, counsel and direct them whenever required."

"Sir, I thank you for the confidence you have shown in our ability, but I do not know if we are competent enough for this task," Nayan said humbly.

"Nayan, I agree with Professor Aditya," said Deshpande.

A silence followed Aditya's pronouncement, which was broken by Mansukhani who said, "Nayan and Sathe, both your families have been unfortunate targets of the Pride Group. This should be your call now. You guys have to take it up and make it your own agenda, your personal war. All of us have to play the big game in life some day or the other, and what better time than now when you have complete backing from us all?"

"Do not run scared for fear of failure. Recall what I told you guys in Matheran. Do your duty with utmost devotion and the leave the rest to the almighty," said Aditya emphatically.

Nayan was made the chief of the project and Sathe his associate. As decided earlier, Mansukhani was to carry out the initial investigative work. A broad schedule was decided. Concluding the meeting Aditya said, "Nayan and Sathe, this battle against Indrajeet will do your confidence a world of good. It will help you to contribute ably towards your friends from Nigeria, Indonesia, China and Oman. Before we leave, I'd like a candidate to take up the responsibility of documenting our success stories and sending them to our friends all over. They would most certainly benefit from our experiences." This task was given to Naidu.

It was also decided that small booklets be published, presenting these stories in different languages to arouse public awareness. Aditya asked Nayan to coordinate with Bhadralok on the Pride Group Project and take the project to its completion.

Mansukhani began his spadework by hosting a party, using the pretext of his daughter's birthday to invite some of his old mafia clients. His intention was to revive his links with the underworld, and thereby get to the source of Hyper Wealth. As his connections began to develop, he made visits to Hong Kong, Dubai, Jeddah, Karachi and Paris. He even approached the offices of some internationally known mafia outfits in order to rejuvenate rapport for legal services. He knew the initial groundwork would pay dividends. The first break came from Dubai, where two rather small and inexperienced outfits, handling investments of Dubai based Sheikhs via Hyper Wealth, contracted him for some professional work. While working for them, Mansukhani was able to unearth some very vital details about the nexus between a few Dubai based terrorist groups, the Sheikhs, and the liaison officer of Hyper Wealth in the Middle East. Some of the documents and CDs that he could lay his hands on were codified using advanced digital encryption techniques. Not knowing how to crack these codes, he passed on all the data and information to Nayan and Sathe using the established secure channels.

With his work done in Dubai, Mansukhani went to Hong Kong since all clues pointed there. He was in touch with a Chinese agent working for Hyper Wealth, who upon accepting a hefty bribe parted with vital information about the fund. This bribe he gave by using his earlier payoffs in the form of diamonds and precious stones from the likes of Indrajeet and the underworld. The agent passed on useful bits of information on Hyper Wealth's business and its modus of operation, with the names of key investors and agents with their coordinates etc. Mansukhani committed an error.

He called up Nayan in India from his hotel room to share his joy. He should have realised that an advocate hovering around gathering information would be a subject of suspicion and phone tapping was the first step. Mansukhani returned to India that very night, met Nayan and handed over his catch. The next evening, as he relaxed in his garden toasting his success, a bullet made its mark killing him instantly. After a police post-mortem, the reason for his death was confirmed—a bullet fired at close range through his neck. It didn't escape Nayan—the similarity between this murder and that of his father Dil Bhojani. His mind was made up – the style was that of Pride Group. When powerful people turn hostile, where there is fear of business interests getting compromised, the solution in mafia terms is simple termination!

Nayan, Sathe and Wadia flew over to New York with all the data and information Mansukhani had managed to put together. Mike arranged a meeting with two retired Jewish operatives from the American intelligence bureau who had closely interacted with Mossad, the Israeli intelligence agency, during their tenure at the bureau. Shini and Robert were also present at the meeting, which was brief, and at the end of which, documentation, CDs and all relevant material was handed over to the operatives. It took them three days to crack all the codes and to ascertain the authenticity of the contents. Nayan and Sathe were very elated to know that the information collected by Mansukhani was authentic and could be used as evidence against Indrajeet. But they needed more to nail him. There were gaps in the evidence collected and it was perhaps not enough to get a conviction, especially in India.

The situation was very delicately poised. Conscious of the shortcomings in the evidence collected, Nayan called for a brain storming session with Sathe, Shini, Mike, Wadia and Robert. He knew they had to come up with something completely out of the ordinary to fill in for those inadequacies in their evidence. Nayan pushed Mike to let the American intelligence operatives slip the evidence on to Mossad, hoping that Hyper Wealth's involvement in financing international terrorist organisations would trigger their interest in the subject. Then, if Mossad were to get involved in the matter, nailing Indrajeet would become that much easier, since the issue would instigate a new dimension to the story of Indrajeet from a global angle. Hyper Wealth would be branded as part of an international conspiracy, no more a domestic matter within the confines of corrupt and corruptible Indian justice.

Mike and Robert were not in favour of Nayan's suggestion as they both thought it to be a little farfetched. Wadia, though, doggedly supported it. In fact, Wadia had a few examples of a similar kind where certain issues private to a country got international exposure. He insisted that bringing down the fund was very much in the interest of Israel, America and India alike. Slowly, but surely, Robert saw light in Nayan's proposition. He took it up seriously and promised he would lobby with the Mossad branch in the UK and urge the agency to take up the case. Eventually, Mike also got persuaded into accepting it as a workable solution, and finally, they all agreed to take it forward from there.

After a brief presentation to the American branch of Mossad, it was decided to do a full-length presentation at the Mossad headquarters in Israel. The American branch had found the prima facie evidence against Hyper Wealth adequate. Nayan, Wadia, Mike, Shini and Sathe flew to Israel the following week. The presentation by Nayan and Shini was excellent and was extremely well received. Mossad, in principle, agreed to take up the case, and decided to assign a small team to work on the missing bits of evidence. Sathe expressed a desire to work with this team as it would give him exposure to the finest methods of investigation, being an ace at it. Indeed, an organisation of the stature of Mossad never hires untrained or outside help. But, at the behest of Professor Aditya, they agreed to let Sathe and Ranjan Rishi play an entry role.

After their successful trip, Nayan and Sathe returned home. That night, Nayan called up Professor Aditya and gave him a detailed update on the developments of the Pride Group Project. The professor was happy and encouraged Nayan to keep up the good work.

The Mossad unit completed its job well before the projected time. All breaks in the evidence against the Pride Group were filled in. Now there was convincing evidence about Hyper Wealth being a fund used by terrorist groups. The unit also established the fund's role in cross border speculation leading to enormous volatility in the American metal and currency markets. This was achieved by using petro dollars of some of the powerful speculators from the oil producing countries. Nayan and Wadia visited the US at the request of the American Mossad. They needed their findings to be endorsed by those knowledgeable about the case. The picture looked poised for the finale against Indrajeet and the Pride Group.

Although the evidence against Indrajeet was quite solid by now, Nayan and Wadia were not convinced that it was good idea to file a case against him in the US courts. The reason behind this apprehension was his considerable influence in the Indian government. They were almost certain that he could get any case filed in the US against him, transferred to Indian courts, where he would be able to manipulate the evidence and evade arrest. In the worst-case scenario, if the US courts did not allow the transfer and insisted on trying him there, it would have to be in-absentia, he being in India and not in the US. As physical arrest wouldn't be option for the US courts, the only punishment for Indrajeet would be penalties or fines, which would not matter to him whatsoever. He would happily pay up the penalty rather than be arrested.

The apprehensions voiced by Nayan were taken seriously by Mossad who agreed that filing criminal cases against Indrajeet in the US was not the answer. His physical arrest in the US would have to be their goal. They would need to plan every possible strategy and tactic to the minutest detail. The smallest error would completely nullify all their efforts. Nayan and his colleagues returned to India and approached Aditya in search of a solution.The American Mossad completed its investigation of Hyper Wealth and was ready with the report, which even included details about the Pride Group's illegal businesses in India. Seeking American help in the matter, the Israeli government directly requested the American President for a meeting to present its report on the fund. The regular bureaucratic channel was intentionally avoided, fearing a leak and Indrajeet getting wind of what was happening.

Nayan, Mike, Wadia, Shini were a part of the team that made the presentation to the American President. They managed to convince him that the activities of the Hyper Wealth Fund were against the interests of America, Israel and India, and that it was critical to seize the fund and take legal action against its promoter. They also managed to convey the fact that a few mid-sized American companies were also involved. Terrorism, being the most touchy, delicate subject, the American President did not, and could not, ignore the issue. In fact, he ensured that all possible help by the US would be given to take stern action against Hyper Wealth and its associates.

The President instructed the national security secretariat to coordinate and work jointly with Mossad on the case. Nayan and his colleagues were overjoyed at the spontaneous reaction of the

American President. However, the Mossad team leader remained sombre. He said to Nayan, "Don't start counting your chickens as yet -- this may well turn out to be another wasted effort. Before long, the national security secretariat will consult the trade and commerce secretariat. Time will elapse as they assess the commercial impact, and of course, we mustn't forget the vested interests of mega American Corporations, linked to Pride Group. At the most they may close down Hyper Wealth operations in USA, impose a heavy penalty on the fund managers in America and end the story there. We'll have to come up with an alternate strategy most probably."

Nayan's hopes were dashed and he decided to call up professor Aditya. He updated him about their meeting with the President and the apprehensions of the Mossad leader. They both agreed that there was cause for concern. America is rumoured to always put its business interests above everything else, unless directly affected. The Pride Group's activities in India or any place else, save in America, were of no consequence to USA. With that in mind, Aditya suggested that they wait a couple of weeks for a response from the security secretariat and then formulate the next course of action. If the outcome was contrary to their expectations then perhaps they could resort to exerting some pressure by roping in prominent Indians in USA and urging them to take up their cause with the Americans.

After two weeks, there was still no reaction, either from the secretariat or the President's office. Nayan and Shini called up Professor Aditya for comfort and advice. Aditya, if he had a strategy, did not pronounce it fully. However, he asked the GRG members to go ahead with the alternate plan and collect the smallest detail on the President's hometown. What they found out was that the President, in his younger days, had been an active member of the Young Americans Society's local branch in his hometown. 'YAS' was the codename for this society, which was known to do commendable social work. As the President of the US, he was still quite a champion of YAS, but was now more a sympathiser than an active member of the organisation. Of course, both Nayan and Shini did not miss corroborating on the matter with their global pals who were called to New York for the finale.

Shini, Sathe and Nayan visited the small, quaint hometown of the President and met some of the members of the local YAS outfit there. They followed it up by giving them a presentation about the philosophy and the past and current activities of the GRG. This served to invoke interest among the members and paved the way for exposing the Pride Group and Hyper Wealth issues as well. Nayan openly appealed to the YAS leader to support their cause with the President. Since the president could not be swayed away from his economic stance, this was an emotional ploy used by them.

Impressed by the presentations, the YAS leader agreed to help. All details regarding a brief casual meeting with the President were finalised for the following Saturday. YAS asked Nayan to pack in a lot of emotional appeal in his plea, knowing the President to be a very passionate man. Nayan knew that this was perhaps his last and only chance. At the appointed time, the YAS members, along with Nayan, Shini and Sathe called upon the President. He was casually dressed and relaxed. He had done his homework on GRG and the famous professor.

Nayan said, "Mr President, my colleagues and I, along with the Mossad unit in the US, had called upon you earlier regarding the Pride Group and the Hyper Wealth fund. Unfortunately, despite your assurances and best intentions the matter did not make much headway. The secretariats seemed reluctant to see merit in the case though Mossad and YAS both did."

Nayan went on at length with the story of Salunke against the Indian rural backdrop and the American president stayed fascinated and gripped, interjecting solely to clarify certain indigenously grown political terms. When Nayan was finished, he lavished praise on him that would have brought a twinkle in the eyes of his mentor – Aditya.

Nayan was smart to ascertain that all this was fancy rubbish if the main point was not taken home by the President. He paved the way for Shini to pick up, and she, in her controlled and persuasive way spoke of the Pride Group, their nefarious activities and the funding of the terrorist organisations through Hyper Wealth.

The duo worked on the psyche of the President in such a way that he could not help but pledge support. He offered to set up a new link for the GRG through his PA, Lavina.

It was the tenth anniversary of the Pride Group's New York branch and all the employees were quite excited. The branch had been the best performing export branch of the Pride Corporation, accounting for almost twenty-five per cent of the group's exports. Indrajeet, being the Chairman of the group, was present to take part in the festivities that had been arranged at the branch office. At the stroke of eleven, he made a grand entry, and was received by the manager with an exquisite bouquet, to thundering applause by the employees. The media was also present and Indrajeet, who seemed to be in good mood, interacted well. After the spate of civil and criminal cases in India and abroad, with its reputation severely tarnished, Indrajeet had plans to use this media exposure to do damage control.

After exchanging a few words with his branch people over a cup of coffee, he was led into the banquet hall where the celebrations had been arranged. Those invited for the grand function were Pride Group's customers, business associates, agents, bureaucrats, advertisers, media representatives and other dignitaries. The special guest for the day was the Sheriff of New York city. The festivities were to be started with the traditional Indian custom of lighting the lamp. Indrajeet was walking towards the lamp when there was a small commotion. A couple of men in plain clothes brandished their badges, pulled out a pair of handcuffs and pretty much in Hollywoodian style, the business tycoon was whisked away! One of them said to Indrajeet, "We are from the Central Center of Investigation. Sir, you are under arrest for abetting terrorism against American soil. You have the right to remain silent, and anything that you say or do will be used against you in the court of law. You have the right to consult an attorney and to have your attorney present during questioning."

There was shocked silence all around the hall. The other man produced an arrest warrant, which he read out to Indrajeet who was too stunned to react. He tried putting up a defense but knew it wasn't going to be of much help. He was in the US and not in India, where one phone call would have these officers of the law crawling on their knees begging for his mercy. He nevertheless put forth an argument saying, "This had better be some mistake. You cannot arrest me based on some incredulous charges that you have read out to me. Moreover, I am not an American citizen. I have a certain status in my country and I have an international standing. I am here to celebrate the tenth anniversary of our export branch in New York. Certainly, I am not here to indulge in some terrorist activity and harm the Pride Group that my father has cherished and built. You cannot humiliate me like this. You could have addressed the matter to my attorney rather than slandering me and staging an arrest which will cost you dearly…" Indrajeet was clearly angry and thought that going on the offensive may scare the officers and stall his arrest. His secretary and the New York branch manager, both non-plussed and stunned put up some good arguments to the CCI officers, but in vain.

They replied, "Gentlemen, kindly do not interfere or you will be held in contempt of court." Then, turning to Indrajeet, they said, "For now to the car please, we'll put you in custody and our job ends there. Matters of the court are not decided by us."

Indrajeet realised it was futile to argue and quietly walked away with them. The guests gathered in the hall were still in shock. Of course, there were frantic calls made and innumerable deductions amongst the audience. Nobody said anything while the boss was being led away, handcuffed and humiliated. The news of Indrajeet being involved in terrorist activities was beyond anybody's imagination. The New York branch manager was clearly a nervous man as his boss had been arrested on his turf and he had no clue of what was brewing. His job was at stake and he would have to do a lot of answering.

Meanwhile, the CCI men presented Indrajeet before the special magistrate's court. A brief hearing followed where Indrajeet's attorney tried his best to avert the arrest. However, the magistrate was in no mood to listen, and straightaway remanded Indrajeet to judicial custody until the next hearing. The media was in a frenzy. The next day, Indrajeet's wife, a few close associates, and a panel of Pride Group's elite lawyers left for New York. Ministers in the ruling party in India and the Indian ambassador to the US were hounded by press reporters. A few well-known NGOs supported by the Pride Group, and a mob of angry protesters put together by the corporate communications division of the Pride Group staged demonstrations outside the American consular offices in New Delhi and in Mumbai. This was hot news, a plot right out of a thriller novel.

As the sensational story spun around all over New York, the GRG members and their International friends, all chanced to be in NY, thanks to the Bhadralok Group sponsoring.

After one of the brainstorming sessions, Manzar said, "Nayan ol' chap, its time you and Shini took your vows. We are not indefinitely going to hang around in New York. You folks please wake up and let us all rejoice in the fact that good things can be born out of vile and villainous circumstances! In the search to nail a wicked rascal two souls toiled, stuck their necks out, almost died executing their assignments and in the end were blessed, kindling eternal love and respect for each other. Bravo man you're truly blessed!"

Within three days, the international, inter-religious, cross-cultural marriage got arranged and for all those who mattered were present – professor Aditya, Deshpande, Mohite, Modi, Rajan, Seetabai, and of course, Robert from UK. It was a simple ceremony with close relatives and friends.

The two were blessed in matrimony by a Hindu priest, a Jewish rabbi and a Christian priest. The ceremony was a tribute to professor Aditya's concept of Universal Religion.

The Pride Group hired the best defense attorneys and tried to put pressure on the special court through all channels possible. CEO Lubert of the notorious Global Oil, and CEO Lynch of Western Coke lobbied aggressively with powerful senators to seek intervention from the President to withdraw the case against Indrajeet. The corporation agreed to pay hefty penalties and compensation for the release of its Chairman. It declared that the Hyper Wealth Fund would be closed with immediate effect, and if directed by the court, it would also suspend all business operations on American soil indefinitely. However, all efforts to get Indrajeet released got nowhere. The Pride Group offered millions of dollars in bribes to Indian ministers to have them convince the American President, and the court presiding over Indrajeet's case to transfer the matter to India. A very senior minister of the ruling party even visited New York and tried his best to get the case dropped.

Ultimately, tardy justice managed to overtake the crime, and all efforts proved futile in getting Indrajeet off the hook, or to get the case transferred to India. It was clear that he would be convicted for the many crimes he was charged with. On that cue, shares of Pride Group companies crashed worldwide. Slowly, but surely, those ministers who were seen frantically lobbying for Indrajeet, made a volte-face and refused to comment on the case. In today's world, there is no one so faithful or foolish to stick his neck out in a losing battle. The Indian Prime Minister remained equivocal stating that he had full faith in the American judicial system and that nothing but justice would be done. Pride Group's American partners remained tight-lipped, not wanting to upset the apple cart.

On the judgment day, the courtroom and its precincts were full of reporters from all over the world. Nayan and Shini were also present answering the media questions about how they were trained to fight corruption at all levels. The judgment was seen by one and all as a victory of virtue over vice, of truth over falsehood, of all things good over everything bad. The message conveyed was that if goodness were to survive, then bad elements necessarily needed to be eradicated and defeated. It was possible to get rid of demons like Salunke and Indrajeet by an honest, collective, persevering, dedicated effort.

The court read out its judgment that ran into several pages, and which sentenced Indrajeet, for his various crimes, for twenty-seven years in American prison. There were a few pending cases against him too that were expected to add another six to seven years. For all practical purposes, he was condemned to life imprisonment. Hyper Wealth was closed with immediate effect. Besides the prison sentence, a hefty penalty of five billion American dollars was imposed.

Indian and foreign media went ballistic over Indrajeet's imprisonment in the US. Indian politicians preferred to keep mum.

What could they say after all? Nayan and his colleagues became the new poster boys of all TV channels. By trouncing Indrajeet, the GRG did not bid goodbye to corruption, but showed the world a way to say farewell to sleaze, dishonesty and fraud in the future.

The American President called on Professor Aditya to congratulate him for the phenomenal achievement. The president asked: "What next, professor?" The Professor replied, "Nigeria, sir! We march to Nigeria … aren't you with us?"

***